3/24

Ellie Haycock Is Totally Normal

Ellie Haycock Is Totally Normal

Gretchen Schreiber

WEDNESDAY BOOKS
NEW YORK

First published in the United States by Wednesday Books, an imprint of St. Martin's Publishing Group

ELLIE HAYCOCK IS TOTALLY NORMAL. Copyright © 2024 by Gretchen Schreiber. All rights reserved. Printed in the United States of America. For information, address St. Martin's Publishing Group, 120 Broadway, New York, NY 10271.

www.wednesdaybooks.com

Designed by Donna Sinisgalli Noetzel

The Library of Congress Cataloging-in-Publication Data is available upon request.

ISBN 978-1-250-89216-4 (hardcover)
ISBN 978-1-250-89217-1 (ebook)

Our books may be purchased in bulk for promotional, educational, or business use. Please contact your local bookseller or the Macmillan Corporate and Premium Sales Department at 1-800-221-7945, extension 5442, or by email at MacmillanSpecialMarkets@macmillan.com.

First Edition: 2024

10 9 8 7 6 5 4 3 2 1

To my parents —
Thank you (it may not be an Oscar, but I hope this will do),
for always being there believing in me
and the writing thing I do —
even when I didn't believe in myself.

Author's Note

Ellie's story is one I am very familiar with, as it's largely—medically—based on a moment in my life where I, too, faced a mysterious illness. This story is highly specific to my experience.

This is one story and it cannot be all things to everyone. I know what it is to hunt for yourself on the shelves and the betrayal and frustration that comes from a story being close but just slightly off. The only way to fix that is for more books by disabled people to be published.

When I started writing this book, I made a vow to myself to not sugarcoat the hospital/medical experience. I wanted to write a story that says this *is* what happens and this *is* how one teenager can deal with it. I also wanted to write a story that was about love and friendship and how both things can exist at the same time.

That also means this book goes to some heavy places. From being ignored by medical professionals to people dismissing your experiences and even who has final say over your care when you're a minor.

I know these things can be hard to read when you also have to deal with them in real life, so if you need to skip my book—that's okay. Taking care of yourself is the most important thing.

Ellie Haycock Is Totally Normal

Prologue

Three Months Ago

Early rounds at speech tournaments are my favorite, because there's still so much promise in the air. No one has settled in yet, we're all live wires hoping all our practice—the hours spent talking to walls—will pay off.

It's also a time where nerves for my competitors are the highest. Time to step off the ledge, people. And that sort of bravery I have in spades.

I walk back to the random lunchroom at whatever high school Coach has carted us off to this weekend. The thrill of performing well only increases when I see Jack, as if he were that extra shot in my coffee. A few students huddle together, but most have gone off in search of their rooms, leaving behind piles of stuff—pillows, boxes of research, comfy clothes to wear between rounds.

Picking my way to our table, I find Jack bent over a comic. His suit jacket's been laid across a backpack, tie lolling out of a pocket. He had the first extemp draw time, so of course he's already been there and back.

"Hi," I say, resting my chin on his head and my hands on his shoulders. It's a comfort to come back to this. Jack, Brooke, and I have been on the speech team since our freshman year, and now as juniors we're at the top of our game.

He reaches up for my left hand, grabs it, and pulls me down to sit next to him.

"How'd it go?" he asks as I slip into the seat. He gives my hand a squeeze, a simple sign to let me know he's there and will look up after just one more page.

"Killed it," I say with a smile. We were friends first long before we dated. I was so lost in our friendship that I missed the fact he'd asked me out, only to have Brooke sit me down and explain that *no*, Jack did not ask if I was going to the dance with the group of us, but with *him*.

He shuts the comic and turns to face me. His focus is what hits me first. Maybe it's what makes him a great extemp speaker. How he can zero in on you and make you feel like the only person in the world. He doesn't push but lures you in until you're so drawn to him that it doesn't matter what he says.

"Pity the others who will perform for a dead judge."

I laugh. "They should learn to start earlier," I say with a wicked grin. "How'd you do?"

Extemp speaking is an art unto itself: you draw a subject and get thirty minutes to prep a seven-minute speech. Jack loves the thrill of it, the never knowing what you'll get and how you can speak to it.

And he always figures it out, even if he has no idea about the topic. It's the reason he's state champion two years running and has gone to nationals since he was a freshman. There is no question that Jack cannot find an answer to and speak like an expert on for seven minutes.

"They couldn't have given me something easier." He talks me through his speech, the pieces that he pulled, and I just relax. I pull on a hoodie over my dress top and put in some earbuds to listen to music as Jack goes back to his comic. He's there holding my hand, like it's the most natural thing in the world.

My phone pings and my stomach drops as I see a notification about Mom's blog. She's written a new post. I close out of the screen as fast as possible, afraid Jack might have seen it. The last thing I need is for any of my friends to put their research skills to the test and find out just how much of my life is on the internet.

Policy debaters start trickling in, carting tubs and cases of research. Jack gives me a poke and I look up. He holds out the comic.

"You should read this," he says.

I look at it dubiously. "Have you even tried watching *BSG* yet?" It's one point of contention, that I will enjoy my boyfriend's preferred media but he doesn't always reciprocate.

Brooke sets a tub full of perfectly filed research on the table. She pulls out a yellow legal pad from under her arm and chucks it on the table. The flow of her debate round is all over it. Circles where someone dropped a counterplan, stars where she knows the information to pull, and notes from her partner.

"Have you still not watched *BSG*?" Brooke says, hands on hips.

"Why is it important that I watch this show?" Jack asks. He's all focused on me, meeting my eyes, not willing to budge. "We watched that other show."

Brooke and I exchange looks.

"Yes, but this one, it's different. It's . . ."

"It's her favorite," Brooke says.

"I'll get to it, I promise," he says, his gaze flicking between Brooke and me.

I fit here. Between my friend and my boyfriend, doing something I love. It's easy to forget the million little cuts that go along with speech, the small looks of shock on the judges' faces when they see me for the first time, the way some competitors like to say *It's great that you compete*; as if I'm here as some charity project. I keep these slights to myself; neither Jack nor Brooke ever sees them, and I don't let them because it would ruin some part of the experience. I know they would stand up for me and that's enough.

We go through the rest of the day, performing and speaking—until the three of us are standing on the stage each holding a medal. We crowd in for a picture and I upload it to my social media page.

"Who's Caitlin?" Brooke asks when we're on the way back home.

The sky edges toward black, and despite feeling good this morning, I have a scratch in my throat that feels like an oncoming cold.

"A friend," I say, hoping that Brooke'll drop it.

"'Kay," Brooke says, drawing out the word but not pushing for more details. Knowing her, she's putting a star by it, making a note to circle back around later.

In the morning, my sore throat had blossomed into full-blown painful swallowing and brought along a cough that never left.

VATERs Like Water

This is #TeamEllie

Age: 3 yrs. Entry #14

Comments: 15   Bookmarks: 2   Shares: 1

Sometimes when you have a sick kid it feels like all you talk about are problems. The insurance company. The school district. Other kids and their parents.

But today I want to talk about the bright side. The better side, our side.

You've seen me use #TeamEllie. We're so lucky to have a group of extremely talented physicians who make sure our baby girl is in tip-top living shape. I think it's finally time you meet the team!

Mom: fearless leader, general in charge, and all-around caregiver.

Dad: support system, calm in the face of a surgical storm. The only one who can make Ellie laugh after surgery.

Dr. Carlyle: the one who keeps everyone on track—internist, always and forever wrangling doctors in prep for surgery.

Dr. Williams: specialist. Hand surgeon, the one who talks us through all the ins and outs of surgical choices.

Dr. Anthony: specialist. Orthopedic surgeon, who can stand eight hours to put my daughter's spine back together. Who monitors her growth and sets a plan, even if sometimes he doesn't understand why a three-year-old doesn't want to wear a brace.

Dr. Lee: specialist. Heart guy. The first person to fix my daughter.

Dr. Moyer: specialist. Nephrologist. When your kid only has one kidney you have to keep it healthy!

And that's just the main team. I could go on and on about the nurses and support staff who make every hospital visit, every surgery, as comfortable as possible. Without you there really is no #TeamEllie.

We're in this together!

Gwen

Chapter One

The nurse injects radioactive material into my vein. She smiles at me, and I want to feel some side effect. As if at any minute I'm going to be blessed with superpowers.

But there's nothing. Just the slight sense of cold as gallium slides into my veins.

My first clue that superpowers were not in my future should have been when the nurse asked me if I was pregnant. I'm pretty sure the spider did not ask Peter Parker that. And I'm pretty sure that spider was just randomly radioactive—like Peter didn't know that it was, say, gallium being shot into his veins to look for illness in his body.

At least that's according to Jack. His comics fascination is finally getting to me. I suppose this would be something to tell him, and the thought is briefly comforting.

The nurse tosses the needle into the red box. "That's it?" I ask. Being shot up with radioactive isotopes should be more exciting.

Her smile comes in warm and comforting. I want to tell her that's not needed. I know the score here. "That's it. We'll take this IV out and you're free to go." She wiggles her gloved fingers, ready to tackle the tape holding the IV to my inner elbow.

My stomach starts its floor routine, because I know what all of these tests *could* mean.

Cancer.

Brain tumor.

Cancer.

Lung tumor.

Organ failure.

Broken spine.

Cancer.

Stop, I tell myself firmly. *Body, you've fucked me over a lot. A. Lot. You don't get to grow any more tumors.*

That's right. More. I have one. It's normal, or a "benign cyst" in doctorspeak. Tumors are malignant. Cysts are benign. But they're pretty much the same thing—things that are growing in your body that shouldn't. It's fine.

Ping! goes my cell phone.

Mom's head shoots up, ever ready to be the MVP of #TeamEllie. "Want me to reply for you?" Her hand is already on the zipper of my backpack.

"No," I say. My chest tightens and I curl the stubby fingers of my right hand in as far as they can go. Only the pinkie is able to touch my palm, rubbing the smooth skin there. There was a time, when I was younger, that Mom would have answered my texts while I was hospital-ly occupied.

Mom freezes, concern crinkling her brow. I put a stop to this sort of "help" the moment she started sharing these "cute" details of our relationship with her audience, details like my full text conversations. The audience loved to know how Mom would type out my texts to my friends—those friends, however . . . not so much.

"I mean, uh, it's probably just Jack checking in on a passing period." Lie. Total fabrication.

"Jack . . . haven't heard that name in a while."

Well, we're not exactly in the same city anymore, and whose fault is that? I say in my head. I'm tired from the early morning and little sleep thanks to this unknown illness; the last thing I need is Mom on my case about my boyfriend.

"Knock yourself out." I gesture to the nurse, moving my elbow so she'll get back to taking this tube out of my arm. Gloved fingers probe the tape, looking for the loose edge. IVs—needles in general—are my least favorite torture device. Strange, given that I've had around forty surgeries. Doctors kept saying I'd get used to it.

That was the original doctor lie. They said I would get used to a lot of things: shots, surgery, the Milwaukee brace, physical therapy. . . . Hasn't happened yet, and it's not trending up. My "normal" is what everyone else might call abnormal.

Wrong.

Messed up.

Disabled.

Words that made up my life from day one—just don't let Mom hear them. She shifts in her seat, eyes ostensibly on the quote she's cross-stitching: *The only disability is a bad attitude.* I should make one that says *Keep your attitude out of my disability.* Really, her eyes are trained on the nurse, watching every move, ready to step in. Amazing how protection can feel like a noose. I take a deep breath. For all my frustrations with Mom, she's fiercely protective. And at this point, after dealing with me since I was born, Mom probably knows enough to pass the medical boards.

The nurse sets to work untangling the layers of tape while inflicting as little pain as possible. I want to tell her it's okay, she doesn't have to worry. Removing the tape and pulling at tender skin—skewered with the IV—is never completely painless. Tiny zings of pain race down my arm toward my fingers. I fight to keep my face neutral, to not make her apologize any more than she already has. I don't need anyone's pity. I just need the tests my doctor ordered, each requiring its own set of contrasts, dyes, and drugs, to come back with a clue to why I'm sick this time. I've always seen doctors for VACTERLs, but this . . . *thing* is new, persistent, and completely stumping the fancy Coffman docs.

Ping.

Ping.

Each notification feels like a direct hit. I simultaneously want to run to my phone, cling to a lifeline in my normal nonhospital life, and smash the offending object under my boot to fully stop the hospital from corrupting my normal life. The nurse pauses, silently questioning if I want to go deal with my friends.

Nope. I shake my head.

With practiced care she starts to undo the layers of tape, searching for the tube beneath. I allow myself one flinch and a quick inhale. Mistake. My lungs do not like that. They crackle, and a cough sparks deep inside me. I pull away and the nurse backs up, hands raised, and I cough. A constant dry stream that racks my body and stings my lungs. Right, the reason I'm here. Not because I'm about to join a secret government agency that really wants its acronym to be SHIELD.

DARPA would even be preferable to what I have now, which is: *Unknown. No conclusion. We can treat the symptoms.* I'm used to medicine with clear results. You have VACTERLs. Do this surgery, you get to live. Need these functionalities? We can do X, Y, Z procedures.

But now my lungs have me missing speech competitions, time with friends, and weeks going between my bed and the couch. And the only explanation is a fancy way of saying *We don't know.*

Bright lights flash at the corners of my vision, and I strain for oxygen. Just when I think this is it, my lungs cut it out and suck in a long, slow breath. I relax back in the chair, looking anywhere but at the nurse.

Ping.

Ping.

"Shouldn't Jack be in class by now?" Mom asks, testing the edges of my lie.

Ping.

She reaches for my bag, unable to stop herself from interfering with my life. Just because she can dictate my medical care doesn't mean she can meddle in my love life.

"Mom, it's fine." I try to lace *Back off* into every word. I should have put my phone on silent and then no one would know about those messages.

Shock ping-pongs over her face. "Sorry," I say, trying to look contrite. "Brooke's probably checking in to see if I can spot any potential holes in her 1AC," I add to my lie. Well, mostly. Brooke does have debate prep and I do help her out with casework, but it's tomorrow.

All my friends at Evanston High School want to know what's wrong with me. *Why are you at the hospital? And not just the local one? Weren't those doctors enough?* Because when I was twelve my dad got a new job and we moved to Evanston. It was the fresh start I'd desperately needed. I wasn't Ellie the girl always missing school for surgeries, or Ellie the star of her mom's popular, award-winning blog. For the first time I was just . . . Ellie. I've worked hard to keep it that way, hide everything as much as I can so they won't poke and prod as much as the doctors. Their support is meant to be a balm, but their questions feel like shots and their inquiries like exploratory surgery.

Mom's look softens, like she knows what I'm giving up. "I'm happy to answer for you. I can read the texts—"

"Brooke can wait just a few minutes." She wants to be helpful, wants to make sure that I can still coexist with my friends even though I'm at the Virginia-Ruth Coffman Memorial Medical Center and they're four hours north in Evanston.

I hyperextend my left arm and give it a little shake, indicating the nurse should carry on with her duties. The last piece of tape is pulled free and she presses gauze over the IV and then pulls.

I hold my breath, grateful for the distraction from my phone as every cell seems to focus on my arm. I hate this part. I swear it hurts worse than going in, which is no picnic either. She lays the used IV on the tray and presses hard on my arm, helping my blood stay in my body. Gauze is wrapped tight around my arm and she tucks the end under the layers.

"Wait at least fifteen minutes before removing," she says, practiced words that she probably says a hundred times a day to a hundred different people. With measured precision, she collects all her accoutrements, needles, IV, and tape, and disposes of them in the red medical waste bin before chucking her gloves in after.

I stand up and Mom hands me my coat and then busies herself with wrapping up her cross-stitch pattern, leaving me to my own devices. The nurse watches with strange fascination as I struggle into my coat. Her question is written across her face: *Why isn't your mom helping?*

Because I don't need any help, I want to snap.

I stick in my left arm—the one hampered by gauze but fully functional otherwise—and pull out my phone, which takes some interesting maneuvering. The screen flashes Jack (4) at me before I can lock it away.

"Here, let me," the nurse says. Impatience dots her words, which she tries to mask as a "good deed."

Mom and I share a look, and she presses her laughter into a tight smile. Just like that, we're a team again. Maybe when I was a baby it was nice for her: someone grabbing the door, another person holding the elevator. Things that are actually helpful, that you might do for any person, not just because I'm disabled and they want to look nice.

"I got it," I say, adding a glare that translates to *Back off*. Mom rolls her eyes. She's better at handling these things now, but I still have a tough edge. The nurse backs up, waiting for me to tackle my own issues.

VACTERLs left me with fewer bones than the average human. Most of those missing in action were located in my back and right arm. My back is mostly held together with leftover bones from someone else, and my right arm is what doctors and I like to call medical-grade crap. But really, everything below my right elbow is basically not good tissue, which I guess is why it looks like a cross between a claw machine and a child's attempt at making a hand out of clay.

After setting the bag on the chair I was in, I bend and loop the strap over my shoulder and stand up. The nurse leads us back to the waiting area—freedom in sight! There have been no other cues that she may know more about my life than just what is in my medical chart.

Ping!

"Brooke must really have something to say. Or is it Jack?"

"Uh-huh." I reach into my pocket and flip my phone to silent, ignoring Mom calling out my lie.

"Um," the nurse says, causing both Mom and me to look up. Embarrassment crowds the corners of her smile, turning it sickeningly sweet. I want to curl into a ball because I have a feeling I know what's coming next. "I just wanted to say, I used to read your blog, *VATERs Like Water*. I love all the work you do for families."

Yup. Just let me hide among the medical waste receptacles.

Mom practically swoons; she puts a hand to her heart and wraps the other around my shoulder like we're in this together. "Oh, thank you."

I head for the door, escaping her grasp, done with this entire conversation.

"Eight a.m. tomorrow," the nurse calls after us as Mom hurries to catch up with me. Does this nurse think we're amateurs? That we need reminding of the schedule? *Pfft.* I turn around and smile at her, giving her a finger wave. Our medical career is longer than this nurse's.

Chapter Two

Mom hovers close, her energy filling the space like the moment before a storm, where the air gets thick, trying to cradle you, protect you from what's to come. At any moment she could split open and just drench me in love and support. She turns to me, her mouth open, but then seems to think better of it and huddles back in her seat. I sink into my puffy coat and pull out my phone, forming a barrier between us.

> **Jack**
> How's it going?
> What about this for Brooke's party?

There's a photo of a llama planter and I click to enlarge it, ignoring the last text.

> I miss you.

I swallow the panic that spikes with each text, that he'll come back and want more. My response is short and positive. Just a quick All's good! But then I delete the exclamation point because I don't want it to look too forced. I round it off by telling him the planter works. Brooke loves llamas.

I'm protecting Jack from the disappointment of not knowing what's wrong with me, and myself from having to be the one to let him down.

Me, I can handle the unknown the doctors give me. But I don't know how to handle what Jack could make of the truth. That I'm not fixable. I am still just Ellie, not Ellie who needs to be handled with kid gloves. If Mom's blog has taught me anything, it's that there's only so much people outside this world can take before they can't handle it anymore.

SOS, I text Caitlin Barrie, my best hospital friend and fellow VACTERLs teen, because while Jack is spared Coffman's gory details, Caitlin gets it in full.

Dots appear almost instantly. God bless Caitlin and her phone that's permanently attached to her hand. She's one of the few people in my circle of friends who understands the ten thousand kinds of weird my life is. Except Caitlin would go into a spiel about what actually causes VACTERLs and I would just glare at the person who asked. I don't have to explain doctorspeak to her or worry that she's going to pity me or freak out—with Caitlin I can breathe.

> **Caitlin**
> Boyfriend or Mom?
>
> > **Ellie**
> > Both.
>
> **Caitlin**
> ETA?
>
> > **Ellie**
> > 5 Mins.
>
> **Caitlin**
> Copy that.

Caitlin is an anomaly of the best kind. Our moms found each other in the blogosphere when we were babies and got thrown together mostly by parental association. We were casual friends, until one of our trips to Coffman overlapped and we became hospital best friends.

Since I've been confined to a couch for the better part of the last two months with only my cat, Tok'ra, for company, Caitlin's constant texts have kept me sane. She understands so much, especially why I keep my friends from the realities of hospital life. Every time I try to talk to Mom about how my friends react when I bring up something like my hand straightening or that time they moved a tendon from my ankle to my hand, Mom gets real quiet and she'll say something like *I'm so sorry.* . . . She takes the blame for my life as if she were single-handedly responsible for my disability, even though not even doctors can tell you what causes VACTERLs. Caitlin never makes me feel bad for what I say.

When I'm not in the hospital we can go months without speaking, and then *boom!*—one text and we're right back in the thick of it. It doesn't matter that her VACTERLs and my VACTERLs are barely alike. We both hold different letters. At this point, I couldn't tell you what the other letters are, but my letters are Vertebrae, Limbs, Renal or Radial (depending on your doc), and Cardiac. Things that for me were largely structural and required a string of surgeries before graduating into maintenance mode. Caitlin's letters are a bit more intense, and her maintenance program is more invasive than mine. No matter our letters, we're both joined forever by an understanding of how an acronym can turn your life upside down.

To avoid Mom, I scroll through social media, catching flashes of Brooke at debate practice and Jack at choir rehearsal. Pangs of loneliness shoot straight through me at being left behind. Brooke and I have done speech since freshman year, when we were thrown together as debate partners. Turns out I hated policy debate and switched to oral interpretation, but our friendship stuck. You can always find us in the speech room, Brooke surrounded by stacks of information and me going through another piece. I would give anything to be back there. Physical pain I can deal—I do deal—with, but no hospital pain scale can measure being left behind.

A picture of Brooke holding a debate plaque stops me midscroll.

The last time we got to hang out was after school in the speech and debate room before my cold went from annoying to debilitating. I laid on top of one of the tables like a lizard under a heat lamp. Brooke was nearby. "Are you actually going to run your piece?" Brooke asked.

"I'm absorbing it," I said, adjusting the script on my face. "Osmosis." My whole body felt like a sack of potatoes. My throat was raw from the previous tournament, but I was pretending that this cold was on the way out. *Come on, body, hold together.*

"Diffusion," she corrected.

"Huh?" I pushed myself up on one arm, script falling off my face.

She flipped her brown ponytail over one shoulder and leaned her chin on her hand. "Osmosis is the passage of water through a membrane. Diffusion is for everything else."

"I know you took AP bio last year," I said, flopping back down on the table.

"And got a five on the test," we finished together, devolving into giggles. Brooke is the brains of our friendship. She could be a doctor or an engineer or anything she set her mind to, but she's still undecided.

"You have a good shot at nationals and can dominate state—*if* you don't wait to step it up."

Post–mysterious illness, it's maybe nationals but not state. I cough again and Mom tenses in the seat next to me. I try to swallow them, the burning sensation in my lungs growing until I'm forced to let them out.

Unlike the colds everyone else deals with, mine just refuse to go away. My lungs would hack until blood and tissue came out if I let them. I spent nights coughing, sleeping only when Mom gave me Benadryl. Not exactly Ambien, but it gets the job done.

I would seesaw between my couch and school. Miss a week, go back, mostly better, and then be out for two days. The process repeated until Mom finally forbade me going back until I'd been well for a whole week.

Even with Mom's new rule, I still didn't improve. Local docs would suggest this and try that but didn't have the patient breadth to understand my complex case. So here we are, pulling in the big, fancy docs at Coffman, trying to figure out what's up with my body, because they got it in one last time. I want Dr. Darlington to have the answers, even though deep down, I know he doesn't.

The bus drops us off at the Family Care Home and I sprint for the entrance. They really try to make this house nice: fake winter flowers in the pots by the door, meals, art. There are plenty of long-term places to stay around Coffman—the transplant house, Gift of Life House for adult cancer patients, and Family Care, which is all about families with sick kids. There's just something forced about it, as if this is their way of handling our lives. I fish out the key fob from my pocket and wince as I bend my elbow, the IV site threatening to royally bruise.

I swipe us through the inside door, letting myself into the large lobby that tries to be a bit of everything. A check-in desk, a living room, a catchall for things families can check out.

A stylized quote in the shape of a house hangs above the fireplace: *Through this together.* That's the only piece that seems made for the space. You take what you can get—what a motto for hospital life in general.

The desk volunteer looks up from her textbook and breaks into a smile. Bright and fake like plastic plants outside meant to withstand the harsh conditions. I ignore her.

Caitlin stands in front of the fireplace, her phone out, trying to get the best angle of her and the sign. This is complicated by her height. Whether it's a product of VACTERLs or just normal genetics, she barely comes up to my chin. Her platinum-blond curls frame her pale face, giving her an extra few inches of height. If her mother didn't forbid it, Caitlin would wear three-inch heels every day even if she has a tendency to fall in them.

"Ellie," Caitlin says, waving me over. She has a full lower arm and is missing only her thumb—which you couldn't tell unless you looked closely. Lucky her. The L—limb defects–is the only letter we share.

Mom hangs back, sliding the X next to our name from OUT to IN on the house board. There are twenty-four names on the board, twenty-four families staying here while their kids go through the medical wringer.

"Come be my photographer," Caitlin says, and the tightness in my chest lessens as the normality of my hospital friendship with Caitlin settles in.

Caitlin shoves her phone into my hands, several photos that are basically the same already captured. Being a photographer is as close as I come to being a part of @APatientLife, Caitlin's handle across social media where she chronicles her life as a constant patient. Despite her many attempts at trying to get me involved, I . . . refuse. Facing that spotlight again—to have people poke and prod at me? No thanks.

I capture Caitlin's poses and then hand the phone back to her. "You don't mind if I steal her, do you, Mrs. Haycock?" She loops an arm through mine and bats her eyelashes at Mom. "I only get her for a few days."

"You can have time for yourself," I add, because that seems to be the collective number one complaint on the blog: no time for yourself because your kid requires it all.

Mom eyes me, and I think I've overstepped, but a smile creeps in. She holds out her hand for my coat. "Enjoy." She kisses my forehead and I squirm away. *Am I five?* She takes my coat and heads for the elevator.

Once she's out of sight, Caitlin and I sag, shrugging off the parental-approved upbeat veneer. That's when Caitlin strikes, turning the camera on me. "What is your one piece of advice about life at Coffman?"

I hold a hand up in front of my face like I'm avoiding paparazzi. "Caitlin . . ."

Hits on *VATERs Like Water* always come with photos of me

postsurgery or in hospital situations. Mom's camera sometimes seems glued to her hand. It's kind of put me off the whole photograph thing.

And then there's the comments on those posts — they skew more gross than normal.

> **Poor Ellie! You're doing the right thing!**
> **She'll definitely thank you for this one day!**
> **We're praying for you and your sweet precious**
>   **angel.**

These posts were always me at my most vulnerable, barely post-op, and she went on to talk about how terrible it was to watch me be in pain but knew it was for the best. Her strength her love, me just an object.

"Humor me. I just saved you from your mother. Plus you want to be an actress — consider this your debut."

Shock filters down my spine like pain meds through an IV. My dream disperses quickly and leaves behind the brutal reality. As much as I want it — to be onstage under the glittering lights — I know that's not in the cards for a girl like me. Or if it is, it's gonna be an endless round of rejections just for the way I look. Which is normal, but I'm not sure it's a battle I want to fight.

I lower my hand, the camera lens as sharp as a scalpel.

Caitlin peeks out from behind the camera, concern creasing lines into her forehead, as if she can see the fear in me. "Pretend you're at one of your speech competitions, then." Her smile is cautious, barely holding back her excitement. I adjust the clip in my brown hair; reaching for that part of me feels like slipping into familiar shoes. Speech competitions are to me what @APatientLife is to Caitlin. My outlet, my *thing*, the closest I can get to my dream. A place where it's talent over looks. "Just try it."

I take a deep breath: *What can it hurt?* I'll comply even as the emotional fallout threatens. What Caitlin has—that captive audience that listens to what she says—I want that.

Big smile, shoulders back—just like at a competition.

I allow that part of me free, my body shifting ever so slightly, adrenaline picking up steam in my blood. This is what I live for—to be in front of an audience. I can almost see Brooke sitting in the front row giving me a double thumbs-up. The vision is both a comfort and a stab of sadness. I miss Brooke.

A small smile that spreads for the camera: I can do this. A deep breath and my lungs crackle.

And as coughs leak out of my lungs, I eke out, "Beware of social media and the nurses who follow your parents." The words come out before I can stop them, probably a solid sign that today was too much.

That makes Caitlin drop her phone. "I'm sorry, what?" Her outrage soothes me. Brooke would have a million questions: *What do you mean your nurse follows your mom? What does your mom do?* It would mean letting her into a place I'd rather keep hidden.

"My nurse today read Mom's blog. She was a big fan of all the work my mom does with families."

"When did this place go so downhill? You'd think with the money we're paying they'd do a better job hiring the staff." Caitlin flips her blond hair and pauses for breath, and a new voice sneaks in before her rant can truly start.

"Are you two interested in the house dinner?" Caitlin and I both turn in what I feel like must be slow motion. The perky volunteer behind the desk, her bright smile exposing as many teeth as possible, gives a little wave, just to show us it was her. Her blond hair falls in soft waves around her heart-shaped face. Her skin is trying desperately to hold on to her summer tan. "It's being hosted by a sorority. They're bringing spaghetti." Her voice is heavy with syrupy concern, the sort that masks itself as medicine. This dinner would be *so good for us.*

"Sounds like just the thing for *A Patient Life,*" Caitlin says, stepping in and saving the poor volunteer. Perky beams at us like she's just done her good deed for the day. Internally I roll my eyes. She's one of *those* volunteers. Much like the commenters on Mom's blog, this type of volunteer has a voyeuristic need to see our lives, if only to save us from ourselves. Usually, the Home is better at fishing them out, but no system is perfect.

Caitlin and I exchange looks.

"We have to eat," Caitlin says. "Or we could always go find your mom."

"Fine."

Perky beams, and at least when surgeons give you bad news you have the satisfaction of knowing you've mooned them at least once.

Chapter Three

House dinners are meant to instill an air of familiarity and family. The food is not exactly Michelin starred, but after a long day of being poked and prodded, I'm glad for an easy meal surrounded by lots of people. They provide a barrier between me and Mom. Can't have a meltdown in a public place.

Caitlin and I load our plates with noodles and red sauce and steaming slices of garlic bread. Her phone dings about ten times before we get out of line.

"So many loyal fans," I say, trying to figure out where exactly we're gonna sit. It comes out harsher than I mean it and I look away from Caitlin. Her whole page is about education. Whether she likes it or not she gets to teach people about disability—and not just what you might find in a medical school textbook. This is her life, but she's not the specimen under a microscope, she's both scientist and specimen. Unlike me, Ellie in #TeamEllie, who is just constantly served up for others to study.

Caitlin eyes me over the top of her phone. There's a question in her eyes, like she's trying to see if it's worth telling me the truth. Panic eats away at me, and for the first time I worry that Caitlin is pushing me away.

"You're sure you want to know?"

"Yeah. I want to know about something that takes up your whole life."

She looks down at her phone again and then back up at me, trying to decide how truthful I'm being. "It's a post on maintenance checkups. Dr. V agreed to be involved." I don't miss the smile that pulls on her lips, unable to hide the pride she has in her work.

"Ah," I say, knowing that type of post all too well. Mom's directed me through several at different ages. Posts that chronicle our days at Coffman, which doctors we saw and how long the wait times were—usually accompanied by photos of me having a complete toddler meltdown—or how many times she had to drug me because Coffman was running behind on certain tests. Those posts too went viral and it was one of the many times she got invited to some local morning shows. It gave her a chance to launch her fundraisers to bring families like ours together. To share knowledge and resources on how best to live like we do. As much as I want to be supportive and promise myself that I will be, my face can't hide the grimace.

I was so sure I could take it. No matter what I do, I can't escape how my mom has put me on display.

Caitlin's mom smiles at us from a group of other moms. Like mother, like daughter; both of them can go anywhere and instantly find friends. Sometimes I'm jealous of how easily Caitlin just slips into the world. There's no crooked spine or missing bones in her arm to snag the eye. Caitlin can blend in. And even though I know it's ridiculous, sometimes I wish I could too. I love who I am, but that doesn't change what people see when they look at me.

Caitlin steers us away from her mother. I raise an eyebrow. No parentals. Check. Instead, she chooses a table with a single occupant. A boy with brown skin and a beanie pulled over his ears sits on the other side, reading a book. His thick eyebrows sit over dark eyes. But neither the book nor the beanie can hide his bald head underneath. Cancer.

I take a step back, not because I'm scared of him but because of germs. Cancer is a pretty common reason to come to Coffman, but usually you see everyone but the kid—parents, friends—the kid is locked away in their room recovering from or prepping for a round of chemo. Cancer treatments wreak havoc on the immune system, not exactly a patient you want mixing with the Home's gen pop.

Caitlin sits without even noticing Cancer Boy, too busy with her fans. I sit, trying to angle us away from him. "How's Elijah dealing with everything?" I ask, teasing her but also wanting to draw her out of this online world and the dangers it poses.

"Good. He wants to know how everything is going. So I tell him everything."

"And he doesn't mind that?" When Caitlin says she'll share it all, she means every thought that runs through her head while she's seeing a doctor. Fears, hopes, and statistics. @APatientLife is Caitlin with a filter.

"Does Jack mind hearing about it?"

"I don't tell him anything." That gets Caitlin out of her phone and she looks at me like she can't believe the words coming out of my mouth. "You and I both know this place isn't exactly conducive to long-term relationships."

I've thought about telling him and even went so far as to script it out and practice. But I chickened out when he draped an arm over my shoulders, unable to believe that telling him would make him see my disability as just me and not a part of me.

Plus I've seen what "sharing" does to Caitlin's relationships. They say they're all in and then she shares this part of her life and they dump her. She has not figured out that maybe her oversharing is what's killing her relationships, but I have enough evidence to prove my theory. Reveal too much about the hospital to your significant other and the doomsday clock strikes midnight.

"Um, and what are we?"

"This is different and you know it." A cough rumbles in my chest, and I clench my mouth, refusing to let it out. My breath rattles the pleurae in my lungs. Closing my eyes, I will the cough away, but the force only grows and I lose, doubling over, catching the cough in my elbow.

Families tense around me and shoot me daggers of *Should you even be here?* That's always the tension in the Home, between community and survival. I come back up, drawing a deep breath. My hair falls out of its clip; it's been months since I had a cut and my brown hair falls in useless sheets around my face. I stand up to go find a wall to help me put it up again.

Cancer Boy's brown eyes follow me while Caitlin's on her phone, and those thick eyebrows rise when I go to do my hair. I know it's weird, but Mom decided that me being able to touch my face with both hands was overrated. And honestly, my right hand is better now. So while the surgery might have ruined my social life, score one for the long-term function.

"They need to"—Caitlin motions toward my chest when I come to sit back down—"figure your shit out. What do you think insurance is paying them for?" *They.* There is only one *they* at Coffman. Doctors. At any given moment they are either your savior or your warden. "They'll be able to get a better picture, at least—see something your other doctors didn't?"

I want to laugh, but a cough stops me. Yeah, my at-home doctors who looked at clear X-rays and the number of cough medicines I went through and were stumped—their only solution was that this was my doing. No amount of me complaining or Mom backing me up would change their minds.

"Not sure the ones here are any better." I don't mean to let that out, and Caitlin bristles at my words. Despite knowing me since I was six weeks old, they always side with Mom. I grew up with those doctors, my life and their careers intertwining; they all asked Mom or listened to her when she wanted something done to me, but no one—not even those I knew so well—asked me what I wanted. At least Darlington is open about his disdain for me. He has zero interest in what I have to say or what I'm experiencing, probably because he thinks I'm about as smart as his prescription pad.

But now he's my only hope. Too bad he's also a . . .

Torture device.

Liar.

Pompous SOB.

Those titles don't require one hundred thousand dollars in debt and twelve years of your life to obtain. For what he's putting me through, he better be worth it.

Please be worth it. I'm not willing to place all my faith in his plan, but I can't abandon all hope. I cling to what I don't think will happen, just to quiet the panic inside my head.

"They know what they're doing," Caitlin says.

I arch an eyebrow at her. Really? We've been through enough to know doctors get it right eighty percent of the time. You have to be your own best advocate when you step into their lair—I mean, office.

"Sometimes the doctors here forget they aren't the gods of all medicine."

She relents. "If you need someone to chew them out and set them straight, you know where to find me."

Caitlin's smile presses flat and I know there's only hard truths ahead. I want to lay my head on the table, block my ears, and pretend to be normal. Go back to the way I am most of the time when I can forget about Coffman and just be me. But being here makes you face reality pretty quick. There's no time to hide when decisions have to be made.

"They don't teach apologies in med school," Caitlin says.

We know the score. You want to have faith in those that care for you, but sometimes it's so hard when they tell you things like *You'll thank us for this one day. It's not that painful. Just one more.* All done in the name of what is good for you. I just wish what is good for me wouldn't break me.

A noise somewhere between a snort and a cough comes from

Cancer Boy, who carefully turns a page in his book, but he's smiling. *Huh, you are listening to us*, I think. A closer look reveals his long eyelashes and thick black eyebrows. So not cancer? But his brown skin carries that deathly sick pallor.

"The doctors here are the best in the world," a voice pipes up from behind us.

Caitlin and I both swivel around to see this intruder. He'd almost have his back to us if it weren't for the circular table. From the authority in his voice and the fact that his thick black hair skims his collar—I'd say sibling. No time for a haircut when your brother or sister is hospital bound. Even in profile he wears the ease of someone comfortable with his body, but he sits stiff in his chair like he's been strapped to an IV pole.

Sibling, definitely a sibling.

I should let the boy have it. Unleash a stream of *Don't even get me started about the medical-industrial complex.* But I pull my words in, hold them tight against my tongue. No one going through this hell in any capacity deserves a full takedown.

But a minor one wouldn't hurt. His sibling can thank me later.

"You can be the best in the world and still not be right about everything. World-record holders don't set new records every time."

"But they have more wins than average." He turns around, fixing me with his wide-set dark brown eyes and a look that says he's ready for a fight.

"Well, if you have a non-world-record-needing case, sure, I suppose that works." This metaphor has gotten away from me. Sports of any kind were never my strong suit, but I think I made my point anyway.

"Maybe if you trusted your doctors—had some faith, you wouldn't be here," he counters.

"So I can just be another case for them to write a paper on? *Look at this anomaly I found among humans.*"

"But they did fix you."

My face drops, and anger runs hot through my veins. Clearly, I shouldn't have held back at first. What would a sibling know about this experience? Sure, it sucks to be the one dragged along, but their life is only mildly fucked up. Me and kids like me, we get majorly fucked up by this system.

"If the doctors had done their *job* right the first time around, I wouldn't be their candidate to try on every test to figure out what's wrong with me."

Anger pounds on every word I want to say, loading them up like a cannon, but before I can let them fly, Cancer Boy cuts in, his large frame pushing me and Team Doctor Boy farther apart.

"Hi," he says. Cheerfulness clings to the edges of his words, which are a sheathed knife that says *We're done here.* "So, doctors are neither good nor bad, they just are. And we're scaring the newbies." He nods toward the other tables where young families eye us with alarm.

"And why should we listen to you?" Team Doctor Boy asks.

Cancer Boy takes a deep breath. "Because I have cancer and my list of doctors is longer than yours."

And there is no comeback to that. Except maybe *I'm sorry*. But even then, hiding under the *I'm sorry* is *Thank God that's not me.* Cancer is no joke, and you don't need just yesterday's miracles; you need all the miracles past, present, and future.

Cancer Boy cracks a smile.

I look to Caitlin to share a *What the hell is going on?* look. But she is just as shocked as I am. We haven't battled for our lives in years. Sure, I hate being sick, but Cancer—with a capital C—is not even close to what I face.

And he's smiling.

The boy opposite me fishes for words, his mouth opening and closing before he finally catches some. "I—I—then . . ." Unfortunately, he didn't get enough to make a sentence.

"It's minor cancer."

"What," I manage to spit out, my mind still racing to get past *cancer.*

"I just wanted you both to stop arguing."

"So, you don't have cancer?" the boy asks. His words come out slow, as if he's worried that Cancer Boy might be a few cc's shy of a full dose.

"No, I do. But it's, like, small cancer. Little c. Totally curable. My parents are just overly cautious."

I look at Team Doctor Boy and he's just as unsure as I am. What do we say to that? It's still cancer—capitalized or not. I quickly look away because I don't want to focus on the boy's rich brown eyes.

"Uh-huh," Caitlin says, the first one of us to overcome the shock of his announcement and then the amendment to his announcement.

"You know, if you have cancer you might as well go to the best place in the US for treatment."

Team Doctor Boy across from us looks like he might want to say more but mercifully remains silent. Cancer trumps just about everything in the hospital.

"Exactly. Glad we had this talk. Enjoy your stay." Cancer Boy gets up and returns to his place at the table, picking up his book once more. Point made.

VATERs Like Water

This is that surgical life

Age: 11 yrs, 4 mos. Entry #836

Alt text: Ellie's crying, her right arm—four fingers, shorter than normal—is propped up, bandages being removed postsurgery, exposing the six titanium pins going through her arm attached to a frame. She's pulling away as the doctor attempts to change the dressing.

I wanted to share this photo because I want to be real with you all. To not just show you the happy moments, but also the ones of deep struggle. Watching my child hurt is something no parent wants, but what is a parent to do when the thing that will give your child freedom comes at such a cost?

If you've followed along since the beginning, you know that we're no stranger to surgery in this family. In fact, this one here is just the start of a long process that will cover at least three separate surgeries and take up the next four to five months of our lives.

Ellie's having her hand straightened. I'm sure this sounds strange to some of you, because your arms were born that way. It will give her so much freedom—she'll be able to go through life with two hands instead of one and another that's basically useless.

My daughter was so scared for all of this, but I kept telling her all the things she'd be able to do once she was done.

Focus on the positives to get through the negatives!

Gwen

Chapter Four

Gallium scans are simple: you lie on a table while the machine tracks the gallium in your body. You can't move. Each image takes at least an hour.

I had four. All that time it was either sit and imagine what I would be doing if I were back home—hanging out with Brooke and going somewhere with Jack—or I'm mentally yelling at Team Doctor Boy. It's easier being angry at him. *Trust, have faith*. What does he know?

I strip off my gown and shove it hard into the trash. Mom's waiting for me when I get out and I just keep going before she can even mention the word *photo*. Blogs are basically obsolete, but it hasn't stopped Mom. There's just enough time to grab food before we have to see Darlington. Despite the fact I've been lying down all day, I'm starving. My phone goes off while I'm stuffing a sandwich in my face.

> **Caitlin**
> He broke up with me

Those words are a punch to the gut, even if it's not surprising. I've been through this dance with Caitlin too many times to count, and each time my anger simmers just below the surface.

> **Ellie**
> Shit. Cait.

I'm so sorry.

Ice cream and movies tonight?

Caitlin

Why would he do this to me? Why do they never
stick around? What's wrong with me?

Ellie

Nothing. They're jerks.

Heading into a doctor's appt.

Be back soon. Hang in there.

Caitlin

Remember Drs are there to help!

I shake my head; even in the middle of her breakup, she has to remind me of that.

"Everything okay over there?" Mom asks.

"Yup." Clenching my phone, I can almost feel Caitlin's last words to me: doctors are there to help. For my other Coffman docs, this is true. I love seeing them once a year just to prove I'm still my own brand of normal. From our first meeting a few days ago, I know Darlington is not like them and this is not going to be like other visits.

"They're going to find something," Mom says. She has the absolute faith of Team Doctor Boy. I guess it's easy when you're not the one being called a liar by your GP. I've never trusted GPs beyond their ability to follow directions from Coffman. When GPs want to play in the big leagues, my body becomes their ground to prove themselves. They stop listening to me, and even Mom has trouble reining them in. At that point the only way to get them back in line is to sic a more powerful doc on them or move GPs, and in a small town there are only so many.

Have faith. If only they had faith in me.

Pulmonology takes us to a new floor, but the waiting room looks the same—as if someone thought they were designing a library and then were like No, *make it a medical facility*. The familiar hardback wooden chairs and dark wood-paneled desk offer a strange sort of comfort.

We're called back fairly quickly, shown to an exam room. Mom and I both make sure the nurse flips on the colored lights outside our door, which signals patients are present. One time they forgot and we were stuck in the room for hours until Dad had to go to the bathroom. It was a rare trip when Dad could come with us. The nurses were so startled because they thought the room was empty—turned out the doctor had already gone home because they thought we were no-shows. Now we always make sure the lights go on before the door closes.

"Ready for this?" Mom asks, her voice shaking slightly.

I give her a weak smile.

As if on cue, Dr. Darlington struts in wearing a suit, like every other doctor here, and a look that says *I know best* mixed with *Listen to me, mere mortal* that some doctors must pick up somewhere in medical school.

His smile is plastic, all hard and shiny. Absolutely zero feeling. He bypasses me, holding out a hand to Mom, saying, "Mrs. Haycock." She takes his hand and then grabs her phone, ready to record everything to relay to Dad.

"So, Doc, what's the diagnosis?" I ask, putting myself out there. Can't let anyone say I didn't try. His cheeks pull so hard on his smile I think they might crack, but he says nothing.

A few taps on the computer and he pulls up the gallium scans; my insides are barely there ghosts.

I do not have a medical degree, but those scans make my stomach sink. "Shouldn't there be bright spots?" I ask, because this test was supposed to find the infection making me sick. I bite the inside of my cheek, trying to quell the panic rising that this has failed again. Maybe I am losing it. As if to prove a point, my body grows a cough that goes until my lungs sting and I cradle my chest because of the pain.

"We were hoping the gallium would show us if there was an infection.

But as you can see . . ." He pauses to click through the different scans, each one as bland as the next. "There are no signs of infection."

Tears prick against my eyes. I won't cry. Not in front of Darlington. In no way was I prepared for this outcome. Deep down I had hope—I told people this was pointless, but even further down, buried under loads of fear, I knew it was possible. This is Coffman! And somehow this letdown, this confirmation that I was right all along, just makes me feel worse.

Mom shakes her head, getting back in the game. "So what are the next steps?" she asks, taking control. That's why we're a team here: she can have it together and I don't dare open my mouth, because if I do, some very nasty words will spill out.

Darlington leans back in his chair, and for the first time, he fixes his gaze on me. I sit up straighter because I won't fold under his scrutiny. Not since the first time I sat in one of these exam rooms and he listened to my lungs has the man even looked at me. I know I can't trust him, but that doesn't change the fact that we're in this together.

"Given all the tests we've done, and how each comes back looking good, we don't see anything that would suggest a cause."

Any hope I had for a diagnosis buckles under those words. This is why I don't have Caitlin's or Team Doctor Boy's faith in the medical profession, because when you need them to do their job, they let you down. They know numerous procedures and the science behind why it all works, but when it fails? They pass the blame and wash their hands of your case.

They're not the ones who have to live in the fallout of the unknown.

"How school's going, Eleanor?" Dr. Darlington asks. My skin prickles because this is exactly what my GP started with before pulling out the *this is all in your head* diagnosis.

Mom looks at me because we both know where this is going and neither of us is on board for it.

"I haven't been there in, what, two months?" I turn to Mom, looking for confirmation.

"And before that? Maybe something happened last year?"

"Excuse me," Mom says, butting in, "I'm not sure I'm following this line of questioning."

Dr. Darlington sighs. "We have to consider all the options with no clear cause, and at this age I think part of this could be psychosomatic."

I swear the room goes so quiet I can hear the nurses' gossip down the hall. My blood has to have stopped in my veins because I don't even feel the pounding of my heart. I can't think. Dr. Darlington thinks I'm the problem too.

"I'm sorry," I say, gathering myself enough to spit out words. The world comes back hard and fast, like I've stepped on the moving sidewalk at the airport and I'm moving through the world faster than normal. Both Mom and Darlington look at me. "You think this is in my head?" The edge in my voice could crack a rib cage wide-open.

"I think there is a problem, but your mind is making the symptoms worse."

"So there is a cause?" There's an edge to my voice that hacks off the last of my patience. Can he keep his story straight?

"As I was saying"—his tone is meant to cut me down to size—"it may be *part* of the problem. I think we also need to look at this cyst on your bronchial tubes." He hits a few keys and the images on the screen shift from my gallium scans to a CT scan where the little bubble my body's decided to grow sticks out among the spray of my lungs. "We were hoping the gallium scans would show us if it was gathering infections, but from what we've seen, it's not. Considering your lung function, I think removing it could be beneficial and will alleviate some of the symptoms."

He *thinks*. Doctors all talk like that. *Think, maybe, our best guess . . .* Language meant to protect them and give answers to no one. Medicine is a hypothesis.

I sit up straight. Surgery. Absolutely not. Not when he *thinks* this is the problem. When he speculates that *I* am the problem.

Mom's fingers still.

"You want to do surgery," she says.

"Laparoscopic, yes. It would be a way to go in and remove the cyst."

"But what about a course of inhaled steroids or a long-term working inhaler. We haven't tried one of those since I was a kid, but it worked."

My lungs have never been model organs. Certainly Coffman and Darlington know some hidden med that could work. A medicine that small-town doctors wouldn't know to pull off the shelf. Or maybe an experimental drug that could do the trick.

"Surgery would be the fastest course of action."

I desperately want to go home, but surgery in my chest won't do that. It will take time to heal. Even going in laparoscopically, they still have to puncture my chest wall and dig through muscles to even get to my lungs. And who knows how long recovery will take. It will hurt so much. From my last surgery I remember Dr. Williams telling me it couldn't be that bad as he pulled cotton from my wound that was stuck to my skin with my own blood. Doctors are excellent at doling out pain, but they have no idea what it feels like.

And on top of that, what will it do for Mom's blog? Readership has been slowly falling off; she doesn't pull in the numbers she used to, which means less money to support the charity bringing families together. I know surgery is gonna turn it all around for her, for the cause. Stats always spike when I have surgery.

Mom shoots me a look meant to zip my mouth shut. "What are you suggesting?"

"Here—" He indicates the cyst at the branch of my bronchial tubes with his ring finger. I don't know why that bothers me, but it does. Why can't he just use his index finger like a normal person? "Removing this cyst, we hope, would remove pressure on the bronchi and allow for an increase in oxygen flow. And there's a possibility that some pathogen is being harbored in the cyst that we just can't see."

Mom nods. Clearly she's considering throwing me under the knife. I want to get well. I do.

But when? And when will I actually feel like myself again? Six months? If I'm lucky.

"And will this fix me? I thought you said there were no clusters around the cyst."

Both adults turn to look at me. I feel like waving my arms in the air and being like *Yes, still here,* but I resist.

Dr. Darlington takes a deep breath, because he's about to explain his reasoning in childspeak and that's beneath him. "There is no infection that we can see in the cyst."

"So why do surgery?"

He looks to Mom for help. She looks down at me with a tight-lipped smile. I cross my arms. I have a say in this and I am putting my foot down. No way am I trusting Darlington to cut me open on a hope and a prayer. I hate surgery enough as it is. The way you just drop out of the world, remembering nothing, only to wake up baked in pain.

"Can we put a date on the books?" Mom says, not even pretending to consult my feelings on the subject. Mom doesn't understand the guttural reactions I have to surgery. How the smell of anesthesia is a viselike grip on my heart. The chill of the OR that seeps through even the warm blankets they pile on top of me. The split from my body as I get pulled under, where the only certainty is *if* I wake up, everything is going to hurt.

And then I go into recovery.

Chapter Five

I fling myself onto the bus back to the Family Care Home, anger punching at the undersides of my skin. Surgery—they're just going to shove me under the knife without even asking me about it?

Mom and Darlington have it all planned out. My fingers shake when I pull out my phone to distract myself.

For her part, Mom is calm. She's made the first hard choice for me because that's what always happens. This visit, this *plan*, is the first real answer we've had. There's still a lot to go through before surgery can happen. Doctors, tests, not to mention the worst enemy of all: insurance.

There's a click to my left and I see Mom with her phone out taking a photo. "How you feelin', kiddo?" Mom asks. The nickname is supposed to be loving. A rope to string us together, remind me that we have an unbreakable bond, and all I want to do is hack it to pieces. There's nothing Mom wouldn't do for me, but sometimes I just want her to chill.

Words swim in my mouth, but I can't catch the right ones. How am I supposed to talk about the absolute cold dread that's taken my body hostage? When she wants to show this fear inside of me to the world?

And just like that, I'm drowning in the past. Walls flash between the pale green of the OR. A strange smell like permanent markers coats the air and a sweat breaks out over my body. I'm fighting through the memory of being alone, strapped down, knowing pain awaits me when I wake up. The memory is so overwhelming that I freeze up.

Messages from Jack blink up at me, a lifeline. His questions puncture the dread, bringing back the dream of my normal life—friends, speech tournaments, classes—my life-life. My fingers hover over the keys. The last thing I want to do is have to explain why I am this way, to lay bare all the remnants of surgery that aren't bound by scar tissue.

"Ellie?" Mom asks.

"I'm fine," I say, trying to pin down the chaos inside me, ball it up, and shove it away. Jack's texts are like a siren's call. I can't look away, and more than anything I want to go back to the place where it's just us. Normally I can manage something—a few lines, an emoji, just a tap back. Enough to let him know I'm alive, but not enough where he feels the need to pry up the boards and discover my hospital secrets. Now, it feels too raw. His texts are just a reminder that I'm stuck here.

Caitlin's open with her boyfriends, and look how that turns out. Heartbreak.

I delete Jack's texts, unable to look at them any longer. Even his mundane tasks remind me that I am somewhere I shouldn't be. I belong there—at school, with him. That is my life and this—hospital existence—is just limbo.

I flip over to my conversation with Caitlin. The tightness in my chest loosens as I settle into something I can do. Caitlin needs me, and if there's one way to avoid my problems, it's to fix someone else's.

Ellie

Almost back—where you at?

Nothing. *Come on, Caitlin,* I will her text bubbles to appear.

Ellie

Caitlin.

I'm coming up to your room when I get back.

The plan is already forming in my mind, pushing out thoughts of Darlington, surgery, and Mom's blog—I'll soothe Caitlin's broken heart and forget whatever just happened in that doctor's office.

Hang on, Caitlin, I'm coming.

"Ellie," Mom says, pulling me close so I can see her phone screen. "Say hi to your dad."

She FaceTimed him? I must look shocked because concern replaces exhaustion in Dad's eyes. His smile is strong but sags on his tired face. I can tell his day has been stressful. He's in the middle of a major project at work and that means long hours, which is why he couldn't get time off to come be with us on this trip. Besides, Coffman has always been a Mom and me thing.

"Hey, kiddo," he says quietly. If Mom is the one who's always put together, always ready for the audience, my father is the stage manager—never meant to be seen but secretly keeping the whole thing running.

She fills Dad in on the appointment. The plan. Through it all I smile, but it's a sickle carving me up internally. The fear of surgery has not left, the cold realization that brings with it the phantom smell of Sharpies—what the inside of an anesthesia mask smells like. I start to freeze up again.

"What do you think, Ellie?" Dad interrupts Mom's eager TED Talk. I don't know if it's the distance between him and the hospital, but he seems to remember this is all happening to me. He gets it.

Now all eyes focus on me.

Just say something.

Anything.

"I don't want it." The last time I had surgery it ruined everything, and I don't think we're moving again anytime soon. Dad is not surprised by my response, while Mom tries to shake off what she heard. No ignoring it this time.

"Ellie, this is what Dr. Darlington is suggesting. He thinks it will alleviate your symptoms."

"Did you hear anything that you just said? Alleviate my symptoms — not fix me. Not ensure this fuckery doesn't happen again."

"Ellie," Mom hisses. Cursing's approved for hospital floors only, and even then the door must be closed.

The phone can't hide Dad's warning look. Parents gonna parent, I guess. "Back up for a second, I wasn't there, but I do have some questions."

Coughs bubble out of me like water from a fountain. My lungs to the rescue! Mom rubs my back, adding a few hard thumps to dislodge mucus that isn't there. I double over and hate myself.

Dad grimaces; worry hangs on him like an old sheet, just making me feel worse than I already do.

Great. Just great.

I force out a few more coughs, not ready to face them yet. Dad just gives me a look like he knows I'm faking. Mom scoots closer. I'm boxed in, nowhere to run.

"We held a date for the surgery," Mom says.

"No." I cross my arms over my chest and pull away from Mom. "Can't we get a second opinion or try a steroid?" I'm grasping at treatment plans. This is sixth grade all over again, when Mom said it was going to fix everything and it tore apart my life.

"Darlington *is* the second opinion," Mom says.

The bus lurches to a stop and I fly down the aisle and out as fast as I can, not caring that I left my parents hanging.

"Eleanor Ruby Haycock." My full name snakes down my spine, turning it to rock and planting me straight into the ground. I don't want to talk about it. Not what Darlington said about me. Not about the surgery he proposed. Unless it's about me cheering up my best friend, I just don't want to hear it.

I turn around.

Mom studies me like cleaning our house, trying to find the next task to tackle. We're going to talk about the surgery. I'm sure she and

Dad will be all about getting on the same page about my health. Being underage is *great*.

"Mom, please?" I deploy an underhanded move. My voice even cracks when I need it to. I focus on the ground, as if I'm trying to be brave to hide my nonexistent tears. She wraps her arms around me, and I shrink away, pry myself free.

"I know this is scary," she says.

She hangs there in space, her arms holding on to a ghost me. Her face darkens, but only for a moment before she realizes, hopefully, that maybe I need a friend right now. "Ellie, we should—"

"Caitlin and I are hanging out," I say, pushing through the doors to the House. As the words leave my mouth, I can feel the ice in my body start to melt. She frowns but leaves me to it, heading up to our room alone. My stomach does flips, trying to dislodge the dread Mom has put there.

I tuck that problem away for later and turn to the desk. My luck is nonexistent today. Perky Volunteer Girl's smile is pressed in place and as brilliant as ever. Did she not just see what happened? Could she tone it down?

"How was the dinner last night?" Perky asks. I glare at her, but she's undeterred. "It smelled delicious," she presses on. I've known too many girls like Perky. There's always at least one every visit to the Home. The ones who offer advice without a medical degree, who think organic vegetables and scented oils can reorganize the body to its proper state. People who make themselves feel better by caring about sick individuals.

"It's been a really terrible day. Dinner was fine. I just want to check out some movies, okay?" I use the same voice I use with nurses and doctors at our local hospital. The ones who still have to Wikipedia "VACTERLs" every so often.

Perky's smile falters like I've slapped her, but she recovers. "Of course." Her voice is apologetic and it doesn't even touch my heart or make me feel bad. She motions for me to come around the desk.

I wave her away when she tries to come open the cabinet. I know where all this stuff is. She hovers and I can almost hear her thoughts churning in her head. *Should I apologize? What did I do wrong?*

Ignore her, I tell myself, and open the doors to the display of movies. There's the full collection of Disney movies for the little ones and then plenty of teen movies and current blockbusters.

Perky sits back at the desk and I try to focus on my task, but a scent carries through the air and I freeze, my hand tightening on the cabinet door. I feel the faint impression of a mask, the one used to funnel anesthesia into my body for surgery.

I turn and see Perky at the desk working on flyers with a large permanent marker.

"Could you—" Perky turns around, the offending marker half ready to spring into action. "Cap that, please?"

She looks at her marker, then back at me. This feels stupid, ridiculous, but the panic racing through my blood is real. I can practically feel the chilled OR air creep in around me.

I grab Caitlin's favorites and sign them out, wanting nothing more than to sink into the floor and disappear.

"I . . . are you okay?" Perky asks. Her voice has lost its helpful edge, lost that sheen of happiness. This is probably the voice she uses to talk to her friends.

I look her in the eyes. "If I was okay, I wouldn't be here." No chink in my armor—nuh-uh. I'm supposed to be some brave soul—at least that's what all my teachers and adults in my life-life say. If only they could see me now.

She flinches as if I slapped her. She reminds me so much of Brooke at that moment, who just wants to know what to do and what to say to not step on an emotional land mine. There is no rule book on how to be a friend to a person like me.

A deep breath clears my lungs of any remaining marker fumes. *It was just an irrational reaction,* I tell myself. *Focus on the things you can do. Movies. Ice cream. Caitlin.* "It was a really bad day," I say, not sure why I open up to her of all people. "And I got some terrible news from my doctors, and my friend here—her boyfriend broke up with her. So she's devastated and I have to pick up the pieces while telling both my parents and my doctor that I don't want surgery."

Perky dives under the desk and I can't believe I actually made her run for cover, but a moment later she comes up with her backpack and digs through her books, coming up with a bar of specialty chocolate.

"Here, I can't . . . I can't fix the surgery thing, but breakups should always have chocolate."

"Thanks." Now I feel bad because she's being nice. Less shiny and showy than her volunteer nice. It's a nice that has heard me, seen me, and just wants to offer a place for me to rest. Not to push me up and make me into a poster for her to look at later.

"And . . ." She looks around and then pulls a key from under the desk. "Follow me."

I follow her around the desk and down a hallway where all the staff offices are. The hallway is dark because everyone's gone home for the day. Perky inserts the key into a door and shoves it open.

I anticipate a kill room, plastic sheeting, scalpels . . . I dunno. Instead, there are just shelves of quilts and blankets.

"Take one. Take two, in fact."

"What . . . what are these?"

"We're supposed to only give them to new families, but we have so many they won't miss two."

"Why are you doing this?" I don't step into the room, unsure how to treat this shift. She's not responding how the commenters do—she doesn't just want to view, she might do something that's actually useful.

"I'm just trying to help." There it is, that volunteer edge to her voice.

"Cool." I pick out two quilts with wild color patterns and Perky shuts off the lights and ushers me back down the hall. I collect the movies and chocolate, trying to keep everything in my arms, but I can't and the movies clatter to the ground and the bottom quilt spills out from its neat folds.

I curse and Perky sprints around the desk.

"I've got it," I snap, and our uneasy truce is over. She backs up and I collect my stuff. The chocolate goes in my pocket and the DVDs fit in the large pocket on the chest of my coat. Wrap the second blanket around the first and force my arms to grab it. Sometimes I have to position my right arm around objects, and because it lacks normal bones and muscle groups, it just snaps back into place like a clip.

"Need any help?" Perky asks.

My arms are full of blanket and Perky is standing there like a scolded child. I don't want another person feeling anything toward me today. Mom, the doctors, I swear I can feel the prickle of Dad's reaction all the way from home. "Can you get the elevator for me?"

She leaves the desk again and we cross the lobby to the elevator. "I'm Veronica, by the way."

"Ellie."

"Have a better night." Her turn of phrase catches me off guard. Like she understood that all these words, all this pressure to help us, can't actually fix us or make it even bearable.

I nod my thanks and the elevator closes, separating us again. I fail to suppress the urge to block the door to invite her up, wanting another partner to face Caitlin with, another person to field questions that I'm not great at answering.

It pops open. "Hey," I call out, "I don't know when you're done, but if it's before seven—come up and join us on the third floor. We have ice cream."

"My replacement should be here in thirty minutes," she says hopefully. There's no trace of Perky here. I smile at her, feeling like we could be anywhere—and not two kids on the opposite sides of a hospital line.

"See you then."

At least with Veronica there, all the focus can be on Caitlin and not my surgery.

Chapter Six

It takes the full first act of Caitlin's favorite Best Picture winner for her to come up for air. When I feel like shit, I want funny, simple fluff. The latest Marvel film would have been top of my list, but Caitlin is art house and fancy cinema all the time.

And her mask cracks. The one that is always in place to hide the sort of stuff that will never go up on @APatientLife. Before the world, we all wear a mask. Each disabled person I've met does this; it's like a mask that makes you accessible to the outside world. We're happy, our pain is bad—but not too bad. We take up space but not too much space. Our emotions are never allowed to stray into territory that might suggest the world at large has no desire to accommodate us. These questions surface only briefly and are then swallowed up by who she thinks she should be.

I give up on trying to follow the story, my mind happy to miss the finer points of filmmaking, and hunker down under the quilt. Perky—I mean Veronica—hasn't shown up yet. Maybe that's a good thing. Caitlin in her normal state keeps a leash on her tongue; Caitlin in survival mode cares very little about who lives and who dies under her verbal lashings. And I'm not sure if Veronica has full control over her "perky" tendencies.

I nudge Caitlin with my feet. Just a way to tell her I'm here. Her watery eyes flick from the screen to me. I smile at her, shoving all the warmth, love, and affection I have for her into the gesture.

She just stares right through me. "What's wrong with me?" Caitlin asks.

I flinch, not with it enough to answer this question. It's branded on my heart, under my skin, on the insides of my eyelids. Sometimes I think when I was born this question was my first breath. *What's wrong with me?* Not a diagnosis, not an acronym that no one understands, but what's wrong with me that I can't find a way to fit into this world?

Her gaze floats back to the screen. "I wish life was like the movies." If we were girls in movies, her question would be referring to her relationship, but we're not in movies, and this breakup—every breakup—always leads us back here: Is this all tied up somehow in how we look? In what we are?

"Solved in an hour and a half?" I say, trying for a joke that falls flat on its face.

"Solvable. Nothing goes wrong in movies that can't be fixed." Caitlin runs a hand—the one missing a thumb—through her frizzed-out curls. They spread around her head and in the glow of the lights look like a lopsided halo.

"Because." I stop myself there. *Because life's not fair. Because we are this way. Because you keep going after and getting boys who don't treat you right.*

My phone lights up with a new notification from Jack. An arrow of warmth pierces my heart and I can't help but be grateful that he's separate from this. He puts up with my wild moods that come and go. Nothing may be simple, but he holds on. I just need him to hold on a little longer—until I'm back and the idiot doctors have finally figured out what's wrong with me and I can return . . . to what feels normal.

Jack
See you soon!

I stare at his text. *That's weird. Maybe it was meant for someone else?*

"I hate that answer," Caitlin says, drawing me back to the present. She deflates around her bowl of mostly melted ice cream.

"Yeah," I say quietly, tucking my phone and all thoughts of Jack away. There should be better answers. Better reasons for why things happen.

I shake my head. What am I saying to my friend? She is the one thing I can fix, the one thing I can save even as my own life crumbles. And in that moment, the mask that holds me in is stripped away and I find the words to this pit of unknown feeling.

"No, sorry." I sit up and throw the quilt off. "The world is fucked up. There's nothing wrong with us—but there's something very wrong with the world. And something particularly wrong with that asshole."

I pace, if only to give my anger an out, and there's Veronica standing in the doorway looking like she's about to run away. What was I thinking inviting her up here? She is definitely not ready for this side of the Home. There's a reason volunteers are supposed to stick to the first floor.

Caitlin sits up on the couch, her head popping up over the back. She spots Veronica and I can feel the lasers in her eyes. Not happy, but no longer on the verge of tears. I have approximately five seconds before she lets Perky have it.

"You came," I say, shock sliding out in between the words. Caitlin's head snaps back to me. At least I've managed to get the attention off Veronica. But now those lasers are firmly on me.

"You said . . . If it's a bad time . . ." She backpedals like she can't get out fast enough.

Oh no, you don't. She can't leave—this is the distraction Caitlin and I need. And what a blessed relief it is. I draw in a breath, frustration and anger tamped back down for another day.

"No, no, come on in, we were just getting started." I will forcibly drag her back, shoving my people-approved mask back on. Because I don't have time to go down that road into my own feelings. Better to put the mask back on and get on with it.

I wave a hand toward a chair and Veronica sits. She fingers the arms like she may use them to push herself up and sprint for the door.

"And to what do we owe this honor?" Caitlin's words are knifepoints meant to skin both Veronica and me alive.

"Veronica," I say, taking my place on the couch, "was the one who gave us the chocolate and these blankets."

"What's your favorite film?" Caitlin asks, and I hold my breath. *Come on, Veronica, nail this question.*

"Oh." She looks to me as if I'd have an answer. "Umm, well, I've always had a soft spot for *Citizen Kane*, but most recently I've found the films coming out of foreign markets to be more interesting than what we're doing stateside."

Caitlin leans back, and a smile creeps in—Veronica couldn't have given a more perfect answer.

I'm good for film discussions only if the topic is the finer points of comics vs. movie adaptations. Caitlin considers my lack of film appreciation her greatest failing as a friend.

"I hope you can catch up; we're not starting over."

I sigh in relief, and Veronica and I exchange a smile. We made it through. Caitlin un-pauses the movie. The addition to our pairing changes the mood. Caitlin picks herself up, slotting back into her @APatientLife self. I nudge her with my feet and she gives me a waning smile. She's not perfect, but she's holding it together.

Little C lets himself out of his room, passing by the cutout opening in the wall, his beanie in place and book in his hands. He wears a surgical mask, but otherwise he looks like he could be one of us.

"Hey, Little C," I say, "join us." Inviting Veronica was a good move, so why not continue to add to the party?

He pauses at the opening, resting his book on the ledge and draping his long arms over the edge.

While not able to be completely open-concept, the Home does try to have lots of visible points into each room. There are "windows" in the kitchen that open onto the hallway and cutouts in the family room walls so that it's easy to see which rooms are free for use and which ones you may actually have to fight over—or have an awkward conversation about.

Little C watches the screen. "Movie night and no one called me."

"Sit and shut it or move on," Caitlin says. She can be a little strict when it comes to her movie-watching experience. I didn't know how low it was possible to get in a movie theater chair until she went off on a girl texting during the show.

I hold out the popcorn bowl, trying to tempt him into joining us. He taps his book on the ledge but then leaves it there. He drops into another chair. "Eh, why not. This is one of my favorites."

Caitlin glares at me. I have now brought not one but two people into her inner sanctum. I incline my head and plaster on a smile. I did—but at least they can speak her language.

"Even if I prefer his earlier work—before he got famous. Lesser-known but brilliant cinematography."

Caitlin's head turns slowly, like a monster in a horror movie distracted with new prey.

I could kiss Little C. Except now I am trapped between three film nerds. My kingdom for an action movie lover.

"I saw those," Veronica says.

And that's all it takes for Caitlin to pause the movie and cement the three of them as friends. They start a conversation about the merits of this director's early work versus his current films.

Where is a white flag when you need it? Giving up on their conversation, I check my phone, but there are no more mysterious messages from Jack.

"Ellie—" Caitlin tries to include me but then sees my phone. "Just tell them already."

I click my phone closed.

"Tell who what?" Little C asks.

I open my mouth, but Caitlin gets there first. "Ellie will stare at her texts from her friends at home for hours—and never reply."

Veronica and Little C trade looks that say I've officially been labeled as "the weird one."

"Ooooh yeah," Little C says, nodding as if he gets it but is really just being polite.

"See?" I point to him as someone on my side—even if it's forced. "I'm not the only one. He—Little C—gets it."

"Luis," he says, holding a hand to his chest. "And for the record, that's awkward as hell."

"I take it you don't give them the Big C versus little c talk?"

"Wait—" Veronica stops us, cocking her head to the side like she's trying to understand a foreign language. "Little c?"

"Like the cancer that is curable," Luis says, looking a little apologetic. Veronica stares in wide-eyed amazement.

"Those exist?" Veronica says. I try to hold in my eye roll. She just had to go and let Perky off her chain. And here I thought Veronica could hang.

"She's the normal one," Caitlin says.

Red stains Veronica's cheeks, but Luis just smiles.

"Can I interview you? For my channel? The whole online disability conversation can be real white. Would love to hear about your experience—if you want." This launches into a whole thing about @APatientLife and I tune out when the three of them take a hard left into a conversation about *The Elephant Man*. I know Caitlin's diatribe on this film and could probably give a decent TED Talk about *The Elephant Man*'s failings even without having seen the film.

I'll gladly accept being left in the dust if it means Caitlin's no longer on the verge of tears.

Team Doctor Boy rounds the corner and we lock eyes. I bet he won't be able to turn around fast enough. He stops, probably unsure if he wants to step into this pool. The last time we all faced off, it ended in a draw. There's a score to settle.

But he just raises his eyebrows, a silent challenge that seems to say *Go on . . . say something*, and walks on through. The corner of his mouth quirks up and I only just stop myself from throwing my phone at him.

"Still here, I see—guess you're still hating on doctors?" he asks, casually talking just to me since the others are still locked in conversation. He stops by my head on the other side of the couch.

"That's not how this works," I say, and inwardly flinch because what a pathetic comeback.

"No opinions, Ellie?" Luis says, pulling me back into the cinematic conversation. The film crew are now fixated on Team Doctor Boy and me like we're up for a major award.

"Ellie is more of an explosions and super-suits kind of girl," Caitlin says like she's talking about a mean commenter. A little self-righteous, a little condescending, and fully disappointed.

Luis pulls back like he can't quite understand how Caitlin and I go together. And the shock on his face only makes me laugh. Caitlin and I make very little sense on paper, but that's what can be so special about hospital friendships. They don't have to make sense and can be forged from the simple fact that we're going through something extraordinary.

"What I'm hearing is that she should be thanking us for expanding her horizons. She can join Ryan's crash course," Luis says. The three of them break into giggles and I roll my eyes. I'm used to the crap about my movie taste, but do they have to do it in front of Team Doctor Boy?

"Very funny."

"*Thor: Ragnarok* was one of the best pieces of cinema," Team Doctor Boy—excuse me, Ryan—says. The three film snobs stare in amazement, or probably what is complete horror. I'm sort of impressed. Jack dragged me to each and every Marvel release. While I do love a movie with super-suits, I'm just . . . particular when it comes to action. I want to be able to go there and not have read the five hundred comics that came before it to understand the nuances. Not even Jack can get me to wade into that mess.

But *Thor* remains one of the best movies I've ever seen with Jack. I guess Ryan isn't all bad.

Mom comes in and there's no more time to process Ryan's love of action movies because unless I am hallucinating, Jack is suddenly there.

My Jack—Jack, who likes comic books. Jack, my boyfriend, is standing next to my mom.

I sit up straight. Blood drains from my face. I try to take a deep breath to make sure my brain has enough oxygen, but it just sets off my lungs.

"Jack?"

He smiles and gives a small wave to the room. Mom looks like she just delivered the best present. My brain fires off a series of thoughts piecing things together.

Mom.

The surprise.

This. . . .

How dare she.

Chapter Seven

I have to be dreaming. I'm going to wake up and find that I'm still in Dr. Darlington's waiting room, where I fell asleep before our appointment. Because what I see is my boyfriend standing in the one place I never wanted him, and that is an absolute nightmare.

"Jack?" My voice shakes, hoping this is all stress. Lots and lots of stress.

He smiles, but his body seems to curl in on itself, hands shoved deep into pockets, shoulders hunched forward, as if he's protecting himself from this place. From us. No smile can hide the fear in his eyes. "Hey." It's so simple, and my chest contracts. His eyes skip like a river stone over my friends, seeming to bounce off their differences before settling on me.

I scramble up from the couch, trying to dislodge myself from this scene. Before he can learn to look at me with the shock he shows to my friends. Jack doesn't fit here, the Ellie he knows doesn't fit here.

Ryan backs up away from the couch as my actions send popcorn flying. Luis just nods from the chair, that single jerk of the chin that boys use to communicate.

Before I can get to Jack and shove him out of the room, Caitlin is ready for a fight. She's never been one to make excuses for people who don't understand us. Just because you grew up in an ableist society doesn't mean you get a free pass. At least, not in Caitlin's book.

"Jack? I've heard so much about you." Her voice and demeanor are @APatientLife Caitlin, warm, welcoming, and definitely meant for an audience. She holds her hand out—the one missing a thumb, as if to test him.

Jack nods and keeps his grip on hers featherlight. "Uh, hi. Ellie doesn't—hasn't told me about—you are . . . ?" He grasps for words, trying to fit them in an order that makes sense.

"This is CaitlinVeronicaLuisandRyan," I say in one continuous word, before I slip my own hand into Jack's and drag him toward the door. We need to be anywhere but here, where my lives are literally colliding. An explosion is imminent.

"Nice to meet you all," Jack says over his shoulder as I pull him from the room. "Ellie, Ellie, stop," he says before I can throw us both into the elevator. Mom hangs back, giving us some space. There's a shift here; he stands taller, with the posture drilled into him by his choir teacher.

With a cautious look toward my mom, Jack steps closer, compacting the space around me, and coughs rip into my lungs. I want to hold it in, because that look—the one he doled out to everyone in the living room—I live in fear of being on the receiving end of that look of pity and hidden joy. Pity that this is the way someone like me lives and hidden joy that it's not him. I know it's not his fault—I can make excuses for him all day.

He steps closer and I want to lean against him. To let the Home fade to gray behind me and exist in his world of brilliant color. As if to prove himself, he takes my right hand, his thumb tracing the ring of scars left over from when my finger became my thumb, as if he can gain experience by association.

It takes everything in me not to rip out of his grasp. The memory of the first time he did it slams into me.

"Please," he said, catching my hand again, his thumb tracing the slightly S-shaped scar running down the back of what is supposed to be my thumb. Whether because I don't let people touch it or a lifetime of surgeries has rearranged the nerves, I saw his thumb travel over my skin, *but not until it reached the base did I feel it, and the shock of it ran all the way up my arm.* "I'm not scared."

He wasn't scared like Mom's commenters, he wasn't scared like Caitlin showing off how she pees standing up to her followers, he wasn't scared because he knows that the world is going to be okay.

I rip out of his grasp, folding in on myself. As with everything in the hospital, it has to be done alone. I draw a shaky breath, my lungs settling back into their regularly scheduled breathing pattern, and Mom, sensing me floundering, steps in.

Jack stands there, hand still outstretched like he doesn't know what to do next. As if a sudden move will irrevocably break us both.

"I was just going to make his mom some tea," Mom says.

Great, I mentally bite out as if I'm shoving the word into a Milwaukee brace. Mom just gives me a big smile. She thinks this is helping me, that this was what I wanted.

Deep breath. And then I manage to say, "I'm gonna show Jack the game room." It's hopefully the emptiest room in the house. Mom nods eagerly and seems to shoo us away. Why does she never check in with me before making these decisions?

Because she's always the one in charge of those decisions, my mind supplies.

My phone buzzes in my pocket and I can only imagine it's Caitlin going THE FUCK, GIRL? But there's no time to verify. Jack's silent behind me and my head is screaming questions as we get on the elevator. He leans back against the wall, hands tucked into his pockets, his gaze possibly giving me a sunburn.

We wait to go down to the first floor and I ask the most basic question. "How's it going?"

I reach for normal. That feeling that I have when I'm home, where everything fits. I'm just Ellie. I do things my friends do—speech and debate, choir practice, and swim team. I study for tests and don't have them performed on me.

That's the Ellie that Jack understands.

"Oh, um . . ." Jack flounders for words, as if he can't process how I could just throw down a question like that.

"Tell me about school," I say, not giving up on the idea of being who I am back home. Jack may be here for the first time, but he isn't joining my hospital crowd.

Jack runs a hand through his hair, catching the back of his neck. "Is that really what you want to talk about?"

The elevator hits the bottom floor and I hold up a hand. I don't want to do this where we might be overheard. Lucky for us, the game room is only a few steps from the elevator and blissfully empty. I close the door—breaking the rules, but I hope the staff understand.

Jack stands there in the middle of the video-gaming chairs, foosball table, and pinball machines, looking as uneasy as if he were in Darlington's office.

I pull my shoulders up to my ears and shrug. "Look," I start, because where exactly do I begin? And I choose to tell him exactly nothing. "I know it may seem strange to you, but yes, I want something normal. Something familiar. I want to know about everything I've missed." In general I've found this is the best way to blend back into my life-life posthospital visits. Learn everything that's gone on so that if someone makes a joke or a story gets brought up, it doesn't feel like a punch to the gut.

"Why don't we trade? You get one question and I get one. I'll tell you about school, you tell me about surgery." There's worry in his eyes and he fiddles with the tie on his rope bracelet.

"How do you know I'm having surgery?" I saw his look, the way his body reacted, probably without him even realizing it. What is there to say? I've learned many times over that people like Jack will never understand me. One day, maybe, he'll get half of it. But right now I'm too tired to educate him nicely. So he's now entitled to the brunt of my anger.

"My mom mentioned it and then she showed me your mom's blog."

My blood runs cold and the world narrows to pinpricks around Jack. I always knew the day would come when my friends would find *VATERs Like Water*. But I still wasn't prepared. There are years of my life on that website, all carefully chronicled by my mom. I thought I'd left all of that behind when we moved.

"Did you read it?" I expect my voice to shake, because my whole body feels like it's vibrating. But I'm calm. So calm it scares even me. It's like before surgery when they pump pure O_2 through the mask before flipping on the gas. I know what's coming and am already prepping to let go.

"What was I supposed to do?"

"You could have asked me." A lie.

Jack rolls his eyes. "Ask you—really? That's your response to all this? Do you know how you respond when people ask you about how you're doing when you're here?"

I shift on my feet just to remember I can. To try to knock some life back into me. What can I say? How can I explain something that won't feel like reopening stitches? "There's nothing to say—don't you get it? I don't have answers or things to say."

There's a line. There's a reason I always stay on this side of it, because there are some things he can't understand. That can be understood only after a lifetime of living and struggling with them. Words fail how to capture all of that, to boil it down to understandable moments.

He crosses the space between us and I feel the heat from his body. I want to be able to relax into him, but I turn away. "But I want to understand—explain them to me. You just shut me out. You pull away. What will it take for you to realize I'm here for you?"

"You wouldn't understand even if I tried," I say, finally letting out what's been bubbling up inside me. There are things that people outside this world can just never grasp. Not fully.

The last time I tried to explain this world to anyone—she was my best friend. I was so sure she could handle it, that she would get my personal brand of normal. Her constant glances at the frame on my arm could have worn holes into it. Mom had suggested I just needed to be open about my surgery, tell my friends and show them this world was not scary. I had to be brave even when my friend's stares cut my heart to ribbons. The rumors started after that, and whispers of *freak* and *monster* followed me everywhere. It all came out on Halloween. I was already on the outs with most of my friends, but Mom worked so hard on my costume—I was a fairy princess. My best friend looked me straight in the face and said: *Freaks like you can't be princesses.*

I stopped telling people anything about my life, especially if they were important to me.

His fingers brush my chin, trying to get me to look at him, and I just . . . I can't. Hurt rolls off him and I know it's bad, but it would be so much worse if I tell him. He'd see me as a patient, someone less than he is. "You don't want to try, do you."

I focus resolutely on the ground. Words don't have the weight to bear my emotions on this subject. Do I want to try? No, because he's looking at my life like I'm an alien. He'll see all these things that I have to do to be normal, and suddenly no matter how great I am, I'll be just another sob story. Someone to pity—something less than human.

"Just give me something." He pushes forward. "I'm right here."

He picks up my left hand, intertwining his fingers through mine. My left hand. Not my right. That one is barely touched when there's a normal option. Perhaps that's where all this comes from. Because I see how people look at me every day and always choose the normal half.

When I don't respond he pulls away, reaches for the door handle, and slips out. I close my eyes and feel like screaming, but much like surgery this is something to endure, and so I swallow my hurt and follow him out.

Our moms are seated by the first-floor fireplace, deep in a lively conversation. Mom can fit in anywhere because any scars she has from this experience don't show up on her outside.

"We should go, Mom," Jack says.

"Ohh . . . okay," his mom says, her words dribbling out. She looks between us; I shrink back, wanting to disappear back into the game room. Then she looks to Mom, who also seems lost for words. Silently, they pick up coats and hats. Mom comes toward me and I duck around her. I'd rather confront Jack than Mom.

"Jack, please," I say, and take a step toward him, making the move I couldn't before. This would be the moment to say everything, to tell him what's going on, do the one thing he's asking for. He turns around, defiant; I am not getting off with just surface words and shallow truths. If I want him to stay, to listen, I have to welcome him into this world. And I can't watch him hate my life—so I stay silent. He nods when I don't continue, like he knew I wouldn't be able to and that's why we're here.

He pauses, fingers twitching like he's nervous. We both don't move, but neither can we give in to each other. "I'll see you at Brooke's party. But I can't do this anymore." His voice is soft and I want to wrap myself up in it. Those words are not a final blade but a needle ready to stitch us back together. He shrugs me off and follows his mom out.

"Ellie?" Mom's arm wraps around me, and it's only when she reaches up and smooths away my tears do I realize that I'm crying.

VATERs Like Water

This is the breaks

Age: 3 yrs, 2 mos. Entry #245

Comments: 546   Bookmarks: 202   Shares: 1K

It's surprising the things that will come out of nowhere and hit you square in the face. And while most of you I'm sure are thinking about Ellie's birth, her VATERs diagnosis, and the rather shocking discovery that our child might not make it out of the hospital—there are more devious ones.

I was surprised at how well I could deal with the unexpected from the doctors. Their cool, detached demeanor was somehow more comforting because they're not supposed to be my friend, my family, etc.—they're a doctor. As long as they are the best— it's fine. No, it's everyone else who's a trip.

Coffee dates dried up.

Invitations for playdates were not just postponed but canceled.

Even just casual socializing—*poof*, gone.

My husband worked sixty to eighty hours a week and had a commute on top of that, so it was long days of me alone with Ellie. During her early years my life was just keeping track of all her surgeries and medical checkups. We straightened her hand and that was a minimum eight-week stay near Coffman. Back surgery was another big one. And of course around every surgery came the ancillary appointments. X-rays, CT scans, pre- and post-op checkups, PT, all accompanied by different levels of Ellie's cooperation. There wasn't time for a lot of socializing.

But when Ellie started preschool and suddenly I found myself in close proximity with my old friends, it was strange. I'd try to

set up coffee or lunch and be met with shrugs and maybes. . . .
Finally I pulled aside the woman who had been my best friend—
let's call her Becky for this story. Becky and I went back several
years—we'd gone to the same college and settled down in the
same town. Got married around the same time, and both got
pregnant.

Becky had been one of my closest friends throughout preg-
nancy. We were, after all, normal then. No one, not even the
doctors, could guess what was in store for me. At first I chalked
up Becky's disappearance from my life as just me being caught
up in the new rhythms of being a mom. But when I did resurface
and look for my friend, she wasn't exactly welcoming me with
open arms.

All I wanted to know was what was going on. . . .

She looked around nervously, as if some knight in shining
armor might appear to save her from me. "I just . . . look, we
love you and I'm sure it can't be easy, but . . ."

"But?" I asked, pushing like I'd learned to do in the hospital,
like I'd learned to do in the face of a doctor who wanted to talk
over me. Stand my ground because no one is going to hand you
anything.

Becky looked around, searching for anyone who could help
her, but no one was coming to save her. The other parents raced
for their cars once they saw us square off.

"But what do we have in common? Your daughter . . . the
other moms and I . . . we don't want . . ."

"She's not contagious."

"No, but what if one of our kids is too rough with her and
something happens. . . ."

"Are you running an underground three-year-old MMA
match or something? I can promise you Ellie may not make it in
that ring, but she's not going to break that easily."

"This is not funny."

"You're right, you not wanting to include my daughter in your playdates is not funny."

That made her angry. Her prejudice was just fine as long as it remained under the surface. "What are we supposed to talk about with you? No offense—what do you want us to say when you're like Ellie has surgery *again*. That she's in the NICU *again*."

"I don't know, maybe 'That's hard, do you want to talk about it?' 'I'm sorry'? 'Is there something we can do for you?'"

Becky closed her eyes and winced because she knew, *knew*, that whatever she had just said wasn't right. "We're all struggling and it's just . . . I'm sorry."

She walked away after that, done with the whole conversation.

I'd already been blogging for a while at that point, but I went deeper then. Looking for other parents who were facing the same things, because if my community didn't want me, then I would build my own. That's how we started our charity to bring families together. Host events where we could discuss issues going on in our lives. How to deal with schools, friend issues, medical issues—be a support system that we couldn't find in our everyday lives.

If you're interested in supporting the cause, feel free to check out this link to donate!

In this together,

Gwen

Chapter Eight

I stare at the ceiling and cough.

Mom took pity on me after Jack left. She didn't question or push, just hugged me and hung on the edges of my world, making sure small pieces didn't float too far away. In these moments, our relationship almost feels normal and I can forget about *VATERs Like Water*.

She's just my mom.

I lie on my side and cough.

No doctor here at Coffman can attempt to stitch up the wounds that Jack's visit did to me. What's worse — they may actually be self-inflicted.

I pull a pillow over my face and still I cough. I'm sure if you opened me up there would be bruises blooming all over my insides from the pummeling this sickness has dealt me.

Brooke's party. It's a shred of hope. If I can fix this, if I can get home and show Jack, things can go back to normal — My lungs burn with another cough.

Doesn't matter what position I'm in, my cough doesn't stop and my brain won't turn off. Mom stirs beside me, my illness pulling her out of a deep slumber. Instead of waiting for her to wake, I get up.

Under the harsh bathroom light, I stare at the small bottles of over-the-counter medicine. I could easily take them, but I don't want drugs that will make my brain foggy tomorrow. I settle for my hoodie and grab a box of DVDs from the shelf just outside the bathroom and head for the living room.

The lights in the hall are on the "nighttime" setting, just a few lights on to make sure we don't die if we need something outside our room. Kitchen appliances cast long shadows, and I sit on the counter waiting for water to boil. This is a familiar routine for me, even when I'm home: kitchen, tea, family room. Dad is usually the one to find me the next morning asleep on the couch as he's heading out the door to work.

I pour the hot water into a mug and add a teabag before heading back to my new favorite late-night haunt: the living room. There's no trace of Caitlin or Luis. Light from the streetlamp spills through the large windows, and cold tries its best to get through the leaded glass.

Curling up on the couch, I check my texts. Caitlin's left me a few. Your quilt is in my room. Is everything okay? Did your mother completely murder you—do I need to play detective?

All of which I ignore. What am I supposed to tell her—my boyfriend and I had a fight? No. Because then I'd hear about how it's my fault because I didn't talk to him. Caitlin is an open book for her boyfriends. She has to have surgery every six to eight weeks, so I understand her reasoning. It's impossible for her to just blot out the hospital experience from her life. In my lesser moments, I might think she was "lucky," which is messed up. Except that I see what happens when she shares every detail of our life here—I just spent the evening cleaning up a breakup.

Credits roll and I settle in with *Battlestar Galactica*. A few mindless hours and maybe my brain will chill out. I set the volume so low that I can hear only about every third word, which is not a problem since I've seen it so many times I can tell you what happens in each episode just by being told the number of people left alive on the ships.

My brain quiets as I cough, sip, and repeat until my lungs slowly ease back into clear function.

I am just getting to the part called sleep when I hear a voice.

"Shouldn't you be in bed?" I curl farther into the couch, trying to stay in my warm spot. There's a nagging familiarity in the voice, like an intern on five a.m. rounds or a doctor I haven't seen in years. I know the voice and know for certain I should avoid it.

Ignore him, I tell myself. My mind starts to drift off, but I can't shake his presence. Even with my eyes closed, I can feel him standing there, glaring at me.

"Tell it to my lungs." I push myself into a seated position, hiss when my feet hit the cold floor. Even the heaters can't keep everything warm all the time.

Dressed much like me in a hoodie and sweats is Ryan. His dark hair is hidden under his hoodie and he stands there, arms crossed, decked out in sweats with logos for different soccer events. Perhaps it's the low light in here or the late hour, but I can see the illness hiding beneath his skin. What seemed hidden before—I'm guessing some sort of invisible illness—now collects in the bags under his eyes and the hollows made by the sharpness of his cheekbones. Still, I can see the boy he was, strength and power tarnished by his illness but not completely defeated.

I'm not sure what earns me more disapproval, that I am here or that I'm in his way. Great. Here to hate on me again. I rub the almost sleep from my eyes. The light from the TV changes as one episode ends and another starts to play.

"Can I help you?"

"Why are you up in the middle of the night?"

"Probably for the same reason you are," I respond. I'm not exactly at the top of my witty repartee game. Besides, he's up seemingly for the same reasons I am.

A cough tickles the back of my throat and I reach for my cup of tea, only to find it empty. I suppress the cough as long as I can because I won't show my illness in front of him.

His dark eyes hold on me.

"Umm," I say, and struggle to find the remote to pause the show. What am I supposed to do with him? We're not friends. I'm not sure if he even likes me.

"I couldn't sleep." He lets out a breath and it deflates him. This was his last barrier holding off the truth. You can always tell the kids who are new to it. The ones who don't know how to adapt or regulate their lives to avoid the triggers of exhaustion.

His confession hangs between us. I shift the remote from one hand to the other, just to have something to do. To buy time until he realizes this thing we're doing here—isn't going to happen.

"And you chose to come hang out with me?"

"You said you liked action movies."

"You wanna watch with me?" I ask, because I'm not a total bitch. He looks at the space between us on the couch like it might be contaminated. Which in this house—fair. "I'm not contagious. Promise."

He raises an eyebrow.

Don't just stand there staring at me.

This stare is there to strip me bare. It's entitled. Not just to what's on the outside but what's on the inside, my medical file. Questions come with the stare, serving only to further fillet my sense of self into edible pieces. There are so many tactics of dealing with the stare and I usually go with ignore, but that has yet to work on Ryan. Overshare it is.

"My lungs suck. I mean, so do like half of my internal organs. Except my liver. That is in perfect, better-than-normal working condition. This is all to say sit or leave but just . . ." My voice carries off.

Ryan's already pushed me to the edge with his insistence that I listen to doctors, and yet he sits down, leans back, and puts his feet up on the coffee table. No words. Nothing. So the overshare didn't work in scaring him off. Fine. Different tactic.

"You were probably the only person like yourself at your school, but here you're just one of many kids looking for cures and answers." It's easier to be like this with him. To let truths I've known my whole life just roll off. I don't have to worry about him, the way I do about Caitlin or Mom or even Brooke. Who cares if Ryan likes me? We're just going to spend a week orbiting each other surrounded by rings of mutual loathing. And then *poof*—he'll be out of my life forever. At least right now he's a nice distraction from my problems.

"You come here often?" he asks.

"No, I prefer the couch on two, but I was too exhausted to go down there."

"I meant—"

"I know what you meant." He was a total normal before this happened to him. Any self-respecting hospital regular knows you don't ask about what goes on in the hospital—you wait for it to be volunteered. He was probably one of those kids where nothing was wrong and then one day the big bad strikes and now he gets to experience a new way to live. I hold up my right arm and pull back the sleeve of my hoodie as if to demonstrate *why* I'm here so often. "Only when I can't sleep, and tonight, I shouldn't have even tried."

"It's a lungs thing again?" Laughter hangs off his words. A silent taunt, begging me to rise to the occasion.

I slant a look at him. The ghost of a smile haunts his lips. First he interrupts my almost sleep and now he's laughing at me. This is not what I asked for.

Well, if he wants to open the door, then I am not going to hold back. For some reason, I lay it all on him. Darlington and surgery. My mom and her determination to fix me. My friends at home. And the crowning moment—my fight with Jack and how our relationship is on life support. "And now I just need to go home so I can explain everything. I have some time." I pull out my phone and show him the text Jack sent confirming that we're not together. And the only way to fix it is at Brooke's party.

Jack
I just can't right now.
We'll talk at Brooke's party.

I finish and take a big breath, my lungs feeling easier than they have since I first got sick this fall. I sink back into the couch.

"Nothing?" I press when I feel the silence ready to swallow me up.

He turns to me. "I don't see what the problem is."

"Of course not." I grab my cup and try to leave.

"What I mean," he says, holding up a leg to stop me. I glare down at him, but the corners of his mouth quirk up. "Is that it's obvious, and I'm surprised you haven't thought of it already."

"Was there a compliment buried in that line?"

His stare reminds me of a nurse who can't believe I did something so foolish. The hospital should just hire him to put the shame into incoming patients.

"You want to get back to Jack as fast as possible." That name zings through me, a million electric shocks to my heart, and tears prick my eyes again.

"Brooke's party is in two weeks," I say. I've never been one to cry in public, reserving my tears for those moments where the world cannot see. Where they cannot judge. I bite the inside of my cheeks in order to hold on to my composure.

"Well, I'm sure they can get you in before then."

"Recovery time much?"

"Then don't do it and you never get back to your boyfriend."

"You don't understand." My breath rattles in my chest as if to prove that I still can't go home. That this, whatever this is, will always be between us if I stay here.

I don't have to look at Ryan to feel his eye roll. Or just his general disbelief that I'm being this obtuse.

I've had enough surgery. Certainly more than my fair share. Forty plus. It's not as high as Caitlin's number—she's in triple digits—but certainly my number is more than the average human has undergone.

So what's one more? my mind asks me.

Because it's one more that no one else has to have.

"I don't . . . ," I start, unsure if I can trust these words to the room. "I don't like surgery." I test the words for the first time.

"If you did, we'd really have a problem."

"No." I close my eyes because here is the thing that just might be too much. I bite my lip and try to keep the deep-seated sense of dread at bay. But I can feel it. The loneliness of the operating theater. Everyone masked and gowned except me. Sheer terror because what I'm about to go through will hurt like hell but will make me better. "It's . . . complicated. Every time I think about it I just . . . I want to run away. When I was six, I used to plan escape routes out of the OR, thinking I could just bring in a big enough teddy bear that they'd mistake it for me and no surgeon would be any the wiser. Because I knew how bad it was going to be."

"Explains why you like action movies."

I turn my head to look at him and let out one hard laugh, trying to hide how easily he's crawled into my mind. "I guess." I lean back on the couch and stare at the ceiling. Strange how easily he can connect the different parts of my life together. Brooke can't even do that and I've known her for years. Jack's never even come close. . . .

"But would it help?"

Just when I thought boy wonder might surprise me, he completely missed the point. I shrug. "Do you moonlight as a psychologist or something?"

"When you get my bill, you'll know. But don't worry, I'm giving you a special rate."

"Oh thanks." I let out exactly one laugh, hoping it doesn't set off my lungs. But for once they seem to get the memo and stay silent.

"They can't force you to have surgery." His tone shifts, losing the joking feeling and morphing.

"You'd be surprised," I say under my breath. Not that my parents would. I don't think. I bring my good hand up to cover my face. Ugh, I hate myself for thinking that. My parents love me. They want the best for me. They've done what's best for me. But sometimes, I just want to be involved—to have a say. To not be made to feel like that is wrong. Mom gets all teary-eyed when I say something that seems to question a decision she's made, like I'm just supposed to be grateful for all she's done. And I am . . . but also . . . this is *my* life.

"Which goes back to the original question—surgery and get better, no surgery and don't."

"Why do you trust doctors so much?" Normally, I do too, but this Darlington—I just struggle to have faith in him the way I do with others.

Ryan and I lock eyes, both of us ready to defend our positions to the end. He breaks first with an eye roll. *It takes two to make a staring match. . . .*

"Or a third option, have the surgery and remain the same. Fourth, have the surgery, get worse. Fifth—"

Ryan cuts me off. "When I had my first attack, it was the doctors who figured it out. They were smart enough to say you need expert care. Top doctors only. They didn't sit around and try to work stuff out on their own. They want you to get better."

His words needle me, prick me like an allergy test. I have the urge to correct him, tell him how not all doctors are good. But knowing him, he'd probably come back with *And not all doctors are bad.*

He'll figure it out soon enough.

Ryan sighs. "Have you even listened to them? Like actually heard what they had to say?"

I turn my head, the muscles in my neck straining for more extension, reaching for that normal range of motion. Side-to-side movement was never my friend. His words tangle up in my muscles, pushing them just a bit more. But I'm not made like that. And I just want him to understand that. "They say it's psychosomatic."

"And?"

"And they think it's in my head." For believing everything that comes out of a doctor's mouth, he needs a vocabulary lesson.

"Well, something's in your head. Did he list reasons, explain why they think this?" I grab a throw pillow and hit him with it. "Hey," he says, moving away.

"You can leave anytime."

"That, right here, is the problem." He holds a finger right in front of my face. "You're not listening to what I'm saying."

"Yes I am." I shake my head and look away. He's exactly like them—like Mom and Darlington—well-intentioned but probably gonna hurt me in the end.

"What did I say." Ryan stays in my space, his finger hovering between us. I want to escape from his strange gravitational pull.

"That I should trust doctors. That there's something wrong with my head. You're just like them." A flash of anger and I pull back, I don't need him. I don't need another person telling me how to run my life.

"No, I said that you need to be part of the process—first it was all surgery, then you bring up the psychosomatic thing. But here's the question: Why suggest surgery if it's all in your head?"

I open and close my mouth like a fish. He's caught me. A smile sneaks across his face and he lifts an eyebrow, daring me to agree with him. "Don't look so happy." I turn away from him, crossing my arms.

"Hand me your phone," he says, holding out his hand palm up.

I stare blankly at his outstretched palm, the long, tapered fingers. A surprise even to me, I find myself fishing for my phone in the pocket of my hoodie. I hand it over without asking why.

He types in something and then hands it back.

"What's this?" I ask, looking at the contact information.

"My phone number. You should have the surgery, but you also need to listen."

"And this is for . . ."

"I'm your accountability buddy—a medical coach of sorts."

"What does a soccer player know about medicine?"

"I know more about coaching than you do. Consider yourself in training."

I toss my phone onto the space between me and the armrest. "I know the sport I'm playing."

"You are not ready to go pro."

"You think I'm not already?"

"I think you're about to get benched."

"And you think you can help me?"

He shrugs, way too confident in himself. "Got to get you back to lover boy."

"Please never say that again."

"You in?" He offers me a hand. I wonder what brought him here. Is it cancer—one with a Big C? Or something else? But it's rude to ask.

His eyes widen when I take his hand. I'm just as shocked. His fingers are cold—not just like it's winter so of course your extremities are cold, but cold like there's something really wrong.

Chapter Nine

Mom is an early riser, which makes it almost impossible for me to sleep in. Even when she tries her hardest to close the door as softly as possible, I'm jerked out of dreamland.

Exhausted, but at least free of any medicinal-induced fog, I roll over and stare at the popcorn ceiling. A cough boils in my lungs and I hold it in, playing a game of chicken with my body until a long stream of coughs erupts, cracking my lungs like eggs.

I crash back on the pillow and reach blindly for a cough drop on the side table. Sucking on the medicated candy, I try to persuade my body that sleep is not my archnemesis.

A pitiful cough fights back against the cough drop and I turn over on my side. My phone wakes up, showing me a list of notifications. I scroll through them.

I can't believe it was so easy to pour my heart out to Ryan. I told him things I've never told anyone. Not Brooke, my best friend for years. Not Caitlin, who knows more about my life here than anyone else. Least of all Jack, who came here wanting to share this experience.

My heart lodges between my tonsils, as if those useless organs can stop its escape.

Jack has been part of my friend group for years. We did speech together, and Brooke and I went to his swim meets. I'd never even considered him boyfriend material. Wasn't sure I even thought of him in that way. He was just Jack. But the more time we spent alone, something started to develop. The more I looked forward to seeing him sans Brooke & Co. And the way his eyes sparkled when he talked about comics became the way he looked at me.

And I liked that.

Jack saw me, wanted me. And the butterflies that flew around my chest were something I'd never felt before. Like I was special, and not just in the bad way. He took me to the dance and we'd been together ever since.

And now not only does he know about my impending surgery but he read Mom's blog. I just have to make it to Brooke's party. Then we can put all of this hospital stuff behind us and go back to our lives. I just need to focus on getting better, on getting out of here as fast as humanly possible.

One notification stands out among the rest—Mom's blog. Against my better judgment, I click the link.

This is how you be a parent.

And there is the photo of me from yesterday.

I skim her words, trying to take in as little as possible. It's a recap of everything that's gone on—with the highlight and big reveal being: surgery! I'm the villain of her blog, it seems, being the one who doesn't want to do this, and she's having to pull rank as a parent. The only thing I read in full are her likes, bookmarks, and shares—which are the highest they've been in months.

Not to mention the commenters only validate her decisions.

You're doing the right thing!
I have just the thing that will fix this—email me
to know more.
We're praying for you!

People are always willing to pray for you, as if you're the thing that's wrong and needs help fitting into the world and not the world that needs reshaping to make space for you. I take a screen grab of the comments and send them to Caitlin.

Ellie
Why is this totally normal?

Caitlin
That is definitely 100% absolutely weird.
She has to stop this.
#FreeEllie
I can make that trend if you like.

I start to type a message, How about you trend something if I win state . . . , but I stop because I'll be back to my life-life without Caitlin. *But she could be around,* my mind says. A new message pops up on my phone, and I click over to it.

I stare at my phone—*Medical Coach?* I tap on the contact.

First Name: Medical
Last Name: Coach
Title: Ryan Kim

Well, I guess he really meant what he said last night. I click back to his message.

Medical Coach
Sleep well?

Ellie
Debatable.
You?

The door to the room cracks open and Mom sticks her head in. "Ellie, you up?"

I wipe my face with the sleeve of my hoodie and force a smile, hoping that I come off as natural as possible. The fact that I've been sick for the last three months is probably helping me more than I'd care to admit.

Mom's smile is warm and, bless her, she has coffee—it's the peace offering I need. Plus caffeine is a natural cough suppressant, so in between doses of medicine I can have all the coffee I want.

My lungs do not like the change in position, popping off a few coughs. To her credit, Mom doesn't even flinch at these. She sets my coffee on the side table and retreats to the desk chair. We live in the wreckage of our shattered conversations. Her words still cut like shards of glass, trying to wear me down into accepting her position. The blog says it all to everyone, and sometimes I wish these things could just stay between us.

Everything she's done for me. Her words ring in my ears. A response to a comment I've never forgotten: *My life is Ellie's health. There is nothing left for me.* Eleven words was all it took for me to zip my mouth shut about everything. Caitlin can talk all she wants about how easy it should be to talk to my mom, but how am I supposed to do that?

What took me so long to figure out was that as much as she may want her own life—the only one she has is about me and so she won't let me go. Freeing myself will kill her, and she's the only one who's been here from day one. Even Caitlin can only guess at those early years.

I sip my coffee, wondering why Mom's up because we don't have a list of appointments. The medical coach might call this a bye day. All I want to do is stay in bed, hang out in our room, and plead illness.

Mostly true.

Mom carefully sets her coffee down on the counter and folds her arms across her chest.

I tense, ready for a fight. Last night still hangs in the air and clings to our clothes. Words and their tangled meanings that just drive us further apart.

Now we're both on the defensive. "I heard back from Dr. Darlington's office." Mom's voice is cautious.

I run my finger over the edge of my cup. "And?" I try to keep my voice as neutral as possible. I don't want to rock this boat, but pain and hurt sneak in there, souring my words and turning them into darts.

"I scheduled the surgery—" I open my mouth, but Mom holds up a hand. "Let me finish. I think this is best, but I understand you have questions."

Resentment pushes against my skin, making me feel like I'm too much. What she doesn't say is that there is a choice. I don't get to decide to have surgery or not, I can just be more okay with it than I was yesterday.

I slump back against the headboard. Ryan's words are caught in my sleep-deprived mind. *Why suggest surgery if it's all in your head?* I try to come up with every possible answer to that, but Coffman is not like other hospitals. Here, doctors don't get paid per test or per surgery—so it's not financial gain.

"And Dad okayed this?" It's my last trump card; any hope of putting this off lies with him. Surgery has to happen ASAP so I can whiz through recovery in time to get back to Jack, but I can't shake off my body's natural reaction to the threat of surgery. The world takes on that milky shade of blue green. As if some kid who really liked *Star Wars'* idea of blue milk grew up to design ORs.

Am I really going to do this? Just waltz back into Darlington's office and be like *Yes, please let's discuss cutting me open?*

Ping!

Medical Coach
See reason.
Remember they wouldn't just suggest surgery.
You have to talk to the docs.

Ellie
So terrible. Got it.

Medical Coach
Nice deflection.
But it won't help you.

Ellie
Foul!

Well, all right, then. I take a big breath. *Jack, this is all for Jack.* "I was just hoping we could see him today." Again, no matter how hard I try to sound nonchalant, my words crumble to the ground between Mom and me, separating us even further.

"You want to see him? Dr. Darlington?" Mom asks, her voice heavy with skepticism.

Mom narrows her eyes at me. She comes up to the bed and puts the back of her hand to my forehead. "Are you running a fever now too?" There's a lightness to her question that can't quite block out the concern. In moments like this, I feel like we've fallen back into safe territory.

"I'm fine," I say, ducking under her hand and dropping my phone in the process. I feel secure that we've found this joking manner again. It's back to us facing this together rather than her chronicling my life. There's hope here that we can be that again.

"About last night," I start. It's hard to talk around the tightness in my chest, but I know that the only way to ease this will be to talk. Sometimes I can take this pain, but I can't take every punch.

"Your father and I just want what's best for you. I know that's not always what you want to hear. And trust me, I know you have not always been happy with our decisions, but they are because we love you."

Her words are final and burn off the ache in my chest, replacing the hurt with fury. How dare she talk to me like I'm still four and in need of major surgery? I was a child; I had no idea how to weigh in on what was happening to me. But now I can form words, thoughts, ideas. In two years, I am going to be the person in charge of myself and my parents will have nothing to say about it.

I am going to have the surgery because I want my life back, but I will at least share my thoughts on the subject.

"I know," I say, trying to look cowed, apologetic—things I hardly feel.

"You need this, Ellie. We all want you to get better."

My phone buzzes with a new message.

Medical Coach (1)

I close my eyes. Do I really want Jack back badly enough to go through surgery? Of course I do. I want to go back to hanging out in the halls after school with him, working on our respective speech pieces. The faith he has that all of this is going to work out. I may not be able to see a future for myself doing what I love, but Jack can. That means playing nice.

"I'm sorry," I say, and drop my head down into the blankets, fighting with my own emotions as much as I fight with my mother.

This wasn't how this was supposed to go.

Mom's shoulders sag. "I'm sorry too." She comes over to the bed and pulls me up into a seated position.

"Get dressed," she says. I can hear the humor in her voice. We may have had harsh words last night, but they're all one-sided because they never seem to cut Mom. "I think we both need a break from these walls. Let's do something fun."

Chapter Ten

I hope this *something fun* is actually something fun, like a bookstore or a movie. More likely it's going to be something "fun" as in "FUNctional." This is a term Mom coined when I was five and refusing everything left, right, and center that had to do with the hospital. Calling trips, blood draws, and wearing the brace "something FUN" worked on me.

I was five and naive.

Caitlin and her mom wait for us in the lobby—there's hope for real fun yet. And at least this version of fun includes Caitlin.

Large sunglasses cover her face, but the hint of a smile tells me she's already moved on from her breakup last night. Her corkscrew curls fly every which way, and as soon as I am close enough, she whips her phone out, snapping a photo of us.

A sneak attack.

Her grin is wild and untamed. Caitlin is a girl of big emotions. She swings through them almost as easily as breathing and lives them all out loud.

"Not for social media," I say. I know what Caitlin's feed means to her. I want to love how "out there" she is. She shows off "our" perspective, but every time she gets near me with that camera . . . I just have flashes of what happens on Mom's blog.

I want to be as comfortable in front of a bunch of people I don't know, but I just . . . years of Mom's blog has taught me one thing:

people are not there for me. And there's a solid ten percent that should just be removed from the gene pool. The ones who call Caitlin a *freak* and *ugly* or dare to say things like *If I were in your shoes, I'd kill myself.*

Caitlin pulls down her sunglasses and glares at me. "We look cute." She shows me the photo, and yes, despite being deep into a hospital visit and post-breakup, we do look good. It almost makes me want to say yes. "It could be good exposure for your speech thing."

"It's not about your social presence." Thank all that is good. Hard to be a social media darling when you don't exactly meet the industry standard of beauty.

"Fine." Caitlin draws out the word. "I don't know why I bother—besides, this isn't for A *Patient Life*—this is proof of life. If this were for the media we'd def need a redo."

"What?" I ask.

"My friends want to know that you exist. They're starting to think you're just a figment of my imagination."

"You talk about me to your friends?"

"I mean there's not much to tell them, but yeah."

"Any idea where we're going?" I ask, forcibly changing the conversation as our moms lead the way to our car. Compacted snow and salt crunches under our boots.

"Apparently that is privileged information," Caitlin says. "You doing okay?" There's an unsaid question peeking out from between her words. She saw Jack last night; she saw me leave.

"Are *you* okay?" I say back to her.

She sighs. "He was an asshole." She adjusts her sunglasses and squares her shoulders, ready to take on the world again. "He got scared when I mentioned that this was going to be a regular thing." She waves her mittened hand at the world, but I know what she means. The Home, the hospital, Coffman.

"Is this where I ask about Jack?" she asks innocently.

A lump forms in my throat. All that I did to protect him from this place: trips in the summer, where absences were rarely missed; never,

ever letting anyone see me adapt stuff; being my normal self so that no one could point to me and be like *You're different.* Only bad things happen when they see you're different. Case in point—last night. Jack finally saw this part of my world and it nearly broke us.

My lungs seize. A cough stumbles from my throat and I pull away from Caitlin and her probing questions. She presses her lips into a fine line and sticks her phone in her pocket, focusing all her attention on me. I need her to look away. Caitlin and I know how far to push each other, and I need her to respect my limit. Coffman's already a place that will push you further than most people can imagine.

"Well, let's hope this is *fun*," Caitlin relents, playfully nudging me. I looked after her last night, and this is her reminder that she's here to look after me today. We've both lived with our parents long enough to know that "fun" can mean a lot of things that resemble nothing like the definition of the word.

Not wanting to push anymore, I pull out my phone and see three new messages from Ryan.

Medical Coach
One—clearly you know nothing about soccer.
Two—maybe I like the show.
Thought about actually talking to the dr?

Ellie
He's in surgery.

Medical Coach
And he can't fit you in today?

Ellie
It's almost cute how you know so little.

Medical Coach
That was a joke.

Ellie
Sure it was.

I pause, unsure why I want this information, but I let my fingers go.

Ellie

Do you tell your friends about this?

Coffman hospital stuff?

I hit send and instantly regret it. Maybe I crossed a line. He's a medical coach, not a life coach, not a friend. But still I crave his answer from his opposite view of my world.

"Who are you texting?" Caitlin asks, trying to look at my phone.

"No one," I say, and shove the device back into my pocket. Caitlin would never understand my need for a medical coach. She has always had a complete say in her medical life.

Me, I just sort of hang on with enough knowledge to be dangerous. I can speak medicalese, but when it comes to the dialect of doctor, I'm barely conversational. The difference is I know what's being said and can understand the procedures of medicalese, but I have no clue when it comes to the conjugation, grammar, or sentence structure. Most of the time they seem to pull things out of their asses and pray that it works. Few actually take the time to translate what they mean.

Outside is a blur of colors and ash-gray snow. Caitlin's mom turns around from the front seat; her bright lipstick makes her lips seem comically big for her face. "I read your mom's post last night—how are you feeling about surgery?"

I want to melt through the seat belt. It might be the only safe way out of the car. If Jack was angry at me, I can only guess what Caitlin has in store for me. Surgery wasn't just something I didn't tell Jack, it was something I told no one.

Except Ryan.

"What." Caitlin pulls back and stares at me, and I don't need to look at her to know she's a deadly combination of angry and surprised. We tell each other everything about the hospital. Every appointment.

Every test. Every surgery. Except this one. Last night was a lot, and the last thing she needed was me and my problems.

Her mom flinches and I meet my mom's gaze in the rearview mirror. She seems to offer an apology and I look away—not accepted.

"Oh, um, yeah," I say, words coming out of my mouth in weird bursts that make no sense no matter how hard you squint at them. "I . . . yeah . . ."

I type off a message to Caitlin.

> **Ellie**
> I'll explain.
> It's a long story.

"Not as excited as you are about the *Morning Show* appearance?" Mom chimes in with a distraction. She gives me a wink in the rearview mirror, so proud that she's *got my back* and completely oblivious to the other words that came out of her mouth, but I caught them all.

> **Ellie**
> Oh.
> TV SHOW????

> **Caitlin**
> Don't try to distract me.

> **Ellie**
> A. TV. APPEARANCE.

And that is the final word on the subject until Mom pulls into the parking lot of a JOANN fabrics. I don't know why this was such a secret—it's not like we've never been here. I guess Mom decided to go with FUNctional, because she always knows what's best for me. Someday maybe she'll ask me.

Caitlin pushes her sunglasses up on her head, trapping her curls in a makeshift headband. We race for the store, Caitlin claiming me and dragging me toward the yarn section.

"Two skeins," Caitlin's mom calls after us. This has always been more Caitlin's playground than mine.

"Two minimum, got it!" Caitlin says, ignoring her mother's limits. Caitlin learned to crochet years ago from a night nurse who decided she needed to do something productive. When she's stuck in the hospital, she just does baby hat after baby hat. It's easier because she saves on shipping. The nurses can just cart them down to the natal ward.

Caitlin drops a basket in the middle of the aisle. Around us walls of yarn reach for the ceiling in every shade and gradient imaginable. Caitlin trolls the aisle like a general inspecting her troops.

"Don't think we will not be stopping by the embroidery aisle," she says, stopping to feel the softness of one. Her words are a threat meant for me, that I will be doing the "good" thing for my fingers.

"Don't think I will buy anything." I make a face—that was a weak comeback.

We face off in the yarn aisle, two friends betrayed by each other. Caitlin just points her crochet hook at me. Caitlin crochets, I embroider. The whole holding a needle and hoop thing was highly suggested by my physical therapist around my hand straightening as a way to keep my fingers loose. Apparently one of the potential downsides of said procedure is that you can stretch tendons too far and permanently freeze your hand into a fist.

Not great, all things considered, but Mom still felt like this straightening process was absolutely necessary. I flex, as much as I ever could, the fingers of my right hand; they still work. I can do more things with my hand straight than I could when it sat at a ninety-degree angle to my wrist. I just wish a better-functioning body didn't come at the cost of all my friends.

My phone dings in my pocket and I ignore it.

"A TV show?"

"It's not—"

"If you say it's not a big thing—you're wrong, try again." Despite being hurt that she didn't talk to me about it, that I wasn't an immediate text, I'm so happy for her. It fills me up so much that it stings and hurts.

Caitlin sighs. "Some people think what I do is cool. They want to give me a platform to reach more people." The words come out of her mouth brimming with passion but hidden under a sullen mask. "And what about what you want?" Caitlin turns away from her success without a second thought. She casually dumps two skeins into her basket. "Surgery? We both know how you feel about that."

"Not much of a choice." My voice is so small I'm surprised it can be heard over my heartbeat. How can she bring this back to me, when we should be screaming and celebrating her? Screw two skeins—we are going to buy the whole shop.

And yet my friend just stands there, fiddling with her crochet hook. We're both too good sometimes at hiding what we truly feel. Caitlin may be a girl of big emotions, but that doesn't mean she doesn't know how to bottle things up inside too.

"You need to talk to your mom." Caitlin cocks a hip, whatever confidence she lost now back in full force.

"The hits on her blog are going back up, which will help her organization," I say. The blog is one of those things that I just *get* to be a part of.

"Screw her engagement ratings, and she can find a way to fund her families together project without pimping you out. I mean you can't do that speech thing—"

"Why do you keep bringing that up?"

With precision, Caitlin jabs her crochet hook into the nearest skein. "Don't worry, I'm buying it," Caitlin says, tossing the mutilated yarn ball into her basket. She turns on me, crochet hook at the ready again. "Because I want to feel like I'm part of your life. I say this with all the love in my heart—what is wrong?"

"My friend didn't tell me she got the opportunity to be on TV." I reply, because now who's keeping secrets?

"Trade?" Caitlin says, breaking the standoff.

"Fine."

I motion for Caitlin to go first.

"Fine. I'll start. I didn't tell you because I'm not doing it. It's just nice to be asked."

"You live for *A Patient Life* getting asked to do this morning show — it's like your dream."

"And what do we both know about dreams?"

The hard truth forms a mountain range around us, one neither of us knows how to scale. And here I thought Caitlin had some clue, was maybe a bit further ahead, willing to lay down some sort of scaffolding for me to follow.

We back away from that topic because there is only so much existential dread a person can handle in one forty-eight-hour period.

"Why didn't you tell me about what happened with Jack last night?" Caitlin asks, her voice quiet, as if she's stripped away everything else and is showing me the real cracks in our friendship.

Her wide hazel eyes lock on to me, demanding answers and refusing to take my shit. She's never had a problem with telling people she doesn't want something. It may happen anyway, but not without her voicing her very strong opinion.

I pick at my cuticles, unsure how to answer her question. "Did you know that she thought bringing Jack here was helpful?" Each word grows softer and softer. But each one brings a new level of understanding to Caitlin. "How am I supposed to tell her it wasn't? She thinks she knows best."

"Shit," she says. Her annoyance at my reticence disappears. "But weren't you glad to see him? You disappeared . . ." Her words trail off, because realization hits her.

Hard.

"Ellie," Caitlin says. She takes a step forward like she'll comfort me, wrap me up in her arms.

"Please don't." I press myself back into the racks. The last thing I want is to be touched.

"Is everything good with Jack?"

"If I can make it back by this party, we can make this work."

Ping!

My phone goes off; I don't reach for it.

This time it's Caitlin who looks deflated. "Why am I just finding any of this out now? Come beat down my door and pour your heart out next time." She doesn't come any closer, and I'm thankful that she knows me well enough to give me my space.

"You have a lot going on. Apparently turning down TV gigs." That's my excuse for everything. I don't tell my friends because this is messy and their lives can't handle it.

"Oh, come on. Not that excuse. We both have a lot going on. Have you seen our medical files?"

"Yours is bigger."

She rolls her eyes. "Technicality. Each of ours is bigger than ninety percent of the population." Her smile wavers when her joke fails to cheer me up. Her voice shifts, and she draws closer to me as if we're in this together. Two against the world.

"Why are you turning this opportunity down?"

She looks off down the aisle away from me. "I can't do live on camera."

"You do stories all the time."

"Yes, and I take five million tries before I post one."

"If you need help I happen to be a very good public speaker. Plus I've watched my mom prep for this stuff." I wince—not great, but also not a lie.

"And that's the last person I want to be like." Caitlin picks up her basket. "Come on." When I don't move, she adds, "If you're going for torture, we might as well go to the embroidery section."

"Excuse me?"

"Here's the CliffsNotes so we can get to the real issue: 'I'm Ellie and I think the hospital is the worst. I don't want any of my real friends to know what it's like here. Wah wah poor me. I just want a normal life.'" She rushes on so I can't interrupt. "I say this because I care. I know this sucks, but you need to hear this. Have the surgery and get better. Tell your friends about this place—speaking from experience, it's not so bad. People will always let you down if you don't let them in."

There are so many comebacks I have to that point, starting with *Remember what happened when you let your boyfriend in?*

When I don't respond, Caitlin loops her arm through mine and pulls me toward the embroidery aisle. The tops of her curls tickle my nose.

And because we're back to normal—I offer up one thing. Perhaps it's penance for keeping everything so close, or maybe it's just something I can't keep to myself anymore. And maybe I hope that she can tell me I'm wrong. "Bad things happen when I let people into this world," I say. Caitlin runs her tongue over her teeth like she's trying to swallow the words I spoke. But she doesn't refute me, because inside she knows it's true.

Chapter Eleven

I stop by our room to grab another dose of cough syrup. Mom looks like she wants to talk, so I quickly run out the door again, saying something about meeting Caitlin. I've done the FUNctional, now I can do the actual fun.

Just to spite everyone, I plan on embroidering this project with the words *Darlington Is a Dick.* Just thinking about him pastes images of pale walls, bright lights, and that heavy smell of antiseptic over every thought. This place is safe, and much like our house, as long as I stay here, she doesn't need to keep tabs on me.

Medical Coach (7)

I scroll through Ryan's messages as I go find Caitlin. It was foolish to ask him if he told his friends about the hospital. But I'm curious as to his answer.

Medical Coach
Some
But not a lot
My friend Sarah gets it
Sort of
Her girlfriend has juvenile arthritis

I lean against the wall, taking in what he has to say. There is a whole novel contained in the *some* and *sort of.* An unsure footing, and so you stay quiet but hope that maybe someday—not today and probably not tomorrow, but someday—they will get it.

Medical Coach
Why?
Trying to figure out what to tell Jack?

And just like that, he's overstepped. I click my phone closed and head for the living room.

Caitlin's claimed the couch and Luis sprawls out on the floor, a new beanie covering his bald head. I want to ask why he's bald already if he hasn't had chemo yet—but in the hospital, you don't ask people what they're in for.

"Here to save me or just hiding out?" Caitlin asks when I appear. Yarn loops easily over her fingers and she's already started on a new hat.

"Save you from what?" I ask, dropping onto the couch. Our FUNctional trip has taken its toll and now every movement feels like I'm lifting two tons.

"He's making me watch *television.*" Caitlin pours all the venom that I save for Darlington into that word.

"You do know that this is the golden age of television, right?" Luis says, raising his bushy eyebrows in question. Harsh winter light cuts through the window and Luis picks himself up to close the blinds.

Caitlin holds up a hand. "Please, TV is in the process of cannibalizing itself. There are a few episodes that are decent, but overall— dying art. Film is forever."

I sink into the couch, letting their conversation play in the background. Ryan's words stare up at me from my screen, creating conflicting feelings in my chest.

"Ellie," she says, and squeezes my arm, the one still bruised from my gallium scan IV. I wince and shake her off. She's crouched over me, her eyes fixed on my phone. "Why do you have a medical coach? Do you need me? Is this why you're having surgery? Is this something of your mother's?" Caitlin says. She starts off with mock hurt, but slowly the sense of *You will answer this or else* laces into every word. I feel a pang of guilt because I didn't go to her. Caitlin is a pro at this life. The hospital hasn't torn her life apart, she's made it work for her. She gets me . . . but not how our lives are different. We are not science experiments; I can't just replicate her success.

"No, although Mom would probably pay for the service," I say.

Luis holds up a hand, like he's asking a question. "I'm sorry, medical coach? Is that a thing?"

"No," Caitlin and I say together. Luis nods and motions for us to continue.

"It's nothing."

"How is everything in your life nothing? 'My mom blogs about me'—eh, whatevs. 'I have a rare genetic disease'—you know, it happens. 'I have a medical coach'—doesn't everybody?" Each question is punctuated by a strong jab of her crochet hook. And just like that, she took it too far.

"We can always practice for your TV gig."

Caitlin gives me a look that dares me to cross her and she'll find new ways to kill someone with a crochet hook.

"You can't hate TV so much that you refuse to go on it. I am going to help her overcome that."

Caitlin and I lock eyes, both completely unwilling to move from our position, and for the first time, I feel like we are on the same footing. "Can we both agree that was terrible phrasing?"

"Fine." I wave it away, not willing to get in a fight about the politics of using *overcome* in regard to us. People love to say things like *You can overcome your disability*. Caitlin did a whole month just on the ableism behind everyday phrases. "But you know it would be great publicity for *A Patient Life*."

The words seem to scrape the inside of my throat. I want Caitlin's message out there, because at least it's her life and she's choosing it.

"After everything I found out today—I demand to be told what's going on," Caitlin says, ignoring the conversation and turning the spotlight on me. I just glare at her. Caitlin squares her shoulders, ready for battle, and pulls out her phone. "Should I just call your mom and tell her what you really think about the blog?"

"You wouldn't. . . ."

Her finger hits the button.

"It's just Ryan," I say before the call can even connect.

"Ryan—the guy from dinner Ryan? Newer than me, how can he be a medical coach?" Luis asks.

Caitlin holds up a hand to stop me, as if this news is too much for her to handle. "Ellie, are we friends? What makes you go to *Ryan*—the one who was like *Oh doctors, they're always right!* And you didn't lead with that? Are we still even friends?"

I roll my eyes. Caitlin is one hundred percent overreacting, which for her is just reacting. "Do I need to answer your first question, Caitlin?"

"Yeah, I would like group verification. With witnesses."

Luis gives a two-finger wave to show he's listening.

"He showed up last night and we . . . started talking." I shrug; this is not a big deal. The last thing I need is for Ryan and Caitlin to form a united Team Doctor or something.

"So this is while you were alone—watching that space thing?"

"That *show* is actually brilliant."

"Oooh, which show?" Luis asks.

"*Battlestar Galactica*," I say at the same time that Caitlin says: "Not important."

"Never fear, I am here to settle any and all TV disputes." Luis hits pause on the TV show in progress and turns around to give us his full attention. It's like he's suddenly become the judge in the case of our friendship.

Caitlin holds up her crochet hook to silence him. "Back to the original question. Why is *Ryan*—who you are on a first-name basis with—texting you? And why was I not informed immediately? Did he know you were having surgery first?"

"You're having surgery too?" Luis says, brightening.

I look to Luis for help. Can't he be my way out of this like he was the last time? But he holds up both hands in a sign of surrender. There is no way he's stepping between me and Caitlin, and honestly, I can't blame him. When Caitlin gets on a roll, it's best to just lie down or get out of her way.

Caitlin glares at him. This is no time for interfering, and he seems to fear Caitlin and her hook more than wanting to help me distract her.

"He just sat down, what was I supposed to do—say no, go somewhere else?"

"Yes, you tell him he is not welcome. That doctor's orders say something else. Why would you take advice from him?"

I pick at the edge of my phone case. A message pops up from Brooke:

Brooke
Probably a long shot . . .
any chance of you making Jack's concert at the
Morelands this weekend?

My breath stops when I see Jack's name. It's still a raw emotion, and it makes me miss him and what we had. I'm sure Ryan would be like *Try to figure something out*. There's a small—and I mean small—chance Mom might let me go to the Moreland Mall this weekend.

"He's just helping me with stuff."

"Oooooh, *stuff*?" Luis asks, raising his eyebrows at me. Caitlin and I both roll our eyes and look at him. Luis just holds up his hands in apology, recognizing the line he crossed.

Caitlin turns to Luis. "And do you know how I found out that my friend of five years and over thirty hospital visits is having surgery? My mother."

Luis makes a lemon-sucker face. "That's low." They both focus on me, waiting for my brilliant answer that will excuse all of this.

"It's not a done deal, and if . . ." The sentence dies on my tongue, because it may happen. If I want to get Jack back. If I want my life back.

"Hey guys," Veronica says, leaning over the partial wall.

"What's up?" Luis says as Caitlin and I try to untangle ourselves from our argument. Luis seems to shrug it off without a second thought, his whole body seeming to focus on Veronica. She pulls out a flyer and holds it up. "Anyone feel like a trip to the Moreland Mall this weekend?"

Brooke, you had the perfect timing. . . . This will be just the chance I need to see Jack and clear everything up before I get back home.

"It can be my goodbye tumor trip," Luis says.

"Let's do it."

Caitlin looks at me and shakes her crochet hook, and I swear she's going to ask me if this is about a boy. Because when have I ever been up for Home-sanctioned activities? But after several severe looks she determines I must be sane, because she turns to Veronica. "Fine. Count us in."

Chapter Twelve

My lungs are angry, and sleep doesn't feel like it's on the agenda tonight. I struggle to pull my hoodie on, resigned to another night on the couch—not sure what I'll watch given that Ryan stole my DVDs—or hope he has because they're not in the living room when I came to find them the other morning. I guess it's back to bad late-night TV. This is precisely why I have DVDs in a digital age. I make my way through the semidarkness and discover I shouldn't have worried because Ryan's beat me to the couch.

He sits there, hands buried in his hoodie pocket, his black hair curling over his eyes. I'm sure he's Mr. Popular to go along with his jock status at school. Two cups of tea steam on the coffee table. *BSG* plays on low, and if I didn't know any better, I'd swear he was waiting for me. I waver on the line between the hallway and the living room. This feels like something more. Like if I step across this line, I'll have crossed some Rubicon. I'll be on his side—start trusting doctors or something.

Like getting your life back, my brain supplies.

I'm ready to retreat, but he looks up and smiles at me. There's something like relief there, and now I can't leave. And what's scarier is I don't want to. I want to hang out with him and do one thing that I can count on being great: watch *BSG*.

"This is my spot," I say, plopping down next to him. He's jumped ahead several episodes, already deep into the first season.

"You okay?" he asks.

"Skip," I say. I slump back on the couch to stare at the ceiling. In the last twenty-four hours everyone has been some sort of mad at me. Caitlin. Jack. Mom—I think?

"You only get one skip."

"Who died and made you ruler?"

"Those are the rules for tea."

Deep in my chest my lungs crinkle, the little air sacs heavy with virus or whatever gunk that remains a mystery to my doctors. I want tea, but even the thought of hauling my body to the kitchen to make my own is a herculean task.

I slant my eyes toward him. "Since when are there rules for tea?"

He shrugs. "Since I made them up."

I reach for the cup.

He blocks me with his leg. "Foul."

"I'm fine," I bite back.

"Not an answer." His muscles shake and he can't hold the pose for long. I catch the ghost of pain across his face. Pain mixed with something darker—hatred? disgust? Maybe Soccer Boy is human after all.

"What rule am I even breaking?"

"I can't help you if you don't tell me the truth."

"The truth."

"Rule number one—always tell me the truth."

My lungs split into a cough that leaves my ribs stinging. He leans away, more of an automatic response than anything, I'd guess. "Rule number two," I choke out between coughs. "Don't stand between a girl and her tea." When I can finally breathe without interruption, I sit up. "To answer your question, I'm the same. No worse and no better."

Except . . . I'm not the same, because the same would be me struggling to keep Jack away from this place. There's now a chance I can see him outside of the hospital without actually going home. Morelands can be a sort of safe space where we can both be without the hospital tainting us. Even if I'm not well. Yet. Not well yet. And that curls my lips into a smile.

He offers me the cup—my answer was satisfactory. I accept, our fingers brushing. I pull back quickly; touch is something I avoid. Especially when the person could touch parts of me that are different. I wait for some recognition of what happened to cross his face. Some people flinch, others get curious and want to run their fingers over my skin like it's a priceless jewel. Ryan doesn't even notice.

And it's a relief.

Even Caitlin couldn't help but examine my hand the first time we met. Oh, she offered up her own, comparison and all that, but I've never had someone not remark on it.

"Except?" Ryan studies me and seems to see right into my thoughts.

"Thinking about what's different," I say, abiding by his new rules. The things I will do for tea. And someone who listens.

"Progress, finally." He struggles to raise his arms in victory. Only then do I realize he thinks I'm talking about listening to doctors, and maybe in a way I am. A small lie, because some things should be just for me.

"Not like that. I mean yeah, I want that. But it's more like a brief reprieve—enough to see Jack. Assuming Mom lets me go."

"Hmmm." Ryan nods like he understands, but his eyebrows draw close to his eyes like he wants to say more.

I blow on my tea and want to know what he's really thinking. So I keep adding to our growing list. "Rule three—if I have to tell the truth, so do you."

"You're making all the rules now?"

I pull out my phone and start a new message to him. "And writing it down to hold you to them. So tell me, how are you?" I ask. He wants to play this game, fine, let's play.

Ellie

Rule 1: I will always tell the truth.

Rule 2 (which is bogus): Don't stand
between a girl and her tea.

Rule 3: You always have to tell the truth.

I hit send and watch him look at the message and scowl. He lets out a breath. "Waiting on test results and I couldn't sleep." Not for the first time, I wonder if he tells this sort of stuff to his friends. Does his friend Sarah get to hear this, and what advice can she offer? Or am I the only one who hears his confession?

"Worried?"

"The best doctors in the world are here. They're going to figure it out."

"Not an answer, and I'm pretty sure you're now in violation of rule three," I parrot back to him. Doubt creeps into the corners of Ryan's face, pulling at his eyes and lodging his lip between his teeth. What is going to happen to Ryan when he realizes that medical dramas often leave out that medicine is a science? It's full of hypotheses and sometimes not a lot of answers. Hopefully, he'll get answers. Me, I'm used to a lot of unknowns. That word squeezes in between all the others in my medical charts.

"Why do you hate doctors? What did they ever do to you?" he asks, still avoiding my question.

I run my finger around the lip of my cup. What did they do to me? Where to start—bigger question, where to stop? "You know people always tell you to have faith, but they never tell you what happens when doctors don't figure things out. That's when the blame game comes out. You didn't do something right. They stop having time for you; stop believing your pain is real; stop trying. Doctors stop being gods and leave you in the rubble of their empire."

"How long have you been practicing that last part?"

I scoff. That's what he took from my speech? "Just wait. I'm sure if they can't find answers, the litany of how this is your fault will come out."

"Why is everyone angry at you?"

I cut him a sideways glance. Deflection—again. He motions for me to go on. "My mom wants me to have surgery—and I'm still struggling, but doing it. Caitlin is angry because I didn't tell her about Jack or you. Jack is angry because I'm here." I stare at my hands picking at my chipping nail polish. Is that why Jack's angry? He's angry that I can't tell him things, but I know the doctors' prognoses won't make sense to him. If I weren't here, we wouldn't have this issue. Ryan's gaze weighs on me like one of those lead aprons they give you for X-rays. Somehow, I doubt this will be as protective.

"That's a lot."

"Yeah, I mean . . ." This is what I'm not used to. Someone just getting it, admitting it's a lot, and not trying to talk me down, to make me see the other side—the brighter side. Just getting that, right now, this sucks. A. Lot.

"What's up with your mom?"

"Well, you know she wants me to have surgery—she also blogs about it like she can't handle me, so she has to tell my business to family, real-life friends, and strangers on the internet. She never stops to think what those things might do to me."

"What about what they give to her?"

"This is not a sport." My anger spikes; wasn't he supposed to be on my side? But then again that's the other edge of this whole thing, that Mom has a right to complain. I just . . . wish what brought her happiness didn't ruin mine.

Ryan holds up his hands in a T-shape. "Time-out. There are no sides, but your mom is dealing with a lot. If this were a sport, your mom would be your coach. They talk to other coaches to try to get the best results. They talk to other people to let them know how great their team is."

I squirm in my seat, his words hitting all my sore spots. I know all of what Mom does is about me and this is how she deals with caring for me. "And when you fail, does the coach get to feel as bad as you do? Do you feel bad for letting them down?"

Everyone wants to feel sorry for Mom, because of how hard it is to take care of a disabled kid. And I get it. I'm not easy. "When I was about two, I got my first Milwaukee brace—it's basically some metal and plastic wrapped around my body, meant to teach my spine to grow a new way." Ryan looks lost. Not surprising. "I had to wear it for the majority of the day from when I was two to when I was twelve."

I hated it.

I still hate it.

"What does that—"

"My mom was the one who put me in it. And do you know how many times I've been reminded of how I screamed at her? It's one of her recurring stories. For about five years, I screamed and threw a tantrum every day because I didn't want to wear that stupid brace and she made me." There's every reason why I should cut Mom some slack, because she's done so much and given up even more. And yet every time I get a notification for her stupid blog, I hate her just a bit more. Every time I'm used to make money for other families . . . Just because she saved my life doesn't mean she gets to own it. And then I hate myself for how much she cares about me.

"It was for your own good." There's no judgment in Ryan's tone. No hesitancy. Not so much as a hint of what he's feeling. It's just a statement. A pause that he's forcing me to take to make me think past the anger of old transgressions.

"Yeah, sure, but am I always going to be held responsible for my actions as a toddler?" Anger singes the edges of my words. He can be nonjudgmental all he likes. Me, I'm very much coming down on the side of judgment, and Mom has been failing for a while. Time to make him see that. "She still writes about those stories. When I was in sixth grade my mom wrote a whole long post about me. About surgery—what it was like. There were photos. Do you know what happened to me? All my friends started asking questions. It was bad enough I showed up with a frame on my arm to school—do you know what that is?" The words come out of me in a pile, each one stronger than the next, unleashing years of stored-up rage. I pause, waiting for an answer, trying to catch my breath. I feel like I've just run a race. I push myself forward.

"No, I didn't think so—it's six titanium pins shoved perpendicular through my arm attached to screws. You turn those screws every day."

Ryan's jaw hangs open, but I don't stop. I've never told anyone this, never knew how. But here I am ready to spill it all.

"People tell you to just act normal and no one will notice how different you look. But they never stop telling the stories that keep your differences alive. If I was the monster of my mom's life as a toddler, she made me into a freak in sixth grade. There were some rumors—about what happened to me, what I had—what was wrong with me. If my family hadn't moved, if my dad didn't get a better job, I wouldn't have had any friends."

This story turns my anger into tears. I didn't know how to tell Mom that, or even Dad. Hell, anyone. I read enough books; I knew what happened to kids like me. Writers seem to have only two ideas about disabled people: we die or we're completely cured. The last is not an option for me, so I guess death it is. There are no happy endings for us. Those thoughts I keep locked away, too afraid that if I let them out, I would have to face their reality. I am alive because of a lot of calculated risks, experiments, and the sheer luck of being born in this decade. Kids with VACTERLs even five years before me are not alive. Caitlin knows a handful of others who died or routinely escape death by some miracle of modern medicine.

On top of knowing just how breakable I am, that my life just might be borrowed time.

But talking about that, any of that—only sends Mom into a spiral.

I stand up, wanting to run away as fast as I can. I make it all of five steps before he calls after me. "You're not really a team player, are you?" He pushes himself to his feet and wavers. He holds still, waiting for his balance to return.

"Excuse me?" I sniff and brush away my tears with the back of my sleeve, prepping for a fight. Did he hear anything I just said?

"What I mean is—you don't feel like you can rely on anyone. You *choose* to face everything alone."

"I am in this experience alone. We are in this alone. Does my mom have to go into surgery? No. Do my friends have to spend time at Coffman every year because their genes got fucked up in development? Hard no. What part of any of this is a team sport?"

Ryan holds up his hands, trying to calm me down. "You never played sports, did you?"

I cross my arms over my chest. "For your information, I couldn't play contact sports. Want to know why? One kidney." I bite the words out, each one stoking the anger flaring in my chest.

"Lucky. My parents put me in every sport they could. Basketball, baseball—"

"Soccer?" I supply.

A smile latches on to the corner of his mouth, but he's doing his best to suppress it. "Yeah, soccer stuck. But here's the thing, we all have our roles to play on the team. Some of us are defenders, some of us play offense."

"You are speaking a foreign language to me."

He sighs again and gives me a dark look, his eyes going hard like the blackness of X-rays. I motion for him to go on, not apologizing. He's the one who wanted me to tell him the truth. "Some of us are meant to score points—offense. But we win as a team. Doesn't matter who scored or who defended the goal—we all have our parts to play."

"Are you saying my life is like a soccer team?"

"We're all trying to help you, but we can't if you don't want to give too." He leans back on the couch and seems to pray to the ceiling for guidance. "Ellie, I am on your team. No matter what. You want to yell at me, fine. Cry, I can take it. Because I think you need someone."

I pull back and narrow my eyes at him. "You did that on purpose— the whole 'not a team player' thing."

He ducks his head, his black hair falling in his face. When he looks back up at me, he lets go of his smile. "You're not as complicated as you think."

I gape at him, open-mouthed. No one has ever said that to me. I think Caitlin has tried, but I always wanted to protect her so I just clammed up. What is there to be angry at if I don't let it out?

"Stick with me and I'll get you back for your party."

He holds out his hand like we're making a deal, a bargain. Everything is messed up and he seems to be offering me the only way through this.

"Count me in, Coach."

Chapter Thirteen

You can tell a lot about a doctor from their waiting room. If it's packed full of people, the usual assumption is they're a good doctor.

But break down the crowd before you start giving out that title. Are the patients on the verge of a revolt? Constantly asking the nurses how much longer? Or is it just packed and people are regularly called back?

To the latter—congrats, great doc, keep them at all costs.

To the former—they think they're God, run for the hills.

Dr. Darlington's waiting room is, unfortunately, the first one, as much as I would like to believe it was the second. The dark-paneled walls loom over us and seem to push us closer, a cauldron at the boiling point. Coffman is part museum, part hospital, but someone seemed to have selected the most boring pieces they could find for this floor.

My leg bounces as I try to rein everything in. Ryan's advice is still front and center, and it has to be lack of sleep that I'm actually considering his plan.

Mom eyes me over the top of her cross-stitch pattern but doesn't comment.

"What are you working on?" I ask.

She turns the hoop around to let me see the saying she's working on. *Doctors Are Angels on Earth.*

"That will pair perfectly with my *Darlington Is a Dick*," I say, willing to take another test of if Mom and I can still be okay.

"Why do you think I started it?" Mom and I have a tradition of displaying conflicting sayings we stitched. Hers are always annoyingly positive and mine are more real-world. The best part about this tradition is that they never go on the blog. I guess they don't fit in with her online image, so this thing is completely ours.

A nurse calls a patient back, ending my brief reprieve from impending surgery. Am I really going to trust Darlington? To put my faith in what he and Mom think? Nerves getting the better of me, I open my phone and text my medical coach. Let's see if he's as good as his ego.

Ellie
You there?

Medical Coach
Hit me.

Ellie
Nothing yet. Just waiting.

Medical Coach
Pregame is just as important.
Go in with an open mind.

Ellie
That the best you got?

Medical Coach
Visualize getting back home.
Eyes on the prize.

Ellie
Anything not out of Quotes for Coaches?

Medical Coach
Remember they're on your team.

I click my phone off. Oh. Right. #TeamEllie. It's always been Mom, Darlington, and all the other docs—World Cup hopefuls right here. I let out a breath that ruffles my bangs. Me a part of that team. Sure, that's possible.

I believe that.

Maybe.

At least, I would like to.

Ryan does, can't that be enough?

Mom ties off a string and puts her project down. She's going to say something and I force a smile, hoping she finally has an answer on if I can go to Morelands this weekend. I talked to her about it a bit last night before bed, and she said she'd think about it. Now every time she opens her mouth I live in fear that she will tell me no. No mall equals no Jack.

Jack was on my team. *When you let him,* my brain says. Well, this weekend he can be on my team, because in no way will I let him try out for the hospital team.

Medical Coach
Get out of your head.
How's that for originality?

My name is called before Mom says what she wants. I look down at the message from Ryan. I hope he's right. Mom and I follow the nurse down the hall to an exam room. Lights outside the door are flipped on. She ushers us in and closes the door.

We're doing this.

I'm doing this. My breath snakes in and out and the whole world feels hyperfocused, but I remain jazzy at the edges. Not quite fitting in and only just standing out.

Ryan's message to me blinks up from the screen.

There's no time to question because the door opens. Dr. Darlington enters and shakes hands with my mom. *They're on my team.* I stick my hand out, ready to play ball. Darlington stops and looks at my hand. He sucks in his bottom lip as if he can't decide what I'm playing at. Whatever he decides, he shakes my hand too. I take a deep, steadying breath. *I can do this.* I repeat the words from my medical coach, again and again, trying to calm myself down.

"We are here to talk surgery," Darlington says, seating himself behind the desk. He pulls up my scans. "I've already talked to Dr. Carlyle about getting set up with your other doctors."

I nod along. Dr. Carlyle is my internist. He oversees everything that goes on inside me and is sort of the Ellie-Haycock-organ-know-it-all. And he's maybe my favorite doctor ever. We've been on this wild ride and he never forgets to check in with me. To make a Coffman visit the best it can be.

"Great," Mom says, taking notes on her phone. "We're still good with next week?"

Sweat breaks out over my body. It's now or never. Mom is running this conversation, acting like I've already agreed. Blood tests are being ordered. My kidney doctor wants another look at my lone organ before it all goes down—because I haven't seen her in, what? Five years?

Surgical prep is always a wild few days, going through this checklist, and assuming all things are my brand of normal I'll be cleared for surgery. They don't want to cut me open without making sure I'll survive.

There's always that to worry about. Death. My vision narrows and I'm pulled into that dark place where I'm alone and doctors in gowns are ready to carve into me.

My mouth goes dry. How do I butt into a conversation that is about me? Mom always leads the doctor convos and I just go along. All right, Coach, you're up.

Ellie
What do I ask?

Medical Coach
What does he think the surgery will do?
What is the recovery time?
What happens in the worst-case scenario?

Mom's dominating the conversation, her fingers still going. I hope her notes are for Dad, but honestly I figure they're probably for her blog.

". . . we'll go in laparoscopically," Darlington says. The MRI of my chest is on the screen, and he points out the three places where they'll make the incisions.

"And—" A cough cracks my voice and does a good job of bringing everyone's attention to me.

"She's feeling a bit nervous," Mom says, and as if suddenly remembering, she adds, "Didn't you have some questions for Dr. Darlington?"

My fingers wrap tight around the phone in my hand. This doesn't feel like talking with my hand surgeon or even my spine surgeon. I have known those doctors since before my conscious memory kicked in. Darlington is new. "Worst case . . . what happens . . ." My tongue stumbles over words that my brain can't seem to put in the correct order.

"What's the worst-case scenario?" Darlington finishes for me, an oil-slick smile back on his face.

I nod and force out a cough to cover everything. I don't want him to get the sense that I'm afraid of him.

"Well, if we can't get at this laparoscopically, the alternative is to do a full thoracotomy." He hits a few buttons on the computer and pulls up a different set of pictures. I turn to my mom, accusatory face in place. Dr. Darlington holds up a hand to calm me down.

"And that means?" I ask, not taking my eyes off Mom.

"In a thoracotomy we'd make a larger incision and open up your back."

Jaw drop.

What.

Excuse me?

Does Darlington understand how detached from patient reality he is? That's his plan to calm me down—I wish I had videoed this so I could play it back for Ryan. Darlington should lose his license for his bedside manner alone. The last time they just casually split open my back I was fourteen months old and it was to fuse my spine.

"My entire back?" My words squeak out, but no one seems to register my terror. I don't remember my back surgery, a combination of good drugs and being too young for memories to stick. But I've heard the horror stories, and while my mind has blocked it out my body remembers. I was in the ICU. They opened up my whole back. Carved up under my ribs. I have the involuntary urge to get up and move as far away from Darlington and Mom as possible, as if they're already trying to hurt me.

"It would require a longer recovery time."

With that much trauma—duh. I'll end up in the ICU. If that's the option, there'll be no way I can get back in time for Brooke's party. I'll be stranded in the hospital or the Home until the end of the year—at the earliest. And then? There will be no way to get Jack back before he's just done with me. With all that scarring, I'll miss the rest of speech season, there will be no state, no nationals. I'll be lucky to have a few shreds of a life when I return home.

Mom is still all for surgery and doesn't seem to know how freaked out I am. Without even looking at my phone, I type the words back to Ryan.

"Is that . . . I mean that sounds extreme."

Darlington sits back in his chair, steepling his fingers. He addresses Mom only. "It is a more invasive procedure. Because of where the cyst is on Eleanor's bronchial tubes, there is no other way to get at it if we cannot remove it with the lap."

Medical Coach
What are the chances of this?

My mind is so far gone I don't know how to ask that question. Ryan's clear message blinks up at me, grounding me, pulling me out of the darkness of an unregistered memory and back into this space.

"And the chances of this happening?" I ask. Buffered by Ryan's questions, I feel more at ease inserting myself into the conversation. They help to cut through the shock and noise in my head.

"Given what I've seen of your scans, I think this is exactly the sort of procedure we can do with a lap. Now there's always a chance we would have to do the other, but I would say it's less than twenty percent."

The number feels high. This isn't an X-ray where it's just a few more exposures to radioactive material or another blood draw. This is surgery, and while I've had a lot of them and I know the jargon, when it comes to crossing into the OR, I freeze. I need a push.

> **Ellie**
> Less than 20%.

Medical Coach
Do it.
Nothing's 100% sure.
They know what they're doing.

I'm not surprised by Ryan's response. *Do it.* That's been his MO since he stepped into my life.

> **Ellie**
> I want to believe. . . .

Medical Coach
Try trusting him.
What does your head say now?

I swallow. Trust Darlington? My gut twists at the idea of surgery and all the what-ifs that it holds.

"There's always some risk," Mom says, echoing the words that Ryan told me.

Both adults in the room look back to me. As if I'm finally to be included in this decision.

"Well, Ellie," Mom starts, "what do you think?"

"And this laparoscopic thing—it will get me back to normal?"

"You'll be in the hospital one, maybe two days, and your GP at home can remove the stitches."

I swallow and feel the burn of a cough ignite deep in my chest. This is my chance to be healthy again. To get my life back. Yet my body is screaming no.

My phone buzzes in my hand.

I expect Ryan, but instead, it's Brooke.

Brooke
WHAT HAPPENED WITH YOU AND JACK????????

If Ryan's texts weren't enough, Brooke brought it home for the team. Jack. I need to fix things with him. Seeing him this weekend would be a step in the right direction.

Mom smiles at me encouragingly.

I can do this. I need to.

"Let's do it." I force a smile I don't totally feel but am going on a little faith.

A smile pricks the corners of Dr. Darlington's lips, and my stomach does flip-flops. Is he *happy* that I've chosen surgery? I look down at my phone again and all the positive messages from Ryan. He may be new to this, but he's in control of his medical programming.

"We'll get everything set up." Darlington raps his knuckles on the table and walks out without another glance at us.

"Don't they usually say goodbye?" I ask, stating the obvious to test Mom. Will she side with me or Darlington?

Mom gives me a one-armed hug. "He's very busy, Ellie." I want to sink into her comfort because I want to believe that I made the right choice even if it means facing the nightmares that lurk in the corners of my mind.

Released, Mom gets the new list of appointments and we make our way out of the labyrinth of hallways and exam rooms.

I'm going to have surgery and get my boyfriend back. My life can return to the way it was. Ryan deserves a big high five.

And yet I feel like I just stepped on thin ice and plunged into the freezing water below.

VATERs Like Water

This is the fallout, pt. 2

Age: 5 yrs, 5 mos. Entry #400

Comments: 500   Bookmarks: 178   Shares: 100

By the time Ellie was school-age, I thought I had come across every possible slight. I'd lost friends, my job—so many parts of my identity were just gone, scarred over and left to be dealt with another day. I could and would take on so much for my daughter.

Anything she wanted, needed—I would find. There is nothing scarier on this earth than a mother on a mission.

I thought the worst day of my life was behind me. I thought each time I gave my tiny baby over to doctors and nurses that someday this suffering would end. We would both be able to put Coffman behind us and head for new adventures. Times at the hospital would fade to those rose-colored stories you tell to your friends. The ones you can't laugh at in the moment but later are the funniest things you've ever done.

I was so sure Ellie's first surgeries—those long, agonizing eight- and twelve-hour waiting periods where I couldn't protect my daughter—would be the worst moments of my life. Every one felt worse than the last. Every one had the potential to be the End. Her end. And then if it wasn't, there was the constant question that seemed to lurk behind every step—did we choose right?

I met a woman at the Family Care Home with a child several years older than Ellie. One night, I told her all my fears, explained the surgeries, and we commiserated on how best to argue with insurance agents. I told her these nights, with Ellie in the hospital, were some of the worst nights of my life. The woman, bless her, looked at me over the rim of her glass and chuckled.

When I say I was livid.

She apologized, of course, saying she didn't mean to be rude. It's just that this was the start of a very long race.

I wasn't sure what she meant. I thought I was doing everything pretty well so far. There was nothing that could possibly beat out what we were already facing.

"Just wait until Ellie goes to school" was all she told me.

We didn't talk much the rest of that trip, and I'm not sure what happened to her or her child. Just one of those friendships that comes on quick, goes deep, but doesn't take hold. I didn't think about it again until years later. Ellie was in kindergarten, as happy and as healthy as she could be. It felt like for the first time I could breathe.

Surgeries were down to a trickle, and we only needed to make a trip to Coffman twice a year. A new normal had finally found us. Ellie was in school and for all intents and purposes she was thriving.

An innocent birthday party invitation would be my undoing. Now I'm not that mom who is about to say you have to invite every kid in the class. BUT if you're going to invite every kid but my kid—then yes, you're going to have a problem with me.

Ellie came home in tears, because everyone else was talking about the party—except her. I held my sobbing child and finally understood what the mother meant. The hospital was just the start, and I would give anything to have that be the end of things. This wasn't the last time this happened to Ellie. And every time it broke my heart.

What do you tell your child when she looks at you wanting to know what's wrong with her? Why people treat her this way? My heart shattered because I didn't have answers for her, and even worse—I was probably the cause of it.

Me.

I had done this to my daughter.

And what's worse—I couldn't fix it. I had no answers. Nothing that would heal her broken heart.

Still searching for answers,

Gwen

Chapter Fourteen

Ice cream to celebrate?" Mom asks.

I nod, reaching deep for the same level of excitement that she has. Maybe ice cream will help. With chocolate. Lots and lots of chocolate. I trail behind Mom through the subway to the ice-cream shop that has always been an ice-cream shop—just cycles through different chains and independents. It's back now to the original chain of my childhood.

Ping! I pull my phone out, hoping for a message that will break through my fear.

TUMOR SQUAD
Luis
We are a go for the Morelands trip!

Medical Coach
Huh?

Caitlin
Tumor Squad . . . really.

Luis
The one and only!!
I figured if Ellie can have a medical coach, I can have
a team, a squad.

Medical Coach

What is this exactly?

Ellie

I would actually like that answer as well.

Medical Coach

And who are these numbers?

There's a quick succession of texts with people spouting off their names.

I get a side text from Ryan.

Medical Coach

What is Luis talking about?

Ellie

Isn't it obvious? We're helping a friend celebrate before surgery. Don't you do something similar before big games? Isn't this a sports thing?

Medical Coach

We already covered how you don't know sports.

Ellie

Ah yes, we did.

You're going.

I don't get a reply, but the messages are already stacking up on Tumor Squad.

TUMOR SQUAD

Veronica

I already signed everyone up.

Luis

It's to accompany me on a farewell tumor trip.

This weekend.

Medical Coach
This cannot be doctor approved.

Luis
Caitlin words of wisdom?

Caitlin
I don't think the medical establishment is getting us
out of this.

Luis
Face it—you're going.

Oh Ryan, I think, and add an eye roll. Reading these texts blocks out my impending surgery, but then it hits me again and I get a new injection of adrenaline. Just the flight response kicking in. I force myself to follow Mom through the subway and not sprint for the nearest exit.

Feeling better about the whole surgery thing—or at least pretending to—I text Brooke.

Ellie
I'm coming to see him at Morelands this weekend.

Sunlight filters in through the window high above and I tilt my head back, catching the winter rays. *This is going to be okay. Surgery will not kill me,* I tell myself, even as my stomach flip-flops. I will see Jack this weekend—which is almost all I need to push through this.

"What has you all smiling?" Mom asks, her voice lighter than it has been in a while.

"Thinking about this weekend," I say, testing the waters. Maybe Mom will finally be on board. After all, I agreed to her surgery demands.

Mom presses her lips together, and I hope she's not about to rain on my parade. Again.

"We'll see," Mom says. She wraps an arm around me like I need to be protected, cradled against the outside world.

Caitlin sits at a table inside, finishing up a social media story, and she turns the camera on me. "And um, look, it's my friend Ellie," Caitlin says. I wave my hand in a gesture that says No. But Caitlin drags me into frame. This is payback. "Uh, say hi, Ellie."

I give a wave and duck out of the camera. This is Caitlin's thing and I . . . it feels too close to what I want, but I'll get it only if I parade my disability around.

"Ahh, we're headed to Morelands this—uh—weekend with some of our friends from the Home." She gives her followers a small finger wave. I drop into a seat while Mom gets in line for ice cream.

Caitlin rewatches the story and I see her finger hover over the delete button.

"Post it," I say. Mom once wrote a whole post about that on her blog: how rare and special it was to see two kids with VACTERLs together. And she wasn't wrong.

"There's some bad lighting, and I definitely said um too many times—" She's about to go on about the technical issue when she stops. "Are you okaying me putting a video of you on A Patient Life?"

"Ninth wonder of the world right here. But you have to post it. No filter, no nothing." Caitlin chews her lip. She's used to control, to ordering things just as she likes them. "You want to be more off-the-cuff, here it is. Just like what will happen with your interview."

Caitlin takes a big bite of ice cream, her face taking on a prayerlike quality as it slides down her throat. This close to her routine surgery, solid food becomes an issue for her. Deep bruises dot her skin. Supposedly, Coffman has the best phlebotomists, but Caitlin's veins never cooperate. She comes out looking like a Jackson Pollock and refuses to hide their dirty work.

"Vampires again?" I ask, nodding to her arm.

"Incompetent phlebotomists, but what else is new?" Caitlin sits back in her chair, arms folded over her chest.

Mom drops my ice cream off. "Are you going this weekend, Caitlin?"

I hold my breath; Caitlin can be the deciding vote on this whole thing. One word in the negative, and there is no way that Mom will let me on the bus.

Caitlin drags her spoon around her dish. "Hmmm, yeah. I think so, a few more details to work out." She takes a big bite of ice cream. "But probably yeah."

"I hope you both can go—I wouldn't feel comfortable with Ellie going by herself."

Hope freezes in my veins. If Caitlin doesn't go, then I won't get to see Jack.

Caitlin licks the last of her ice cream off her spoon and sets it down with great care, as if she's setting a dinner table for the queen of England. She does not even try to stifle her eye roll. Of course, *that*. We've fought against parental override our entire lives.

"Don't get too comfy yet," Caitlin says.

"I have a firm date with the sharp end of a scalpel. Comfort is not on the list. The least we can do is get out of this place for a few hours."

Caitlin raises her eyebrows. "And I take it this was the medical coach's doing?" I don't miss the edge in her voice. The one sharp enough to cut into me for choosing someone else over her. And not just someone—but someone with less experience. Who's not VACTERLs.

"It's not a big deal. He's just . . . easy to talk to."

Caitlin grabs her spoon from the table and I know that was the wrong thing to say. She sits back in her chair.

"Since when are you not all in on stuff like this—you could do a whole series on Luis's trip to Morelands."

"I guess we can play it this way." She studies me for a long moment. "Did he have you talk to your mom?"

"What?"

Caitlin checks to see where our moms are, but with us now old enough to not kill ourselves without supervision, they give us some privacy. "Did you talk to your mom about what she posts online?

You keep hiding from this—your mom posts details of your life without your consent. I try and practically get death threats; your mom does it and it's 'no big deal.' Tell me, does your medical coach have an answer for that?"

"She deserves her own space."

Biggest eye roll yet.

"You deserve control of your life."

"The point is, I'm going to have surgery." *Team player*—wasn't that Ryan's advice? "And before next week when I am having surgery, I want to see my boyfriend not surrounded by all of this." I throw my hands up. Jack couldn't take the Family Care Home, there's no way he could handle the hospital.

Caitlin shakes her head like she's trying to fully understand what I just said. "You mean your boyfriend, Jack? . . ."

"Yeah," I say, unable to look at Caitlin. There's a pressure on me, in me, that somehow this too will be too much.

"And I would get to meet him—like a proper introduction?"

"I mean he's not quite up on his bows—" My fingers sweat around my spoon. I just agreed to let my hospital friend meet my boyfriend. That was a line I held for so long, and yet now it doesn't feel so bad.

"Name and Social Security number will do just fine," Caitlin says, tossing her head, getting the curls out of her face. With her pinkie she untucks the gauze wrapped around her arm, exposing the pinpricks that line her inner elbow. "As much as I want to meet Jack—I will go on one condition," Caitlin says.

I raise an eyebrow. *Go on. . . .*

"You have to tell your mom to stop the blog."

Shots. Fired.

"Why can't you just let me live my life the way I want?"

"Because you're killing yourself over this. And I don't like it when people are mean to my friends."

Should have known better. There are lots of things I will do for

Caitlin. Hell, I would donate my one kidney for her. But what she's asking may be a step too far. "It's fine."

Caitlin holds up her phone with Mom's latest blog on it.

"She is two steps shy of going full-on vlogger of your life. How many posts are going up while you're in the hospital?"

"How can I just take that away from her? And what about the good she does? It would be like taking away *A Patient Life*—it's part of who she is."

Caitlin shakes her head. "No, no, no. Do not compare what I do to what your mother does."

"You're right, because my mother would for sure take that TV spot because of what she could do with the exposure."

"This isn't about me—"

"Why does this matter to you?" The question is out of my mouth before I can stop it.

Caitlin blinks and stares at me like I've smacked her. She's always meddled in my life, especially when it comes to Mom's blog. But I'm done. Yes, it drives me absolutely up a wall that she does it. Yes, I live in fear of my friends finding it. And yes, it fixes some small part of my mom.

The community, the venting, it's all part of what sustains her. How can I just come along—*again*—and tell her to scrub it all? Her oldest post talks about when she was pregnant with me and the only thing she wanted was a healthy baby. As a concept, I understand it. But now I feel like I've been a disappointment from day one.

Couldn't even be the only thing she wanted: a healthy baby.

I would rather let my relationship with Mom sour than take one more thing from her.

"It makes you miserable."

"And I've already said what I am going to do about it."

Caitlin jabs her spoon at her empty container; she's not happy. I have always let her have this fight. I have demurred and said the same things over and over again. Maybe Ryan's lessons about listening, about asking the right questions, are finally kicking in.

"She shouldn't—"

"And how did your mom take it?" I shoot back. Our moms may have started blogging at the same time, but only my mom continued.

Caitlin sucks a breath in through her teeth. "Honestly better than I expected. It wasn't exactly a doctor checkup. Below surgery for sure, though."

"Well, I'm glad she understood it." And I am, happy for my friend, that is, but I just want her to understand that what works for her doesn't work for everyone.

"Look, I watch you freak out about this. It's always *This is going to ruin my life. It's going to kill my friendships.* It bugs you so much that it's causing you to freak out over your boyfriend knowing anything— over me knowing anything. You refuse to let anyone in, and we have to have this conversation ten times for you to even stand up to me. Are you willing to give up your life—Jack, friends, and all—for your mom?" Her words hit like a rock on a lake and sink into me fast. She's never made this point before, but the venom in her voice is enough to clue me in to the fact that she's been thinking about this for a while.

"That's an oversimplification."

"When do you get to matter?"

I stir my melting ice cream, trying to find the words. "What am I supposed to say? *Hi—I know this is strange and you started this for me, Mom, but I just want you to stop blogging? Also while we're at it, could you maybe consider deactivating your social media accounts?*"

"I mean if you want to say that, sure, go with that. Anything is better than silence. Just talk to her—then we can focus on Jack and how we can use the Morelands trip to bring him into the fold."

I lay out my plan and how it starts with this weekend. Morelands is normal for us, a safe place that's not the hospital. My plan is going to work: I will be home by this time next week and I can explain everything to Jack. I will be healed. Be back to my normal self. I don't dream of being everyone else's normal, I just want my normal back. That's all.

Caitlin laughs.

I see Jack almost every day at home. He knows what I like. We share the same interests, mostly. He saw me before I was totally ready to see myself.

I'm not throwing that all away.

That may be Caitlin's style, but it's not mine. Long-term. Stability. Normal. Dating another sick kid, that's a whole other layer that I frankly am not signing up for. I have state championships to focus on, and hopefully nationals—fuck, I have to get well myself first.

Ping!

Ping!

Ping!

Messages come in one after another, the screen flashing with *Medical Coach*.

"Shut up, phone," I say, and flip the device over.

"You were saying?" Caitlin says. "You want me to go to Morelands this weekend, talk to your mom. Let her know what you're feeling."

Like they know we just finished, our moms round the corner, smiles in place.

Great. Just great.

Chapter Fifteen

Surgery is scheduled. I'm going to surprise Jack this weekend. Just the thought of Jack spreads warmth in my chest and eases the tension in my body. I'm doing this to get back to my life.

As much as I hate to admit it, Ryan was right. And before he finds out, I want to tell him—that way, there will be zero room for him to gloat.

And maybe I just want him to tell me one more time that surgery is worth it. That I made the right choice. Because every time I think about stepping back into the OR I feel like I'm going to throw up.

Plus maybe he has an idea on how I can talk to Mom about her blog. Because without that Caitlin won't go and I'll be stranded at the Family Care Home.

A little sleuthing and I find Ryan's room number on the check-in/checkout board. We're on the same floor, but his block of rooms is off in the other direction from the kitchen. With every step, my muscles unknot themselves and calm seeps in between the cracks.

His door is propped open by the lock, but I still knock.

"Yeah?" The voice on the other side of the door sounds barely awake, and a strike of regret flashes through me.

You're not the only one going through shit, I remind myself. I back up; this was a ridiculous idea. I should have just texted him. Our relationship requires digital mediation in order to be successful.

And just like that, my body snaps back into pure panic mode. "It's okay," I tell myself quietly. I've handled this before and I can do it again. I have been through more than one hospital stay, more than one doctor's appointment, without Ryan.

Backing away, I'm just about ready to sprint down the hall when the door opens.

Ryan leans heavily against the doorframe. Not leans—slumps, like it's taking everything he has to keep himself upright. The low buzz of the TV carries through the doorway.

I step back and immediately regret it, because I'm shocked. This is the first time he doesn't try to hide his illness from me.

He wears jeans, a hoodie—some soccer team, again. There are deep bags under his eyes, and it's like his muscles just can't hold him up. His black hair hangs in his face and he doesn't even bother to push it aside. I know nothing can make this situation better, and if I say the wrong thing it will one hundred percent make this worse.

"Um, I . . . well . . ." I stumble over words, trying to find the right combination. But I've already messed up this conversation. I made it worse.

"What do you want, Ellie?" His voice is tired—it's a tired that has been put through a shredder and then reassembled.

"My DVDs."

Way to say exactly the wrong thing.

I shift on my feet; this was not how I thought this conversation with Ryan would go. I wanted to surprise him, congratulate him on being an excellent medical coach.

"Your DVDs?" he asks very slowly, which given how I barged in on him . . . fair.

"I'm having surgery." Can he be proud? Spout off some pep talk that would make any sports team win that big game? Give me what's mine and then we can both just go right back to what we were already doing?

"You told me."

Right. Of course I did.

"So, DVDs."

He shifts, a smile playing at his lips as arrogance boosts him back up. "I'm holding them hostage until you come back from the OR. So did you already visit the OR and come back?" His words start off tired but gain sarcasm as he continues.

I roll my eyes and cross my arms over my chest. This was not exactly what I had in mind when I wanted to come talk to Ryan. Here I thought he might want to gloat or even celebrate that his ridiculous plan worked. But noooo, all I get is attitude.

And isn't that what I wanted? Ryan was never going to let me off easy, and I wanted that. Wanted him to be a wall that I would have to knock down, because for once I wouldn't be stuck thinking about my impending trip under the doctor's knife.

"It's on the books, next week." I expect him to be happy about that—to start gloating. Mentally, I'm even prepared to admit that maybe I was wrong.

"See you in a week." He starts to back his way into his room. I should just let it go. *Walk away, Ellie.* But I'm not here to give in.

"Can I give you some advice, patient to patient?" I ask. "Sleeping and lounging around is better done in sweats."

He looks down at his jeans. I purposefully do not. My cheeks heat and I turn on my heels and walk down the hall. I force myself to remain at a walk when all I want to do is run.

"That really why you came here?" he calls after me.

I turn around, walking backward. *Get away, get away, get away.* As much as I wanted to come see him, so he could quiet the fear boiling inside me, I now want to be anywhere else.

He tries to take a step away from the doorway, and for a moment his whole body hangs there like a marionette. Then, like his strings have been cut, he falls.

I run back toward him—I'm not a total jerk.

Ryan holds up a hand, the universal signal for *I've got it* and the disabled signal for *Back off, asshole, I'm handling this.* He pulls himself back up, a sour look on his face.

We look each other in the eye, neither of us knowing what to say. We're stuck in that awkward moment when you know you needed help and got help but were so embarrassed that you needed help. I wish there were great comebacks for this that I could share with Ryan, but this is just how it is.

I recognize that look in his eye. The one that says *No one knows what I have and I'm trying to deal.* Summoning the last of my courage, I meet his gaze. Questions dot my tongue. I'm not Caitlin, I don't have an encyclopedic knowledge of illnesses and medical abnormalities. But I know how this feels.

"You *so* need my help," I say. Ryan raises an eyebrow. He may be able to translate a special dialect of doctor for me, but he is still learning the language of being a patient.

"Come on." I jerk my head toward a common area. Ryan starts, but his muscles refuse to cooperate. "Do you have a mobility device?"

"A what?"

"All that doctorese and you don't know what a mobility device is? A walker? A cane? A thing that makes sure you can move."

He scowls.

Oh, so it's one of those.

"Please tell me you are not, not using one because—"

"I don't need it."

Oh boy.

Caitlin has given me the same song, different verse. I didn't let her get away with it then and it's certainly not going to fly now. I may have been a jerk before, but that doesn't mean he gets a free pass. I have nothing left that will hold my tongue to give him nicer advice. Well, it'll be the same advice, just delivered slightly differently.

"You can barely stand."

"I'm fine." His tone wants to put an end to this conversation. That may work on new parents and old friends, but it doesn't work on me.

I stand in his path. "Rule three—you always have to tell the truth," I say. He frowns, probably regretting the rules that I could remind him were his idea. I stand my ground. When he doesn't relent, I push further. "Have you looked around? Do you see where you are? You need it." This is where I am more comfortable. The needs that will keep you going as a patient.

Ryan goes back into his room and returns with a cane. This is one of the few times in my life where I get a glimpse of what it must be like to be Brooke or Jack. But you never ask what's going on with people here: you wait until someone tells you what they have. No matter how bad I want to know, I'm not breaking that rule.

"You won't judge me?" He leans heavily on his cane.

"Would you care if I did?"

He looks away. No explanation needed; he would care. Very much. Can't say I blame him. It's why we do what we do, the constant need to fit in, to try to make everyone else remember that we're normal. Mostly. Probably.

One of those "totally normal" but obviously toxic things Caitlin always talks about. While the feeling can be normal, the response shouldn't be dictated by others' normality scale.

I wish it didn't make me feel like that revelation mattered. That he'd trusted me with something precious. Most people—I don't care what they think. But my friends? My family? If they ever looked at me the way some people in the wild do, I'd want to crawl in a hole and die.

"Don't you have enough on me to judge in return?" I say, turning down the hall. "Come on."

We find the living room and drop onto the now familiar couch.

"I guess you know my secret now," he says.

"You're not the first boy I know who's used a cane."

"They don't know why I'm here." His voice is quiet but not small. It fills the space, blown up with all the fear he seems to have bottled up. "But I'm sick. I can't . . . my muscles . . ." The easygoing nature gets sucked out of the room. Ryan draws patterns on the arm of his chair with the tips of his fingers.

He seems to be fighting a battle with himself whether to let me in or not.

"Again, if you're trying to win this game of who has it worse: try harder." We're different. Our cases are not remotely the same. He should get to go back to being normal, but I want him to know that he doesn't have to be alone in this.

He looks up at me, like really looks at me. I hold his gaze. The skin on my arms prickles, each hair standing up on end.

"I'm fine," he says, the words barely forming complete syllables.

"Tell me the truth." He started talking about his illness, so now I can pry. At least that's what I'm telling myself, because I don't break hospital patient rules.

"What are you talking about?"

"I mean don't give me the bullshit you give your friends."

He gives me a quizzical look, completely not understanding my words. And here I thought he was smart. "Like you do?"

"I have no less than ten doctors and have since I was born. I've been involved with every medical study about VACTERLs—they practically have my number at the NIH. I have letters V, C, both versions of R, and L—which can also double as one of the Rs. Let me translate that for you," I say, holding up a hand to stop him. "My vertebrae are half formed, my heart also has issues, only one kidney, and no radius, as if you didn't figure that out." I hold up my right hand, showing off what I usually hide.

I hold my breath, unsure how he'll respond. But this is all temporary. Things that happen here, in the hospital, they don't last. So even if I make a big clusterfuck out of this, it's okay. The chances of me ever seeing Ryan again are slim to none.

He relaxes, his cold exterior melting away to reveal the Ryan who watched *BSG* with me.

"So I shared, now you—how long has it been happening?"

He presses his lips together.

Come on, Ryan.

"A few months, I just—it started off small." He waves his hand away, cutting himself off. "They just sent through a battery of tests, so I should have some answers soon." His gaze drifts, as if he's looking into the future now and can see his diagnosis.

Fear hits me, but also something like solidarity. We both have things that doctors, even the smart ones here, aren't sure about. I offer him a smile—we can get through this. And I don't just mean the hospital and doctors' appointments.

"And . . ." I let my voice trail off, waiting for him to take up the story again. He has some time before I have to push him to go on.

Ryan rolls the edge of his hoodie between his fingers. "I used to play soccer. Played soccer all the way through the spring, then summer started. I felt weak at practices. Coach thought it might have been growing pains, shin splints, normal stuff. Then one day, I fell. Just tripped over myself because I couldn't control anything. And here I am, letting myself be poked and prodded by doctors."

"So you can play soccer again?"

He smiles for just a moment and it changes his whole face. Makes it brighten, which is so unlike his sour expression he seems to wear around me. I surprise myself because I want to make him do that again. It makes my lungs feel lighter and ignites a glow in my chest, like I can fill the space. This moment, it's for us.

And that's where I bring myself to a screeching halt.

Ryan Kim does not make my heart do things.

I'm just helping the new kid. Repaying a favor. Because this whole world is different and our relationships are just . . . different.

Jack is the one who's been there for months. Who made me feel special. A lot of my other friends did the whole boyfriend thing early in high school.

I didn't expect high school boys to get the whole disabled thing. College was going to be great, high school—survivable.

Then Jack happened. Suddenly, the future, the one that is always pitched to me—in the future they will grow you a new thumb, in the future they can correct your spine at birth, in the future boys won't feel awkward around you because you'll be normal—that future was then. This now should not exist.

"If you know so much, why am I the one giving you advice?" He gives me another one of those smiles and I want to lean into it.

"Because I need to get my boyfriend—my life—back." The verbal reminder is for my heart and head.

Just like that, the ease we had with each other evaporates. I shift in my seat. There's no reason I have to hide this face from Ryan. After all, he was there for my most epic meltdown, but now it alters the mood, forces us back onto different sides of an invisible line.

"You'll get him back," Ryan says, focusing on his hands, his voice soft. "He'd be stupid if he lets you go."

The truth of his words sinks into me, making me feel warm and safe in a way I haven't for a long time. I want him to look at me and say those words. As if he can sense my thoughts, Ryan looks up, and his gaze daring me to disagree causes butterflies to stir in my stomach.

"I know," I say with confidence I don't feel. "But since you helped me, I am going to return the favor."

"What?" Ryan looks confused.

"You know how to handle a doctor, but you know nothing about being a patient."

"You want to coach me in how to be a patient." Skepticism abounds.

I sit up a little straighter, something I picked up recently when talking to doctors. Act like you know what you're talking about and they are less likely to question you.

"Oh, you need me."

Chapter Sixteen

*R*yan pleads exhaustion and I help him back to his room. Refusing to go back to my room, I hunt for space in the Home. I end up in the game room and spend the rest of the afternoon playing video games that Mom won't let inside our house.

Without something else for me to focus on, the fear of surgery surges back to life, dogging my steps, pelting me with a steady stream of panic.

Trust people. I pull out my phone and open up to my conversation with Jack. But I don't want to ruin the surprise, so I flip open to my conversation with Brooke.

> **Ellie**
> What time is Jack performing?

Her response comes before I can slip my phone back in my pocket.

> **Brooke**
> YOU'RE COMING!?!?
> 3PM
> TELL MEEEEEEEE

Well, now there's no good way to get out of this. *Trust people.* Okay, here goes. . . .

Ellie
Maaaaaaaybe

So it's not an outpouring of my darkest fears, but it's more than I would have given her a week ago. In a rush, I lock my phone and slip it in my pocket.

This is gonna be all right.

I take the elevator back to my floor—not willing to risk the stairs and set my lungs off. I can't give Mom any reason to think I'm not well enough to go to Morelands. In the kitchen, families move around one another, fixing dinner. Ryan sits at a counter and smiles when I start making tea.

"Are you following me?" he asks.

"You caught me," I say, and we both laugh. "Just trying to rest up before tomorrow."

"I can't believe Luis got doctor approval for this."

"Don't tell me you're backing out now?" Luis has provided detailed instructions that can be rivaled only by Caitlin's. I wouldn't put it past Luis to drag us kicking and screaming to the bus. Plus, big cancer or little cancer—it's still cancer. You do the thing.

Ping! My phone goes off and I see it's a message from Caitlin.

Caitlin
Did you tell your mom yet?

Ellie
Yes.

I lie. What's the harm . . . Caitlin won't—

Caitlin
Liar.
Eleanor
I will pull the plug.

Ellie

What kind of proof do you want?

Caitlin

Don't worry, I'll know.

I grimace.

"What?" Ryan asks.

I fill him in on the whole Caitlin thing. Strange how much I enjoy just telling him things.

"If you get out of this, I want out of this."

"What is so wrong with going?"

Before he can answer, a woman who I guess is his mom steps in. She has the same thick black hair that's cut in waves to frame her face and wide-set eyes as her son. "Ryan, who's this?"

We exchange glances. It's one thing for our friends to know, but parents? That's some dangerous, maybe-this-is-permanent territory. His mom waits for someone to speak.

"I'm Ellie," I finally say when it's clear Ryan isn't going to step up.

"Nice to see Ryan making friends, would you like to join us?" She motions to the heavy, well-used dining table. I look to Ryan for a clue—does he want me to stay?

"If you don't have plans," he says with a shrug.

"Sure," I say. Hospital friendships are short-lived, might as well enjoy it while it lasts.

"Ellie?" Mom calls, and comes into the kitchen. Our moms square off.

I fumble my way through introductions, but Mom turns on her hospital charm. The one that she uses to con nurses into extra visiting time and all the Popsicles I can eat. I bite the inside of my lip to keep from smiling. Sometimes she's cool.

"Please join us," Mrs. Kim says. "I'd love to meet the *friend* Ryan has been talking about."

I raise my eyebrows at Ryan as our mothers carry dishes to the table and mouth, *Friend?*

He just shoots me a *get over yourself* look. And I laugh.

We settle in around the table and I'm struck by the thought that my parents never did this with Jack's parents. I mean, sure, they knew each other, were teens in the same grade and Evanston isn't what you'd call a "big city"; most parents know one another on sight. But sharing a meal—never.

Maybe that's something we can do when I'm back? Do I want to do that? The last thing I need is for any future breakup to ruin more things for my mom—even a hypothetical friendship killed by a breakup that's definitely not happening.

"Have you been coming here a while?" Mrs. Kim's question pulls me back into the parental conversation.

Ryan looks like he wants to tape her mouth shut. I guess someone picked up some hospital etiquette. I'm so proud.

"Since she was six weeks old."

Mrs. Kim's eyebrows shoot up. No one really expects that answer. "That long?"

"It never seems that long, but yeah, several years, forty surgeries or so, and a few blog posts . . ." And Mom is off on the story of Ellie's life. I am here just to add nods or small anecdotes when necessary. This is how it always goes. Mom knows more about my medical life than my fleet of doctors. I've committed her spiel to memory, and I just wish she'd let me tell it. She has such ownership of my story—and I suppose for years she was the only keeper of it.

Something taps my foot and I look up. Ryan's staring at me across the table. An unspoken question peers out from his eyes. I shake my head. It's nothing. Some things you just have to accept as a kid with major medical problems, and that something is your parent playing fast and loose with your life.

"So we're friends now?" I ask to distract him.

He pokes at his food. "I mean, aren't we?"

"Oh yeah. I mean, sure." Not the answer I was expecting.

"Just for now—because your rules."

"Right." I tap my fork on the edge of my plate, his answers not sitting well with me.

"His cousin also had an autoimmune issue, that's why we came here," his mom adds as I float back into the parental conversation.

Ryan's hand tightens on his spoon. I think he might actually snap it in two. Parents never realize that sometimes we want to keep our oddities to ourselves.

"Oh really?"

"Hmm, took her forever to get a diagnosis, always in and out of the hospital. But once they figured it out, she's been able to control the flare-ups."

Mom and I fall silent. I turn my fork around. Family history. Must be nice for things to be solved like that. *Poof*, and you can have answers. Some of Mom's earliest blogs wrestled with this exact issue. Who's to blame? And if there's no one, then somehow it must be her fault. As much as I hate her blog, I've read every entry. They were a road map of when my disability stopped being mine and became our family's, like some kind of noxious butter.

"Is Ryan going on the trip to Morelands?" Mom asks. They've carried on the conversation.

He looks up from his soup, caught off guard. I guess he has some explaining to do to Luis. "I haven't heard anything about this. Tell me more," Mrs. Kim asks. Her voice has that mom-neutral edge—the one that makes sure teens everywhere know they messed up. Mom network. They are never going to let anything go down in secret.

"Oh, Luis is gonna be pissed," I say, looking at Ryan and grinning.

His mom looks lost, but she focuses on Ryan. "I was going to tell you," Ryan says.

"It's a trip for our friend Luis—a goodbye tumor party," I say. Mom takes over, and with all the real details.

"I'm letting Ellie go because her friend Caitlin is. I wouldn't let her go alone."

Well, at least that's one hurdle down.

"Do you feel up to it?" is all his mom replies. What a loaded question, but at least his mother is giving Ryan a choice. "You should call your friends—I'm sure they'd love to come see you."

"They all have games this weekend." Anger laced with regret shapes every word. I want to reach out and tell him that it's okay, that I know what he's going through. Watching the rest of the world get on without you, doing the things you love while you're stuck in this limbo of a place, is a real mind fuck.

"I think you should go," his mom says with some finality. So maybe his mom does control his life.

There are of course conditions, most of which I know already. Emergency number plugged into phones, medicine taken, if we feel the least bit bad call and they will collect us.

In the end I'm excited, because I'm one step closer to a bit of freedom and Ryan looks like he's going to go all Joker on me.

"And you have something to tell your mom . . . unless you want Caitlin to pull the plug," he says low enough for only me to hear. *Just when you think a boy is on your side.*

"I thought you were on my mom's side."

"Maybe I'm just on your team."

He holds my gaze and I am at a loss for a comeback.

We help the Kims clean up, and Ryan gives me a pointed look when Mom and I leave. *Now or never.*

We get ready for bed mostly in silence, Mom talking a bit about the next day and what to look out for at Morelands. My phone pings with more texts from Caitlin. Mom stands at the foot of our bed. Behind her, the computer glows. I tuck my knees into my chest and want to bury my head there, but I don't look away.

For Jack.

"What?"

Deep breath, I tell myself. *She loves you.* A small voice says, *Maybe too much.* "Can I—I want . . ."

"Ellie, what is it?" Mom peels back the blankets and starts to fluff the pillows. She doesn't see that there's anything wrong. That I'm not living on a tightrope. This is just a normal night for her.

Spit it out.

"I want you to stop posting about me online." My voice is small and far away, but somewhere in there it holds the weight of a stone.

Her brow furrows. "Those people are our community. They've been there for us through everything. They know what it is to have VACTERLs."

I chew on my bottom lip. Mom talks about *VATERs Like Water* like it's a part of her.

"I just don't want you to talk about . . . about my surgeries and stuff. It's just a lot and I want . . . I want some privacy. I want to be my own person."

"Ellie . . ." And I believe the emotion in her voice. That she heard me. There's hurt, and it feels so close to the voice she used to talk to me in when I was just her daughter and not her daughter and her problem.

Tears catch in my throat, tangling up with a coughing fit that's been threatening my lungs. Hospitals tear us all apart. Mom was the one who brought me here—because it was the best, and it probably did save my life. But now look where we are. Mom sits on the bed next to me and I hide my face in my knees, unable to look at her.

"Ellie, look at me." Her words are gentle, and when she repeats them they strengthen—firm but full of love. They tear at me. What am I doing? Still, I think of Jack reading Mom's words—what must he think of me?

"What's wrong?"

"You just make me sound like I'm still a kid. An infant that you need to take care of. I just want it to stop."

"Oh Ellie," she says, and hugs me. Her weight is comforting, but her words are stones and I fear they may leave bruises. "I didn't know this was how you felt." She kisses the top of my head. "I promise, no more posting about you online."

And just like that, a load is lifted. I look up at my mom, breathing easy because this wasn't as hard as I thought it would be. She's going to change.

"Thank you," I say.

That night I can barely sleep, but this time it's not the coughing that keeps me up or anything to do with my body. I sneak out of bed, grab my hoodie, and head for the family room.

Chapter Seventeen

Ryan's coming in from the other door just as I am and we both freeze, unsure what to do with our once again shared space.

"I thought we agreed this was my spot," he says, humor hidden in the corners of his mouth. "I am new here after all." He shakes his black hair out of his eyes, and I struggle to not tell him to get a haircut already. It's the dare hidden in his words, the one that creates our own world, that stops me. I don't want to break this spell.

I cross my arms over my chest but meet his smile with my own. "You probably wouldn't know what to do without me."

"Who's the medical coach here?"

"Who's the patient coach?"

A full smile is all I get in answer and I just shake my head in an attempt to hide my own. "You make tea, I'll set up the show?" I offer.

Neither of us moves, as if we really are too afraid to cross some invisible line. This is exactly where I want to be. As much as my nights have become a thing I do alone, Ryan's company has been a welcome reprieve.

"Oh absolutely not. I am not letting you have this back until I see you walk through those OR doors."

"Put the disc in, let's see how far you got. I'll go get tea."

In the kitchen, I drum my fingers on the counter waiting for the water to boil, trying to work through how Ryan and I went from enemies to friends in just a few short days.

The water boils and I bring the tea back into the living room. Ryan's already seated on the couch, the show paused on the title sequence.

"How did you get into this show?" he asks as I set the tea down and curl up on the couch next to him.

After catching a yawn in my sleeve, I start on the explanation. "My dad, he watched the original when he was a kid, and when I was old enough he thought it was something we could do together."

"Does he . . ." Ryan lets the question float off into the air, but the meaning of his words is clear. Is my dad around? Are he and my mom still together?

"Yeah, they're still together. He just works a lot. Hazards of having a kid who needs a lot of health care." My dad doesn't always get to spend a lot of time with me because his job keeps him busy. I've never stopped to wonder if he likes what he does or even if this is his life's work. He just . . . does it.

It pays the bills. It makes sure I can go to the hospital. It's completely and totally responsible. Not like my dream. A brief picture of myself onstage pops into my head and I bury it fast.

"You watched this whole thing together, though."

"Multiple times. We do a few other sci-fi shows, but this one always feels like home." Strange how I never trusted Jack with this story. He knew I liked *BSG* but never got into it. But here Ryan is not only loving it but embracing this thing I crave. I crave hearing his commentary or even just the random thoughts he has while watching. Being with him is like being home.

"What?" I ask, touching my face because Ryan looks at me with concern.

"There are like five smiles in this entire show. This is not a happy, comfort show."

"Oh, and what should I watch? What is medical coach approved?" I lean in, invading his space, chin in hand, challenging smile in place, daring him to push me away.

"Hey." He gives me a playful shove at the mention of his nickname.

The contact ripples through my body, making me long for something I've put on hold, saved for someone else.

I want more.

The realization is startling, and—No, I want Jack. This is why I'm doing everything; my body is just confused. I laugh and try to play it off. He is just my medical coach.

Nothing more.

I split my attention between the episode and trying to bottle up these new feelings. We're deep into our second episode when Ryan asks, "Do you think Luis would notice if we just didn't go?"

"If we don't show up I think he would personally hunt us down. That, or he'd put Caitlin on us both. Why do you keep asking this?" He asked the same thing at dinner, and I haven't forgotten that he wasn't excited about this from the beginning. "What's wrong?"

Ryan studies his hands and lets out a big breath, his cheeks puffing out.

"Rule three," I say, reminding him we both agreed to always tell each other the truth.

"You'll call me a hypocrite."

"You're afraid of your friends showing up?" I don't wait for him to answer because I heard him at dinner, saw the fear in his eyes when his mom mentioned them.

"You said your one friend might get it."

Ryan buries his hands in his hoodie pocket and leans his head back on the couch, studying the ceiling. I sit up and close some of the space between us. Everything in me screams to back up, pull away, let him work through this, but I find I can't. I want to know what he's thinking, his hopes and fears about tomorrow.

"Yeah, Sarah would get it. I guess. They're great—I mean Will and Nate—we're on the same soccer team. Sarah's been our friend since forever. . . . I just . . . How did you get out of it?"

"Unfortunately for you, I am going to see my friends tomorrow. Jack's performing and Brooke will be there."

His head snaps up, like he touched a hot stove. There's shock and fear, and hiding under all of that is hurt. Something deep and lasting that I don't know how to respond to. "Does that make me bad? That I don't want them to see me like this?" The look he gives me is somewhere between an apology and real curiosity.

I snort. If he thinks I am going to be a kind and build-you-up sort of coach, Ryan should go find someone else. "No. Were you expecting it to?"

"You're willing to see your friends."

I roll the answer around in my head. "You have nothing to be ashamed of." My gag reflex perks up at those words. I mean them, there's nothing wrong with using a cane. There's nothing wrong with Ryan. Hell, there's nothing wrong with any of us here, someone just needs to tell the rest of the world.

"Thanks." He sounds about as happy as being told he needs a root canal on top of everything else.

Lucky for him, I'm an expert at not letting my friends know about all of this. "Don't let them take control of the conversation. They want info, you change the subject. They ask how you're doing—*Eh, I'm fine*. Or be honest—like really honest, it scares people. Be you, not your medical file."

"You're not your medical file, you know that, right?"

I shoot him a sideways glance. "Obviously, I'm cool."

"But, like, we could do this even if we weren't here."

"We wouldn't be doing this if we weren't here."

"If there's one good thing to come out of it." He holds my gaze, and there's something about the way he looks at me that makes me wish he'd always look at me like that. Here, in this moment, we could be the only two people in existence, and he sees me, not the sarcasm and a cross-stitch pattern that I usually operate on, but me with all those ugly, unidentified parts of me that are not fit for anyone. He sees me and he's totally okay with it.

"I'll be right there with you," I say.

"Promise?"

"Rule number four?" I ask, and pull out my phone to add *Rule 4: We'll always be there* to our growing list. He nods like we've committed to something beyond today.

Chapter Eighteen

Ryan stares dubiously at the door to the Family Care Home. Outside there is a bus. One we are definitely going to get on, which will then take us to the Moreland Mall.

As much as I want to just not be here, at Coffman, about to have surgery—seeing Jack one more time will be the boost I need to get through it. I nudge Ryan forward. We're in this together. He glares at me, his brown eyes telling me to back off.

That's just not in my nature.

"I can't believe I let you talk me into this." He's tense next to me, way more than he was when we parted last night. He's on edge like I've never seen him before; Ryan Kim is losing his cool.

"What is it that you like to say? Teamwork?" He narrows his eyes at me and I just smile. Payback is evil and I quite enjoy it. "You need a break from this before it becomes your entire life." Ryan's fear is not going to stand between me and my boyfriend.

"We're still in the hospital," he grumbles, but inches toward the door.

Starbuck, give me strength.

Mom and Mrs. Kim trail behind us, both of them surprisingly cool about letting us leave the safety of the hospital. There's a new sense of normal between Mom and me—like there's nothing standing between us. I don't have to watch myself around her in fear it will end up on her blog or be used to raise money to support others. If it weren't for surgery in a few days, I'd swear I was living my best life.

"Got everything?" Mom reaches out to adjust the collar of my jacket, and I let her because this could be the new normal, where she's just my mom and not my mom-plus-Ellie-blogger. The bombs I worried about when I told her to stop didn't blow up in my face. She got it. And maybe, like Ryan suggested, I just need to have a little faith.

"Yup," I say, backing up. Faith. But not that much faith yet.

"Cough drops and your extra battery pack?"

I nod.

"Money I gave you?"

Another nod. Plus an eye roll. This is Morelands, not a trek through the Sahara.

"Call if you need me? I can just as easily drive—"

"Mom," I say, cutting her off.

"I know, I know you're a big girl."

I cover my eyes with my fingertips, embarrassed by her comment. "Mom," I say, pouring every ounce of teenage annoyance I have into the word.

"I'm sorry." But her smile peeks through. "Have fun."

I flash her some finger guns and go rescue Ryan, who still looks five seconds away from giving up on this trip.

"Mind if I steal him?" I say, taking his hand, ready to drag him out if necessary. It's a trick Mom used to do when I was a kid and thought throwing a tantrum could get me out of tests. His fingers tighten over mine and he shoots me a look. The touch grounds me, and for the first time the Home doesn't feel like a hotel or just a place to stay, it feels like it could be normal. Because at the end of this trip is Jack. Or so I tell myself. I let go of Ryan's hand just as Ryan looks down at our once entwined fingers. Turning my best smile on Mrs. Kim, I interrupt her interrogation of Ryan.

Butterflies play games with my heart, and all I want to do is squash each and every one of them. I brush aside the emotion. Completely unnecessary.

"Coming?" I ask Ryan through a cough. The sting in my lungs banishes the fluttering in my chest. *Back to your battle stations, body, we have to survive this.*

Mrs. Kim eyes me and looks slightly more relieved that I'm going on this trip with her son.

"Go on," Mom says, waving Ryan and me toward the bus. "Us moms are going to have a day off." She and Mrs. Kim trade looks, but Mrs. Kim seems more wary of letting us go than Mom does. But this is what Mom does—her whole thing is about helping parents adjust to this new way of life.

"Have fun," I call, and practically frog-march Ryan toward the bus. He leans on his cane, and I wonder for a moment if I should be worried about him. Maybe Ryan shouldn't go. Maybe it's too much. Well, he has to learn his limits sometime and no better way to help realign yourself than to overextend. People talk about moderation all the time, but it's almost impossible to practice if you've been running at eighty percent all your life.

"Keep walking," I tell him when I feel he's about to turn back. The comment is for me as much as it is for him. I want to see Jack, but somehow all I can remember is the look of disappointment in his eyes when he left me.

"Wait." Mom pulls out her phone. "I want a photo."

Fear jabs me in the kidney. And I freeze. "Mom," I say, a warning lacing its way through my words.

She winces, probably remembering her promise, and puts her phone away. I breathe easier, my chest returning to its normal crackles.

I don't check to see if Ryan caught that, much less if he has any response to my mother's comments. Instead, I just push him forward. *JackJackJack* . . .

"You did talk to her about the blog?" he asks. "Caitlin's not going to, like, suddenly call this whole thing off?" I glare at him, mostly because of how hopeful he sounds. What could be so wrong about getting away from this place for a few hours?

"If you were holding out hope for that—you'll be disappointed," I say. There is no joke, no lightness, to my words. I am deadly serious. It's been handled—*I hope*, a small voice in my head adds.

Ryan slips back into medical coach. "You wanna give me the play-by-play?"

"Let's just say I've fired a team member." The admission stings, my issues with Mom still too freshly closed. Just because you had surgery doesn't mean things don't take time to go back to normal.

Ryan uses this distraction to try to go back. "I think I forgot something." He tries to do an about-face and I shift, hooking my arm around his elbow. The electricity returns. It's as if it can re-form my body, or maybe reprogram it. Ryan catches my eye, and more butterflies hatch in my chest. Because it's that look like Jack had, as if for one moment, I can make the world spin.

I let go of him fast. What is wrong with me? Maybe because he's helping me, all my feelings are getting mixed up.

"You're coming," I say for what is probably the hundredth and final time. I don't dare touch him again; instead I just wait as he mounts the bus's steps. "Rule number four—I'll be with you the whole way."

"Promise?" he finishes, his tone shifting to serious. And for a second I don't know how to react. I'm doing this for Jack. I want to see my friends, and I think Ryan does too—we need a reminder of why we're doing this hospital thing. It's not because we'll last here but because we'll leave here. We just have to get each other across the finish line, and then . . .

We're done.

Ryan looks past me back at the house and then at his cane. "I never should have made those stupid rules." I just smile and wait for his answer. Not my problem he didn't foresee this. "What if this messes everything up?" There's a haunted look in his eyes, and I can just guess he's imagining something that's already happened to him. Something that proves he shouldn't do this. He shakes it off just as easily before I can counter his argument. "I can't believe I let you talk me into this."

"There is no let, this is practically a kidnapping."

The rest of Tumor Squad is already on the bus. Ryan picks a seat close to the front and drops. He hesitates when I drop into a seat across from him and then puts his cane next to him. I wonder if he expected me to sit with him.

"Are we getting charged with felony kidnapping, at least?" Caitlin asks from her seat. "If not, take him back and do it right. I want a decent criminal record."

"I'm not pressing charges," Ryan says, just to spite her.

"Children," Luis says, pulling down his mask, "settle down."

My doctors may raise an eyebrow or two, but they're not gonna stop me. But if Jack breaks my heart, the docs are not going to be happy.

I stamp out those thoughts; this is going to work. Jack is going to be happy to see me.

Luis grins. "Time to live before surgery and radiation."

"Plus it will make excellent footage for *A Patient Life*," Caitlin says.

"Please tell me we are doing this for something other than Caitlin's weird photo op?" Ryan asks, picking at his seat.

"We're taking photos?" Luis asks. "'Cause I would have worn my good beanie then." He points to the worn-out and pilled stocking cap covering his bald head. Despite the trip and impending surgery, his dark brown eyes still carry a hint of mischief.

"No, we are not taking anything resembling a group photo," I say, putting an end to that. The last thing I need is to tempt Mom with a photo that's blog bait. I can just see the title now: *This Is How a Kid Is Normal!* Gag me with a spoon.

"So no photos," Luis says.

"None."

"If teens go to the mall and don't document it on social media, did it really happen?" Caitlin says. "Plus I have already talked about this on *A Patient Life*." I know that Caitlin will respect my privacy.

"Exactly, it's like Schrödinger's cat but in day form. The day both exists and did not at the same time."

"We know it exists," Ryan says. "Are we the cat, then?"

"Perhaps we are," I say, enjoying this. Caitlin looks at us like we need to be taken to the ER to be seen by doctors immediately. I just smile at her. She holds up a finger to me like *This is a warning*, but her stern look is compromised when she has to blow a curl out of her eyes. Neither of us can hold in a laugh.

Veronica sprints up the bus steps, her blond braid flying behind her, almost out of breath, and walks down the aisle toward us. I don't miss that Luis brightens and sits up a little straighter when she does.

One of the full-time Home employees steps onto the bus. Unlike Veronica, she doesn't have the overly perky face of someone there for the right kind of wrong reasons. She knows this world and knows enough to stay out of it.

Rules are read, times we're leaving, how long we'll be there, and of course tickets. There's a small amusement park in the center of Moreland, and wouldn't you know they give us sick kids free all-you-can-ride wristbands.

As the bus pulls away, we all wave to our parents. At one point on the drive, Caitlin trades places with Ryan so that she can sit closer to Luis and Veronica. The three of them are deep in conversation about some movie. However, I don't miss how Veronica takes any opportunity to touch Luis. She's into the conversation, but something shifts in her when she focuses on Luis. He soaks it up.

"Do you even understand what they're saying half the time?" Ryan asks.

I lean forward, watching the three of them talk animatedly. Words like *cinematography* and *fourth wall* get thrown out at random. "Just nod and go along. Unfortunately, I don't have a film coach to help me through these sessions."

"You could if you wanted," Caitlin says.

I roll my eyes. *Of course she heard me.* Nothing escapes her. She disappears back into the conversation before I can reply. "I will watch whatever movie you want me to when you let me help you with your TV appearance."

"So, truth," Ryan says, drawing my attention to him. His focus is on his hands, like he's not sure I can take what he's about to say. "My friends are gonna be there. I made the mistake of texting one of them last night. After—"

"Ryan not following doctor's orders and getting a full eight hours of sleep? How dare you," I say in mock shock. It manages to crack a smile across his tense features and warmth spreads throughout my chest. So this is why he was so keyed up this morning. Last night it was just a possibility, but now . . . his friends are actually coming. "You don't want them to come?"

"I didn't think I'd mind seeing them," Ryan says, but he shifts in his seat. I think he would very much mind if they showed up. "I mean you'll be off with . . . Jack." He struggles through the word and I refuse to read anything into it. "This isn't exactly a spectator sport, is it?"

"You have no idea," I say under my breath. There's no drug on this planet that will make me forget the way my old friends stared at me. How their points and murmurs of the word *freak* shredded my childhood. Nothing about this is real to them. Science is just a class during the day. They're not the experiments.

"What?"

"Nothing." I flash him a brilliant smile. There's no need to scare him with how much being disabled will make you an object. It's so easy to forget in the hospital, where everyone is some form of messed up. "I mean," I say, backtracking, "rule four."

And I'm surprised that I mean it. I'm not leaving him to face this alone.

"Rule four." His gaze travels over to the others. There's a way his eyes shift like he's balanced between our world and life-life, but this time siding with life-life. He's not worried about them seeing him, he's worried about them seeing us.

I want to hate him for that. Caitlin and I have had our share of judgment from people. Luis too, probably, with his bald head. But Ryan, sans cane, of course, can pass. And what a privilege that is.

This feeling of unease—that maybe he's not fully on our team— trickles down my spine and I can't shake it. I'm not really sure I want to. It's just a reminder to keep my distance.

I was right about the whole hospital situation. It's a real relationship killer. Ryan just doesn't know that his judgment-of-my-life look, the one that still sneaks through his eyes, will be the end of our friendship here.

Ryan sits there and presses his lips together. I can see him on the soccer field doing that as he assesses where to go next. Who to kick the ball to? How to win? *There is no winning this one.*

Not true, for him there is a difference between a win and a loss. People who get stuck like me—we're the losers.

Why didn't I just leave him behind?

When his friends show up, I don't know what I'll do. I don't need another thing to worry about when I leave to go find Jack and Brooke. People change when they leave these walls, like you adopt a certain persona just to get through it. Becoming stronger, more resilient, and sometimes sour just to keep going through all the bullshit.

Ryan is in no way ready to meet his friends again, which means I'm stuck babysitting him for the day.

There are worse options.

Chapter Nineteen

The Home employee hands out wristbands and makes sure we plug emergency numbers into our phones. Caitlin and I do it without being told, but the others sort of grumble.

"Just do it," Caitlin says. "It's not like it will kill you." We share a knowing look with each other that says *Can you believe these people?*

I sigh in response. Whatever will they do when they are responsible for their fragile health 24/7?

"I don't understand why they can't just trust us to take care of ourselves," Luis complains.

Caitlin tenses beside me. After dealing with me and my bullshit, she's roughly 2.5 seconds away from going nuclear on these newbies. This trip is supposed to be about us getting away from the hospital and all its accoutrements for a day.

"Maybe because there's a lump in your neck threatening your life?" I say in a perfectly perky tone. For good measure, I plaster on a smile and look up at him through my eyelashes. I care, and he's going to remember it.

I step up to him and tilt my head back so that I can look up at his face. He gave me the hard truth the night we met, returning the favor's a bitch. "Face it, Big C or little, you have cancer. Your body is literally trying to kill you. The people who let us come here only let us out if we have a direct line to—"

"Major medical support," Caitlin adds. "So put a number in your phone and call if you need it."

With a shrug and a huff, Luis digs out his phone and stabs in the emergency contact. He adjusts his beanie and mumbles what I swear sounds like "I'm practically an adult." Satisfied, the volunteer shoos us off toward the entrance.

Inside, we shed coats, gloves, and scarves, shoving all our winter weather gear into a locker, which takes all four of us to close. I bounce on the balls of my feet, too excited to see Jack.

"We need some kind of plan," Ryan says, trying to harness our chaotic energy. He pushes his black hair out of his eyes and hits each of us with a pointed look.

I give Ryan a look that says *No. You're cute, but no.*

"Since this is my party," Luis says, taking charge, "rides first."

Ryan leads us through the fastest route to the rides, since he lives closest to Morelands. Newer rides crowd the ones I grew up with—aka the ones that I know are safe—and just my luck, Luis drags us toward a new one.

"That needs to be pre-ridden," I say, pulling up short. Luis, Veronica, and Ryan all stop and look as if I stuttered and turn back, confused.

"Yup, most definitely," Caitlin agrees, stepping to the side next to me. "Spinal issues."

Luis's mouth forms an O, our reluctance finally clicking for him.

"I'll hang back too," Veronica says, eyeing the ride with skepticism.

"Okay, Kim, it's you and me."

"What should we be on the lookout for?" Ryan asks, pulling away from Luis and moving closer to me. I guess he's taking his medical coach job seriously. He stops so close to me I can smell the fabric softener on his clothes. His brown eyes linger on me and I try to focus on the task at hand. *Rides.*

Right.

"Does it jostle? Does it have sudden stops? How hard? Throw you against the restraints?" Caitlin rattles off, almost pushing herself between us. It breaks the gravitational pull between Ryan and me, and I step back, suddenly self-conscious at how close we were.

"We'll report back," Ryan says, grabbing Luis by the back of his sweatshirt and dragging him toward the ride.

We find a bench close to the ride and sit down—my body already feeling the strain of the day. Caitlin tilts her face up as if she can catch rays of sun through the opaque windows high above our heads and pulls out her phone.

"Do you have to do that often?" Veronica asks, pulling her braid over her shoulder, picking at the ends.

"What?" I ask, knowing exactly what she means. I share a look with Caitlin. This is such a regular part of our lives that even Veronica questioning it is right on schedule.

"Ask people to do stuff for you?"

I shrug—*Yeah, maybe?* But also it's a balancing act, and everyone is different.

"You have to ask, otherwise people treat you like you're a baby. They help you with the stuff you don't need—" Caitlin starts, but my coughs interrupt her. They double me over and run until I'm not sure there's any oxygen left in my body. Face red and hot, I try to grab air between hacks.

"Whoa," Veronica says, rubbing my back, ignoring what we were just talking about. Startled, I jerk away from her touch. Veronica is nice and all, but we are nowhere near that level of friendship. Brooke has barely earned the right to show concern for me in public, let alone intervene if I'm having issues. It's one of those things that just serves to remind people that I am not like them.

Veronica backs off, one hand raised. "Sorry, I just . . ."

"Okay," Caitlin says, inserting herself between the two of us, ready to fight Veronica.

"I didn't—" Veronica curls in on herself, shoving her hands into her pockets.

"It's fine," I say, waving away her apology and the impending fight.

My lungs calm and I come up for air. "It's not that kind of cough," I explain. Her actions are well-meant but ineffective. "There's nothing in my lungs—never mind."

Caitlin rolls her eyes and mutters something like "Newbie" but follows it up with a louder "Bless your heart." I glare at her. This is not the time. Despite Veronica's perky tendencies, I like her.

"It's like you all have this secret language and I'm on the outside." Veronica says this with the same wistful tone that someone might use when discussing Disneyland. Like she wants to come too. Like this is fun.

Caitlin looks at me as if asking for permission to read Veronica the riot act. And maybe I should let Caitlin do it, but I like Veronica. I want her to be my friend.

"Look, you're cool, and so I don't . . ." I take a deep breath. "You can't say stuff like that to people. I mean anybody, and certainly not to anybody we're here with."

I lean on the bench, certain that she'll walk away. Opening up to people is just going to once again prove that I will end up alone.

Caitlin sits primly next to me, as if waiting to see if Veronica will let her perky side out again.

"I don't want to mess *this* up." The way Veronica says *this*, I don't think it has anything to do with what happened five seconds ago. "Luis asked me out."

I look at Caitlin and her hazel eyes meet mine—things finally clicking into place. Both of us are stunned by this revelation. Sure, both of us date and we have a bit of rocky history with love, but the whole volunteer/patient thing is weird and should be prohibited in any and all volunteer handbooks. Still, breaking volunteer rules wouldn't exactly be my first worry. More like—is Veronica ready for a hospital love affair? Can she handle a romance on cancer?

"Ummm . . ." is all I trust myself to say. Well, that explains the bus earlier.

Veronica has toned down the perky side of herself, but it's still there, as evidenced by two seconds ago. But she's willing to learn. She wants to do better, and that feels different—good different.

"I just, we've been texting a lot," she explains, picking at the end of her braid. "I think he's funny and has great taste in movies."

"It also helps that he's cute," Caitlin adds.

Veronica blushes, her pale skin going red as a honeycrisp apple. "Yeah." She falls silent, and we all watch logs go down the shoot. People throw their hands up and let out shouts of joy.

"Why did you want to volunteer here?" Caitlin asks, backtracking. I nod along, still too stunned to come up with a question. Caitlin is more than welcome to take this over.

"I wanted to help people. I read so many stories about kids in the hospital. Cancer, disabilities, I suppose . . . I wanted to be a part of it . . ." Her voice trails off and she looks at us. I want to hide the shock. Because wow. That's an answer. Honest, at least. But wow. Caitlin is definitely taking this one. Although she may just skewer Veronica with a crochet hook. "I suppose that doesn't sound good."

"None of that ever gets said again. Like. Ever," I say, finally finding my voice.

Veronica nods.

"And why ask us?" Caitlin continues. "My boyfriend dumped me and Ellie's is pissed off she didn't tell him she was having surgery."

"Isn't Ryan your medical coach? He talked you into surgery."

"What are you talking about?" Why is Veronica bringing up Ryan in the middle of this conversation?

Caitlin's eyes go round as saucers and realization hits me. Veronica thinks Ryan is my . . . Caitlin doesn't hold in her laugh. It bubbles out of her and she leans back against the bench, dying.

"What?" Veronica looks confused.

"Do—do you think Ryan is my boyfriend? He is *not* my boyfriend."

But it's scary how easy it is to imagine us being together. Our late-night TV sessions are a bright spot at the Home. I can't believe I'm going to admit this, but I want to see him play soccer, be in the stands when he scores. Or distract him on the days his friends go to a game and he can't.

There are so many places and experiences I want to enjoy with Ryan, but almost nothing when it comes to Jack. I just . . . want Jack back, but I'm not sure why.

Caitlin's laughter finally dries up and she slings an arm around Veronica. "I have to know why you think Ellie and Ryan are dating. I can't remember the last time I laughed that hard."

"They're always together. The way he looks at Ellie . . . I dunno—you fit."

He looks at me a certain way? More than just his usual annoyance—I don't think so. But I don't hate the idea that he might.

Caitlin studies me as if trying to see what Veronica does, how my edges may blur into Ryan's. "Stop it—how soon do you think they'll be back?" The last thing I want is for Veronica to bring up this ridiculous theory in front of the whole group.

"I say we send them a list of rides to check out and then go find something fun," I say.

Caitlin pulls out her phone. "Sending them a list of rides to check out for us." She makes a big show of hitting send. "Done."

"Bookstore?" I ask, wanting to put as much distance between Ryan and me as possible.

"Bookstore," Caitlin confirms.

Caitlin has apparently decided not to kill Veronica and steps into her natural habitat of reading someone into our world. I can practically see her fingers twitch to reach for her phone and record something for @APatientLife. Slowly I can see the lines between my life here in the hospital and my life at home blending together. I learn Veronica is in speech too. This is her first year, so we might actually see each other at competitions. Assuming the surgery goes according to plan. For once instead of putting up more barriers, I lean in, wanting more. Craving it.

We linger over the long tables of new books, picking up titles and flipping over covers, looking for the best books to get us through a slew of appointments.

A little girl comes up to the table; her eyes barely make it over the first stack of books. Her father comes up and tries to lead the girl away. She looks up at me, her brown eyes large and inquisitive.

My stomach drops.

Oh no.

Those doe-like eyes flash from me to the book, to me again. I meet her father's gaze. We both know what will come out of her mouth at any moment. He seems desperate to prevent it. Veronica looks to Caitlin and me, asking if there's something she should do. Fast learner, that one. I shake my head. *Nope, this just has to play out.*

To make matters worse, the little girl starts moving her arm, twisting it and turning it, definitely trying to contort her body into the shapes that come to me naturally and abnormally to anyone else.

"Honey," he says, "let's go." His eyes shoot me an apology.

Caitlin is ready to step in and I reach out a hand and catch her. One thing I've always admired about Caitlin is that she's willing to make a scene to prove her point, but I'd still rather blend into the background.

"Dad, how do I get an arm like hers?" We stop. There is no play-book for this. No rules to follow. Except maybe apologize and run away. The girl's father seems ready to pick the young girl up when she says, "It's so cool."

Satisfied that she was heard, the dad mumbles some apology and finally carts his kid off to the children's section.

Caitlin and I stand there dumbfounded. "Did that . . . ," I say, not sure how I can put into words what just happened. It's not what I'm used to. The one memory burned into my brain forever is the time I made a kid cry just by standing there. Nothing will make you think maybe your friends were right and you were a freak quite like having your existence being a cause for tears.

But that girl . . . I want to give her a medal or maybe congratulate her parents for not raising an asshole. For giving me hope that maybe there are people out there who can just see me without knowing me.

"Was that—okay?" Veronica asks.

"Someone called us cool," Caitlin says. "Kids today. You might just be able to be an actor yet." And just like that, Caitlin ruins my good mood. One kid does not an audience make. The girl manages to turn around once and smiles at us, still trying to manipulate her arm into a shape that resembles mine.

"You getting the book?" Caitlin asks when we both can speak again.

"Later. It'll be good for my dad."

Veronica, who is still struck by what just happened, asks, "You deal with that all the time?"

"Just watch the crowd when we go back out—how many people stare—" I start.

"And move out of the way," Caitlin continues.

"Generally avoid us."

"People are terrible," Veronica says, disgust turning her face sour.

"Now she gets it," Caitlin says, throwing an arm around her as we leave the bookstore.

Chapter Twenty

*R*yan convenes us all for lunch, his need for order overruling Luis's plan to play it by ear. At the food court we split off to different places, coming back to crowd around a table meant for four.

My body feels the strain of the day as I drape myself over a chair, melting into the hard plastic like it's a pillow top mattress. I let out a groan, pushing back a few strands of hair that have escaped their clip. I haven't done this much physical activity in months. Exhaustion wraps around me like a blanket, tucking me in as if to say *This adventure is now over, back to the couch.* No one ever talks about how when you're sick, moving sometimes feels like the air is made of pudding and your limbs may get stuck or even fail to push through.

Ryan comes up with his tray. "You mind?" he asks when he takes the seat across from me. I want to ask how he knows to ask that, because any seat to the side of me is always hard for me. My neck doesn't move very well, so whatever conversations happen around me—they're a bit more difficult. Best to be head-on.

I shift in my seat. I'm not going to read into this. Not one bit. No matter what Veronica said. Ryan and I have just spent too much time together, he's picked up on it . . . it means nothing.

I want it to mean nothing.

Mostly.

Thoughts of last night replay in my head, pushing for more. One more laugh, an inside joke, the touch of his hand—enough!

Forcing a smile, I take a large bite out of my burrito to keep myself from saying something I don't mean. This is just hospital emotions getting to me. Nothing more.

Caitlin has a supersized smoothie but looks longingly at my burrito. "Surgery this week."

"First meal?" I ask. It's a small ritual. Every eight weeks, Caitlin has to have her esophagus dilated so she can swallow properly again. Until then, she goes down to a liquid diet. This time I pull out my phone.

"I thought you said no pictures?" Caitlin looks at me skeptically.

"You need the practice. One take."

"At least give me two."

I shake my head and press record. This isn't so bad, being on the other side of the camera. "First meal?"

"Tacos." The word is a prayer, a benediction, hope in the form of food to one day be delivered. "Salsa. Guac. Chips. So many chips."

I replay the clip and Caitlin leans over. "I don't like—" She reaches for my phone and I pull it away.

"Absolutely not."

Everyone else at the table stares at one another with looks that say they might be running for cover. Caitlin and I aren't exactly normal lunchtime companions. We're a bit of an acquired taste.

"You two realize you're weird, right?" Luis asks.

"This isn't actually weird—this is totally normal," Caitlin replies. Her solemn face breaks into a smile that seems to curl around the corners of her eyes. "Just wait, you'll end up like us."

"Is that part of the treatment plan?" Luis is easygoing, but I spy Veronica's look of concern out of the corner of my eye. She looks like she might say something, but Luis turns back to her and holds her gaze as if to say *I got you*. Well, that's a development I did not see coming.

"Only if you're lucky."

Caitlin and I pull meds out of our purses and line them up on the table. Little soldiers here to help fight an invisible battle. I eyeball a dose of cough syrup and swig it back without flinching.

"What?" I ask, staring at the group's shocked expressions. I drop the bottle into a plastic bag before putting it back in my purse.

"You all need a crash course in how to live disabled." Caitlin says this with all the matter-of-factness of a doctor presenting a case.

"Umm, what?" Veronica says. At least she's taking one for the team.

"You're gonna be doing this, it's not weird, it's just life."

"Just little things," I say, fishing out my bottle of ibuprofen. I dry swallow three without even thinking about it. "Like taking meds. Living your life and assessing risk."

"Learn from us, we're here to help. I've been doing this for years."

"Years?" Luis asks, his eyes going big. Everyone assumes that what we do here is a temporary thing, like we're just passing through. And maybe for some of them—like Luis—it might be.

My gaze shifts to Ryan, who's gone quiet, picking at his food court burger. He's probably wondering how long he'll live in this limbo of not knowing his diagnosis and what treatment plan will make him better. I want to know what he's thinking and I want to tell him he doesn't need to be worried, because I'm right here. I nudge his foot under the table and his head jerks up, his dark eyes finding mine.

I raise an eyebrow. This is what friends do—we pick each other up.

He seems to shake it off and nods to Luis. "You haven't gone through chemo yet. So what happened to your hair?" He flashes me a quick grin. He's okay. Plus he's learned to wait until you're actually friends with a person before butting into their life.

Veronica catches my gaze and just raises an eyebrow. I scowl at her. *This means nothing. Ryan and I are friends. I was checking in on a friend.* She shrugs, but her smile says she doesn't believe that we're "just friends" for an instant. Butterflies come alive in my stomach because maybe I don't want that either?

No. I put a stop to that line of thinking.

"I didn't want to ask, but you're, what, maybe having radiation?" Caitlin adds.

Luis smiles and pulls off his beanie, displaying his bald head. "I heard cancer and thought, *Why wait?* Only later did they tell me I'm not gonna lose my hair."

We all laugh and Caitlin just shakes her head. "What did I say about listening to doctors?"

"Something about them walking on water," I add with an eye roll.

Veronica looks lost. "Aren't they supposed to help you get back to your normal life?"

And there goes the jovial atmosphere, sucked out of the circle. Luis, Ryan, and I all suddenly find our food the most interesting.

"I guess she gets it," I mumble, not really thinking. Normal life — life-life — whatever you want to call it, that's why we're here. This place, for most, is not meant to hold a lifetime.

"It's that kind of thinking that got Ellie into this mess," Ryan starts.

"Yeah, Ellie likes to take that to the extreme," Caitlin adds. I don't miss the shared look between her and Ryan, like they're in on a mission together.

"Excuse me, when did this become the dump on Ellie hour?"

"When you decided to hire me," Ryan says at almost the same time that Caitlin says:

"When I became your best friend."

I feel my cheeks heat, which is probably evidence for Veronica's argument. Two people who have an instant claim to me, and I feel like I'm back at school, caught between Brooke and Jack.

"And when you don't want to explain it to your friends, you'll be like Ellie," Caitlin says.

"Whoa whoa whoa," Luis says — speaking, it seems, for the table, who all look lost. "Back up, what?"

"Ellie doesn't believe in mixing her social groups. Friends at school stay there, friends here stay here." Caitlin preens and I almost want to slug her. I mean yes, this is what I believe. It's what's worked for me for the past how many years of my life? And if all goes according to plan, it will work the same now and I will go back to my life.

I don't miss the doubt and hurt in Ryan's gaze, like he's only now realizing that what we have isn't meant to last. And I don't like how that makes me feel.

"Because how many of your friends at home get it?" I shoot back, wanting to explain my position.

"Some?" Ryan says.

"Most?" Luis adds.

"Right, but you, like, sugarcoat it, right? Dumb it down to make it palatable? It's not like they're living this with you."

"But they're your friends," Luis counters. "They want to be there for you. I have way too many cards from my classmates."

"I used to get cards from my classmates for surgeries, but then there'd be weird questions—*Why didn't they fix you?*" I say. This feels like intentionally showing people my scars. Letting them gape and gawk at what has been done to me.

Everyone at the table flinches except Caitlin, who mutters something like "Assholes."

"So because some five-year-old was an asshole, you just don't tell them anything?" Luis asks. He shakes his head like he's disappointed in me. I press my lips together around the words threatening to escape. What would he know about terrible five-year-olds?

My mind chooses that moment to bring up the girl from the bookstore. Wasn't she different? *It's so cool.*

Luis was right once and only recently did I start to believe that maybe there is still hope for this world. I mean, this is why I am here, right? At Morelands. To see Jack. To try to blend, at least in part, these two worlds. It's definitely not a fifty-fifty mix, but it's something more than I was willing to give.

"Let me guess, all your friends want you to beat cancer?" Caitlin adds. She knows where part of this is going, I think.

"Yeah. I mean the alternative is I die."

I sigh. That question didn't exactly come out the way Caitlin intended it to, but I know the point she's building toward.

"And that's the difference," Caitlin says. "Your friends'll get you back and you might never have to come here again."

"I'll be back here for at least the next five years."

Caitlin and I exchange looks. This is a delicate dance. We're lifetime pass holders at hospitals. Do I want Luis to join that club? Hell no. But also there's a difference between the ones who get to go through this and then rarely look back and those of us who will always come back.

"Okay, I'll be back in eight weeks. And then eight weeks after that. And then another eight weeks after that." She goes on and on, making her point. Luis shrinks in his seat. "Ellie, however, just takes shielding people to the extreme. It's not healthy."

I glare at Caitlin. "That's why I keep—kept—it separate. Because people want an end. They want to say *You beat this, this is done, you are free*—and that's not possible for some of us."

I focus on my burrito. Each word feels like a ton to say, to get off my chest, but even as the weight lifts, another heavier stone seems to crowd in, because the truth is Jack may never understand my hospital self. Because how is he supposed to understand that this will always be a part of my life?

Veronica clears her throat and I look up to see her eyes full of amazement and glossy with tears. So help me, if she says we're all "fighters" or some abled phrase meant to bestow kindness on disabled people, I will duct-tape her mouth shut.

"Eventually you have to trust people." Ryan looks me in the eyes, and the whole world seems to fall away. Trust, sure, I can do that. I trust that my friends know what's best for me. I trust that they trust me.

"And that's why I'm here—because I want to show Jack just a bit of what this is like." Ryan looks away from me like my words were a knife severing our connection. I don't know why it hurts, but I want to reach out. Take his hand, rekindle a version of what we've had, that understanding he had of me.

"I've even been promised an introduction," Caitlin says, adding a flourish to the word *introduction*.

"Okay, but if he doesn't pass our test, you have to break up with him," Luis adds. "Hospital friends know what's up."

Everyone—well, everyone but Ryan—nods in agreement. As if they have a say in my love life.

Chapter Twenty-one

With all the pre-rides done, we hit a riding frenzy after lunch and then my body decides it is done—at least for now. I wave my friends on to the next attraction, and even as Caitlin seems ready to hang back with me, Ryan beats her to it. She hesitates but ultimately leaves with the others. I don't miss the look she and Veronica share. I want to yell after them that this is nothing, I just need to rest up before seeing Jack.

Ryan too seems to be fading fast. He closes his eyes more than once and draws in a deep breath, as if trying to silently talk himself into one more step. We grab coffee because both of us need to get through the rest of the day. I drink heavily while Ryan launches into his running list of *BSG* questions and I find out just how big of a nerd he is. No one at home gets my *you had me at Helo* jokes.

"What's home like?" he finally asks, crossing the line into reality.

I draw my finger around the top of my cup. *Home.* How do I explain a place that he'll never see. A place that feels like it should be as off-limits as asking about why I'm at the hospital. "The usual. A couple of walls, some flooring . . . my dad, a cat." I give him the bare minimum, hoping to satisfy his curiosity so we can go back to where it was safer.

"You have a cat?"

"Hmm-hm," I say. There's so much that I want to tell him—about my cat, Tok'ra, and how he's been my near constant companion these last few months.

Ryan raises an eyebrow, like he doesn't believe that's all I have to say.

So I get brave.

"Tok'ra's great. Especially given these last few months. We're practically fused together—you know, without the actual fusion." My terrible joke pulls a smile from Ryan and I bite my lip, unsure why that makes me happy. Because this feels normal. As if we're not even in the hospital, but just hanging out. As if I could keep him beyond my stay at Coffman.

"So after this," I say, needing to put words to this thing that I feel—this not wanting to lose him.

"After the ride we're definitely not going on?" Ryan says, trying to finish my sentence for me.

"No, like after my surgery." I'm trying to force my mouth to learn the shape of this question. "After they figure out . . ." I motion to him. "We can still like talk . . . right?"

Maybe Caitlin is right, things can be taken out of the hospital, out of this place. They can start here. They can grow. I just have to give it space and care.

"Finally willing to mix your lives."

"If you want to lose my number—"

"Sure." He cuts me off. My mouth goes dry. Did that just . . . work? "Who else am I going to discuss *BSG* with?"

Hope and even excitement bloom in my chest. "I expect a full-on phone call when you get to the end. I can't wait to hear your rant."

"Hey." Ryan holds up his hands over his ears. "Spoilers."

I roll my eyes because who cares about spoilers, but I'm glad that I know he does. It's like a part of him that lives alone outside of this bubble we exist in. It's easy to be with him, to start sharing parts of my life he'll never see. Who would have thought?

Ryan's gaze drifts and I catch the wince of pain on his face. I don't blame him for the fear of what I just said. That maybe there's no end to this. We go through it all, and still the other side could shut us down.

A chill runs up my spine and I pull the end of my long-sleeved shirt over my fingers. Positive thoughts. Only good thoughts. This will work.

Caitlin was the one who always pushed, who reminded me that our friendship, our world, doesn't have to stop at the hospital hallways. And that's what this is between Ryan and me—friendship. I just have to be brave enough to take it outside of Coffman.

"What about you, soccer star? What's home like for you?" I ask, feeling my way across this new and untested ice.

"We only have one wall."

"Oh, modern art house? Lots of windows. Cool." He bumps me and I hold still, making sure he can regain his balance, and then I return the favor. We laugh and stop by the carousel. This could be any time with Brooke and Jack. Old-fashioned Edison bulbs make the world glow around the ride. I'm surprised at how fun today has been and how much I wanted it. We sway to the music, waving at kids who fly by.

Ryan pulls out his phone, flipping it around in his hands like a talisman. I should check the time—see if I need to go find Brooke and Jack—but I don't want to interrupt this conversation.

"You talked to your mom about her blog?"

I smile and stretch back, letting my arms stay on the railing, and pull my hips into better alignment. "Yup, I am a free teenager again."

"But can I have the address—just to make sure you go through with the surgery. Maybe if you need a refresher course."

"If you read that blog, I will consider you a Cylon." My response is automatic, accompanied by a threat that I hope holds weight. I snap back up, knocked out of the normal conversation we'd been having and back into the world where our friendship sprouted.

Other patrons look at us, and a few pull their kids in another direction. Ryan seems to be noticing for the first time that we're out in public and treated like just another piece of art, because he looks around at all the people staring at us.

I sigh. "I don't like my friends reading it. I mean, how would you feel if your mom put everything about your life on the internet?"

"Honestly, I would probably yell at my friends in public too."

"Thanks," I say.

"Why?"

"You're the only person who's ever said that to me. Most people just assume they have a right to my medical file."

"Fuck those people."

"Ryan, language. There are children present." My tone is all false horror, and it's his turn to roll his eyes, but he doesn't. Instead, he goes quiet and studies the phone in his hands.

"You know when you asked me if I told my friends about what goes on here?"

"Not you too," I say, going on the defensive. Didn't we already cover this at lunch? My shoulders curl in and I can feel my walls go up. Ryan has been safe—and I hate how much I wanted him to be my safe place. Who just listened and I could argue with, but who also didn't judge me.

"It's hard," he says, not looking at me, just staring straight ahead at the kids on the ride. Their laughter are tiny pearls of joy that just taunt Ryan and me. "I mean I tell them about you—about Luis and the Tumor Squad. But the appointments, the doctors—I get why you don't. It's so hard to explain, especially after you've gone and lived through it. They want me to get better. But you—you guys get me and I don't want to lose sight of that. So when I try to talk to my friends at home about it, I just . . ."

I reach out and take his hand, because it's something I've always wanted someone to do for me. To not judge or tell me I'm wrong. To just hear me and recognize me, not just with their words but with their touch.

Every inch of contact pings through me. *We're just friends*, I tell myself, and I know exactly where he is. I know what he's going through, and he'll find a way to tell his friends in his own time.

"You're worried this is it." Not a question, a statement. A fear that haunts us all because we know that somewhere, in someone's mind, we're not normal. And we get reminded of that every time we step outside our door.

The little girl this morning aside, people are majorly assholes when it comes to me. When I meet his gaze again, I'm caught. Caught in some kind of force field. Like he's the target that will destroy the Death Star and I'm Luke's shot. We're bound to come together.

The corners of his mouth quirk up and there's a dare in his brown eyes. We could cross this line and it might be worth it.

"Hey, Ryan," someone shouts, knocking us back into the friend zone. Guess I wasn't Luke's shot but Biggs's. Destined to be close but nothing more.

Ryan pales and I'm suddenly nervous. Is this a new development, a new symptom? Where is Caitlin? She should be the one to properly note and categorize what's going on here.

"Ryan," I say, reaching out to touch his shoulder.

"They came," he says flatly. I whip around, looking for who he could be talking about. "I can't believe they came."

"Do we need to go?" I ask, my instincts kicking in. Ryan may be my medical coach, but I'm his patient coach. Step one—only the best of friends are allowed in, and even then, we strike more people off the list.

He doesn't take his cane, choosing instead to try to get along without it. His legs betray him and I run to catch up to him. He grips my arm like it's the only thing keeping him upright. It probably is.

"Wanna read me in, Coach," I say, hoping the nickname will draw him back.

"Ryan!" His name is called by several people, normal teens who hurry to get off the plastic horses of the carousel. Now I understand Ryan's paleness, his refusal to use his cane. These are his people and they know only one sort of Ryan.

"They're your friends?" I ask. "They've already spotted us."

Ryan closes his eyes and takes a deep breath. It's the sort of thing I can see him doing before he takes the field or scores a point. When he lets it out, his breath takes with it his concern, his will to run. I need him to teach me how to do that.

He pivots and I follow, afraid if I don't, he'll fall over. Two boys and a girl greet us, all with smiles that come from drinking a lot of milk. I've seen these types of kids before at school. They're popular. They have that golden glow around them that singles them out. It doesn't automatically make them assholes, just somehow apart from the rest of us. Like they could be the superheroes of the story—or at least what most people would think of as superheroes.

"Ryan, I thought that was you, been texting you since we got here."

"Phone's dead."

No one believes that lie, and it throws everyone off. I was all for hightailing it out of here, but now we're stuck.

The girl breaks away from the two boys and wraps her arms around Ryan's neck. Her close contact means that I have to take a step back. I worry what will happen to Ryan when she pulls away, but he seems to have it under control.

Ryan raises one hand and gently pats her on the back. She releases him and I rush forward again before he wobbles.

"We've been so worried about you," she says.

Suddenly all eyes focus directly on me. Because while I know a lot of people at high school, I for sure do not walk around with that golden halo of excellence.

"Will, Nate, Sarah." Ryan says each of their names but doesn't give them mine.

"Hi," I say, my awkwardness framing the word like an unsure smile. "I'm Ellie, I know Ryan from Coffman."

Recognition spreads across their faces.

"Nice to *finally* meet you," Sarah says, her tone easy, and it surprises me until I remember that Ryan told his friends about me.

"Sometimes they let us out for good behavior," I say.

Ryan barks out a laugh and I smile. His friends just stare at us like we've grown butterfly wings from our ears. And just like that, we have gone from bad to worse.

"We were just leaving," Ryan says. I get the feeling that he too would like a lifeboat. His eyes find mine. "Ellie needs to go see her boyfriend perform."

Right. Jack. The reason I came here in the first place. But if it gets Ryan out of this incredibly awkward friend meetup, I can help him out.

"We really should be going," I add, looking at my phone. There are about five texts from Brooke asking if I'm here and where we can meet up. Definitely going to be late.

Sarah's face falls. "Oh, I was . . ." She stops, and she and the boys exchange looks as if they need to decide if this is all worth it. I want to reach out to Ryan somehow, tell him that I am there, because this friend conference where it seems to be decided if you're still "worth it" is the worst.

"We'll come," the boy on the right says, breaking away from what his friends seem to be doing. The girl just forces a smile.

Great.

I drift to the side of the group, letting the boys pile together, and even Sarah seems to get the feeling that this time is for them and moves closer to me. My body suddenly feels even more outlandish than usual. As if I'm a in glove and I just can't fill all the space and flop around in the extra cloth.

"Always a third wheel," she says as if reading my thoughts. She pushes her chin-length brown hair behind her ear.

"Huh?"

"I wanted to come see Ryan, but I forget how he can be with his teammates." Her eyes drift toward their group.

"Not always, but sometimes," I say, trying that thing again where I'm honest and let people in. Everything in me screams to pull those words back, to cram them back in my mouth and push her away.

We make it to the rotunda just as the choir director raises his hands. Jack's in the middle, and all I can do is stare. There's no way he'll see me in the crowd that's gathered, but just being there sharing space, doing something that feels normal—it's great and somehow makes the heaviness in my limbs feel light, even if for a moment.

"If you don't mind me asking," Sarah says quietly, "you're seeing someone?" There's concern in her voice, like she's trying to get to the bottom of a really hard equation. I follow her gaze to Ryan, Will, and Nate, who have found an equilibrium between their two worlds. They pulled back, leaving the concert so that they could talk. I could see Ryan in school—he'd be just like this, sans cane, of course.

And that's exactly what Sarah is asking about. That she can see Ryan as normal, but me—I'm the one who doesn't fit in her idea of the world.

"I just . . . he talks about you a lot. . . ." She lets her voice trail off but caps her words with a pointed look at me—as if I've done something wrong, and it comes together for me.

I turn on her. "I had a boyfriend. We—he broke up with me." I don't know why I tell her that. I've been so focused on getting Jack back that I haven't even admitted that we're not together. "I wanted to see if today could fix it."

Sarah winces. "I'm sorry. I just . . . They . . ." She nods to the boys. "They don't seem to see how any of this will be different."

Ahh, she's thinking already to when he returns. "I mean, I don't think he's going to come back with a girlfriend," I say, no matter what Veronica thinks.

"But things will be different. Ryan's been keeping a running update with us—mostly just the people he's met. Not so much the medical."

I look back over at the boys; Ryan meets my eyes and smiles. What—how did I misread everything he told me? Or—the case I'm more likely to believe—he's keeping it together for them, but being real with me. Perhaps I'm not the only one spilling my guts to a stranger.

We enjoy the last songs in silence, and I try to pay attention and focus on the reason I'm here. But after everything Sarah's told me, how can I?

Brooke is blowing up my phone, wanting to know where I am. The choir finishes their songs and begins to march off the stage.

"Do you need to go see the *not* boyfriend?" Sarah asks.

I look between my phone and back at Ryan. I want to see Jack. I do, but I think Ryan needs me more than Jack. My *not* boyfriend doesn't know I'm here today, and Brooke won't betray my secret—at least I don't think she will.

"Huh?" I ask, tearing my gaze away from Ryan and his friends.

Sarah studies me like she can't decide if I'm the savior or the cause.

"Don't hurt him," Sarah says. I pull back, but she doesn't say or offer anything more. Sarah goes and pulls Will and Nate away from Ryan. Ryan waves them off and just hangs there like he doesn't want to come back to me, because for a moment he was in his normal world.

Why would I hurt him? Ryan's doing just fine.

"We should actually get going," Sarah says. "Calc test that is going to be murder on Monday. Nice to meet you, Ellie." She gives me a wave.

"You wanna go find Jack?" Ryan asks, rejoining me. The choir is still trailing off the stage, a long line of black robes. I pull out my phone and open Brooke's texts.

Ellie

Hey

got caught up—not sure I can meet up

Talk sometime this week?

I add the last one on without thinking and find that I mean it. Ryan can be nervous about his friends, but he still tells them stuff—maybe I can stand to take a few more pages from his coaching manual.

"No," I say, locking my phone and stuffing it in my pocket.

"You sure?" Ryan sounds skeptical and he looks at me like I just decided to say *Let's go to the moon.*

"I'll talk to him later. We should probably go find the others before they send out a search party."

"You're going to talk to Jack . . . like a conversation?"

"Maybe you're rubbing off on me."

"She finally gets it."

I roll my eyes and drag him back toward the amusement park.

Chapter Twenty-two

Ryan and I meet back up with the rest of the group and Luis herds us onto the roller coaster. Veronica wants to sit this one out—not a fan of high speeds and sudden drops. Luis gives her big sad eyes. He tells her how the plan is for all of us to ride—*together.* Veronica gives in only when he promises to sit with her. He takes her hand and guides her through the line.

I smile. Perfect. *Maybe they do have a chance.*

"What?" Ryan asks. He looks between me and Veronica and Luis.

"Nothing," I say. "You coming?"

"I'm in line, aren't I?"

"Because I can vouch for this ride—doctor and parent approved."

He bumps his shoulder into mine and I can't help but smile. This day may be one of the best I've had in a long time.

"You sure you're okay with not seeing Jack? Like, seeing my friends didn't freak you out? Did Jack say something about you not meeting up?"

"Seeing you with your friends—it was good. I texted Brooke. . . . I'm here with you all and you deserve the same attention, because we're friends." I don't want to run away from them—from Ryan.

The ride attendant gives us the go-ahead and we pile into the cars. For the next two minutes as we race around the track it's like we can outrun the world. I throw my hands up and scream my excitement.

For once, my lungs listen and keep it together. I know my body will crash tomorrow, but for now I feel more Ellie-like than I have for a while.

Next to me, Ryan too seems to have broken the disabled equilibrium. We're just kids enjoying the mall. We land back at the station with a sudden jerk of the magnetic breaks.

Caitlin dances down the steps, Luis waiting for Veronica. Our photos are pulled up on a screen. I've never stopped to look at these before no matter how many times I've come to Morelands—because Mom always stops and, more often than not, she'll buy one of the photos to include in her update—like *Look at us, we can be normal too.*

"Should we?" Veronica asks, bouncing on her toes, still high on the adrenaline rush.

Caitlin and I exchange looks. I mean, sure, we would like one, maybe? But who has that kind of parent money?

"Why don't we take a photo instead?" Luis says.

"We have to get back to the bus," Caitlin says, holding up her phone. But she's not looking at her phone or even really concerned about the time. It's me who holds her focus.

I don't do photos. Caitlin eyes me, because she knows my position. Even if Mom didn't include photos of me in the hospital in every one of her updates, photos just always scream *Ellie is different.* I never look like the others, and normally it doesn't bother me, but when I can't avoid it in a photo . . . it does. I love myself most days, but I dare anyone to say they love themselves all day every day. I just don't need my differences shoved under my nose.

But today I feel brave enough to immortalize this day in digital pixels. Ryan was right—with the five of us, there's something here and we need to treasure the magic we have now.

"Let's."

Caitlin's eyes go wide.

"It's a miracle," she declares. We all pose in front of a display and Veronica steps out to take it.

"Let me," a worker says. He points at me. "You there on the end, can you get a little closer?"

I scoot toward Ryan, aware of how little space remains between us. He's just a medical coach. Nothing more. My stomach ties in knots as we all press together, smiles in place. This isn't the forced photo for my mom. This feels real.

"A funny one," the worker says.

Ryan turns to me and makes a face. I laugh and get called out for it by the cast member. Ryan tries to make his face as big as possible and I do the opposite, squinching my features like I've sucked on a lemon. Photo session over, we break apart and Veronica takes her phone back. She sends most of the shots to our group chat.

Ping! My phone gets an extra message.

How Veronica managed to crop a photo that fast, I don't know. But she's zoomed in on me laughing at Ryan. He's leaning toward me and I have my hand on his shoulder. From the photo, I could be pulling him closer as much as pushing him away.

Veronica
Just friends?

They say a picture is worth a thousand words. So maybe that's why I feel like I'm being yelled at? The photo seems to hint at all the things that could be—the friendship, the ease, the way it feels like we're in sync with each other—and I want it.

"Forget something?" Caitlin asks when she notices I'm not with the group.

I jam my phone in my pocket. The last thing I want is for Caitlin to see that photo of me and Ryan.

She will because of the group chat photos, but when we're all together it looks less like a couple's photo and more like we're just friends.

Veronica is just taking everything out of context.

"Your book—for your dad," Caitlin says.

We're on the opposite side of the park from the bookstore, but if I want to get something for my dad, it has to be now.

"Crap," I say. Yes, I need to. "I'll be quick." She waves me off and I walk as fast as my lungs will allow. Dodging around attractions and displays, I weave my way across the park toward the bookstore.

I walk confidently into the store and grab the book off the table, then make my way to the registers. Purchase in hand, I head for the exit—and there's Ryan. He's almost doubled over, one hand on the table and the other on his cane.

I forget about everything else. What was he thinking? He's pushed himself far enough all day, now he's literally running after me.

"Are you okay?" Everything leaves my mind. The book, my dad, surgery. Ryan takes up all the space in my view.

I rub his back and he slowly stands up, drawing a deep breath. He winces in pain and I want to chastise him for being so careless with his body.

"You just took off. I thought . . . Caitlin might have said something to you. The way you just ran . . ."

"I needed to get one last thing," I say, holding up my bag.

"I was sure . . ."

I take a step closer, pushing into his personal space. "Were you worried about me, Ryan?" I ask, my voice full of laughter. I lean against the table, the book dangling by my side.

I expect him to move back, to retreat, but he not only stands his ground, he leans in. We lock eyes, our faces inches away from each other. His lips are so close, the bottom one slightly bigger than the top.

Wait. Why am I thinking about his lips?

And then Ryan breaks the spell. He scoffs and looks up at the ceiling; using the table he backs up like I've just said the most absurd thing in the world. Secretly, I enjoy putting him on edge. Just a small reminder that he's not the perfect hospital boy he pretends to be.

I reach out and dust invisible dirt off his shoulders.

That was a mistake. The contact. A touch. I of all people should know how dangerous that is. How it can change you. I pull my hand back, as if burned. And maybe I have been.

Perhaps the day has gotten to me, Veronica's words more like it, the late nights, the photo—I kiss him. Just to try it out. To see if this flash of what could be is enough. It's soft—but neither of us pulls away, as if we're both trying to figure out what this is. His hand curls around my neck and his cane clatters to the ground.

The noise has me jumping back. What did I just do?

I pull my book to my chest, as if I can create more barriers between Ryan and me. More things that will fight off the feelings still lingering in the air.

We both stand there glassy-eyed and—at least in my case—wanting to take that kiss back but also wanting it to never stop. What have I done?

Ryan wavers on his feet; neither of us seems to be able to stop this moment or pull out of it. "We should go."

"Probably."

And yet, we don't move.

Ping!

And collectively our phones go off. A string of texts followed by ringtones.

"I think we're being summoned." I hold up my phone to show the number of texts from Tumor Squad.

"Yeah," he says, fishing his phone out of his pocket.

We keep a safe distance from each other all the way back to the parking lot.

Chapter Twenty-three

A stink eye that could rival a nurse's greets us when Ryan and I finally make it back to the parking lot. We make our excuses, staying far away from each other, but getting on the bus forces us back into close proximity and I shy away as if burned.

Caitlin raises an eyebrow, curious, watching our progress. I meet her gaze and then look away, not sure how to answer her question. I drop into a seat, hugging the book to my chest. She shoves her earbuds in and tunes me out, payback. I don't have to share, but she also doesn't have to be available.

I kissed Ryan Kim.

I'm furious.

God, body. What an idiot I am.

That was not in the plan, at all. Period. End of story. And yet . . . I didn't hate it.

I knock my head hard against the seat, as if I can force sense into my brain cells. I was here for Jack and I kissed Ryan. Just to add salt to the wound, I pull up a new conversation with Jack; I should say something.

Anything.

Ellie
I'm having surgery on Wednesday.

I type out the message, and my finger hovers over the send button. I'm doing all of this for Jack. So that I can get back to him. So that my life can be the way it's always been. But now I struggle to hit send. Telling Jack, letting him in, would shatter every rule I've made for myself. They keep me safe—protected.

And alone. It's Ryan's voice in my head telling me that. But I saw him before and after with his friends today. Perhaps he doesn't believe my words, but that doesn't mean they're wrong.

Veronica's giggle startles me.

She and Luis sit close together, bent over his phone. I'm guessing there's a movie playing, each of them with an earbud in. They're figuring it out, and hope glows in my chest. A few weeks ago—hell, a few hours ago—I would have been like *No—don't do this.*

I want them to make it. I want to be wrong. Luis deserves something good. He got a cancer diagnosis. He gets a pass for at least the next year of his life. At least until they've declared him in remission. Veronica has her faults, but I think she'll be good for Luis. And if she's willing to take a chance . . . what does that say about me?

My message to Jack is still there, waiting for my decision. Guilt eats at me, and my teeth gnaw at my lip. Needing to prove that it's still Jack I want, that the kiss with Ryan meant nothing, I hit send. Sticking my phone back deep within my jacket pocket, I lean back. Shadows from the streetlights cast a warm glow over the interior of the bus. It's only five o'clock and I've made a complete mess of my life.

Ryan sits across from me, keeping to himself. I can still feel him near and the kiss that was. I clench my hand around my phone, reminding myself of Jack. Ryan's just some boy who believes that doctors walk on water.

A *boy* who made sure I was going to have surgery.

For Jack.

For me.

So why do I feel like I want Ryan to be more? I look at him again. He's stretched out as much as he can be in his seat, limbs all akimbo.

His eyes are closed and his hair falls gently in his face. The dim light hides anything wrong with him. He opens one eye and then the other to look at me. He smiles, like he doesn't regret a thing we did.

I turn away and pull out my phone, because I am a cliché and cannot survive without it for five seconds. *Please let there be a text from Jack.* Just a reminder of why I'm doing this. But I don't even see a read receipt, and I'm ashamed to say that I stare at this message for a good five minutes.

A new notification pops up. An update from Mom's blog. It just sits on my home screen. I check it again, sure that I misread the alert. But it's on the screen, daring me to click on it. Seeing that stupid reminder that I am just a subject for people to ogle makes my stomach turn.

Mom wouldn't really do this to me, would she? After we talked . . . after she promised. *Only one way to find out.* Deep breath and I click the link. Glutton for punishment: that's me. *VATERs Like Water* was supposed to be over or at least that she'd ask me before sending out something else, that I would have a say in what she said and what she didn't. I thought we had an understanding.

The page loads and there's the new post.

My heart jumps into my throat.

Breathe, I tell myself. Maybe this is just her goodbye post or an explanation. The subject line doesn't give me hope.

This is a new verse, same as the first.

Seconds tick by and anger bubbles up inside me. I am ready to yell at Mom. How dare she do this to me? After everything—she seemed like she was on my side.

I scan the post. There are a few minor adjustments, but I am still the focus of her life. The thing that keeps this whole engine running. She writes about life, the separation between the online and the real world. Fear for me, for having surgery. How this whole thing has weighed on *her.*

She heard me, I guess. But instead of cutting back like I thought we agreed, she made herself the subject of my life. Now it reads like I'm there just as a trial for her.

I don't know if people try to talk to me on the way back to the Home because my whole body feels caught in sleep. Like walking anesthesia. I'm here, but time means nothing.

The bus pulls into the Home and I don't wait for my friends, I flee. They hang back, clinging to one another and the last scraps of fun we had. My lungs hate me for taking the stairs, and I cough most of the way up the last flight.

"How was the trip?" Mom asks. She's in bed, her dark hair pulled up in a messy bun. Concern covers her face as I let out a few more coughs. Serves her right.

"You wrote another post?" My words come out in a sustained hiss that instantly has Mom sitting up and setting aside her tea.

I ignore her calm, happy demeanor. Maybe this morning I thought we could find a new beginning, but now? I am angry. This was not the cap I needed on my otherwise good day.

"I told you I didn't want you to write this anymore."

Mom stands up. Good, we will have this fight on our feet. The press of her lips says she's drawing the lines between us. Normally in the hospital they blur until we're caught somewhere between parent-child and sister-friend. Usually I don't mind this. It makes the long hours go by easier, but now she gets to draw the lines because she's the adult, and I want to scream. These are her rules and I am just forced to play by them.

"There is so much we've done for our community, for other families—raising awareness, funds. You will understand when you are older."

"It's my life." How many times has this been the excuse? But there's not a brace, a test, or even a surgery that can justify what she is doing to my life.

"It is all of our lives, Eleanor." And out comes my full name just to try to kill this conversation.

If she can ignore my direct request, so can I. "Right, because I ruin everyone's lives." That is a dead hit. Mom recoils like I've punched her. "Or what is it—*I'm the hardest trial of your life.*"

Mom covers her mouth with her hand as I spit her words back at her. They've been a poison in my system long enough; it's time she got a dose. Anger dots her cheeks with red, and I know that I should back up. Take the warning for what it is.

I won't stop. This is my life and I'm tired of the way she writes about me—like I've somehow irrevocably changed her life. Ruined it, even. And then she plays martyr. People cheer for her and they pity me. Tell me that I should be grateful for this, for what my mother does for me.

"That—I can explain." She's still caught in the emotional gut punch of her words, and I'm glad. Now she can live with what she's written and realize how horrible it is.

"Sorry to have been such a burden to you."

"Eleanor," Mom says, her voice gaining that mother's domineering edge, but I can see she's fraying at the edges. "That is enough. When I wrote that it had been a long day and I was tired and alone."

"So that makes it okay? To just tell the world how hard I make your life?"

Tears fill Mom's hazel eyes and she fights them back, swatting angrily at them when they fall. "I was just—I shouldn't have said it. I'm sorry."

Her apology has no effect on me. What good are words when actions don't follow? "But you never deleted it." I swallow down the hot tears that threaten to break free. My life has given me ample opportunity to learn to suppress tears. Mom starts for me, like she's going to hug me, but I bolt out of the room.

Wrapping my arms around myself, trying to hold everything together, I wander the halls. And then I remember Caitlin's words: *Come beat down my door.* So that's what I do.

I'm hiccuping back tears when she opens the door. Without

even asking, she stands aside and ushers me into her room. I curl up on the twin bed, because standing isn't something I can continue right now.

Her mom comes out of the bathroom.

That's right—there's no escaping parents here. We're locked in with them. I'm worried she'll make me go back, force me to face Mom again. Her shoulders drop and I see the concern on her face. I don't know how to ask for what I need because there aren't words. Instead I just thrust my phone at Caitlin, who sees the blog.

I just . . . can't go back to my room. Not tonight. Caitlin curls into me, and her mom gives me a small smile before she ducks out of the room. Caitlin turns on a superhero movie and I fear I might cry all over again.

Caitlin doesn't need to talk or ask questions. She just lets me be. I sink into her comfort, that she's holding space around me so I can breathe.

Her mom comes back in with my toothbrush, jammies, and, most important, meds. "I'm gonna make up the trundle, Ellie," she says to get my attention. "I talked to your mom. I said I thought it was best if you spent the night in our room."

I get ready for bed, surprised at how easy this can be. Caitlin and I live too far apart to do the normal sleepover thing. But this feels okay, it feels safe in a way I miss about the Home and Coffman. I could just be hanging out with Brooke. Hospital or not, Caitlin is safe.

I wash my face and brush my teeth. I've never felt so alone. Everything I do seems to bring more people down on me. I crawl into the trundle and pull my legs up to my chest; I cough, turn onto my side, and let my lungs rest. Mom thinks that she's a part of this.

Fine.

She can take the sleepless nights.

I'll stick red-hot needles into her lungs and see how she likes it when they burn. She's a part of this, but she isn't this.

VATERs Like Water

This is the fallout

Age: 2 yrs, 8 mos. Entry #177

Comments: 4.5K   Bookmarks: 8.6K   Shares: 100K

There are lots of things doctors prepare you for when you have a child with special needs. Of course there's the usual suspects— surgery, life expectancy, prognosis—but the one thing they can never really prep you for is what it's like to go back to the real world.

To leave that safety of the hospital, where a team of highly trained specialists is prepared to save the child that you failed. They can tell you all the time that it's not your fault this happened, that it's just . . . the way the cells divide.

But they were my cells.

Mine.

All I wanted for my child was to make sure she had the best start to life and I couldn't even do that.

Those are the things a doctor can talk to you about and probably will talk to you about. They should, and if they don't—you may want to find a new doctor. It's not a fun process and certainly not easy, but as I've said before, finding the right team for you and your child is priority number one!

This was just to be the hardest trial of my life. What no hospital or doctor could ever prep me for was going back into the world and what saving my daughter would do to my life.

Before Ellie was born I worked full-time in marketing. I had clients, went to the office—it was a whole thing and I loved it. Excelled at it. It was a relief some days just to do something that I felt good at—no, great. I had been warned—countless times—that being a working mom would be hard, and some even went so far as to suggest that once I had my baby I wouldn't even want to look back.

But I was so excited to be a working mom. As much as I wanted my child, I loved my job. But nothing prepares you for this, having a child that's not like other children. No book actually delves into how your life is about to be turned upside down and here's how to prepare for it.

As you all know, Ellie required a lot of surgeries when she was little. Many of them were separated by only a few weeks. Enough time to get her well enough to go back under the knife. It ate up a lot of PTO. No matter how well I did at my job, no matter what I said to my boss, there was a choice to be made.

At least that's how my boss phrased it. Because they couldn't fire me outright, that I'm pretty sure is illegal, but he gave me a choice. I could take off for Ellie's back surgery, which would take me out for at least a month between the prep, the procedure, and the healing time, or I could keep my job.

There was no middle ground.

No understanding of what I was going through, because so few could even consider what it was like to have a child who needed constant medical care.

I would like to say the choice was hard—that I was willing to be angry, to fight my boss . . . but it wasn't and I didn't.

I quit.

Or rather I was forced into quitting. I packed up my desk and never looked back.

You got this too,

Gwen

Chapter Twenty-four

*M*om is already up and gone when I sneak back into our room the next morning. I let out a breath, relieved that I don't have to face her yet.

I change my clothes, ignoring the tightness and pain in my hips. The left one in particular feels like stretched-out taffy.

I swallow three ibuprofen and pocket a bottle of cough syrup and leave our room. Technically I shouldn't take the pain meds on an empty stomach, but my body sits at a low-grade six on the pain scale. Not necessarily crying out for more heavy-duty drugs, but enough to say *Hey, what you did yesterday, let's say we don't do that again for a long time.*

All I want is a couch, some *BSG*, and many naps.

I stop by the kitchen, where other Home guests prepare breakfast. Sometimes we catch each other's eyes, but mostly we live in our own lanes. I rummage in the communal pantry for something to eat, and swallow the first dose of cough syrup. First part of the plan—complete. Caitlin has staked a claim on the living room, setting us up for a day of doing nothing but putting our bodies back in somewhat working order.

Then she pulls out a stack of DVDs. What I wouldn't do for Ryan to show up and drop off *BSG*. Not stay—because after our kiss it would just be too weird.

Luis shows up about fifteen minutes into the first film. "Is that *All About Eve?*"

I dig my foot into Caitlin's leg. "You called in reinforcements?"

She smiles at me, all innocent. "Eventually you will understand and give in to my efforts to bring you to a new level of culture."

"Marvel," I say, drawing out the word.

Caitlin looks partially horrified. I guess she did succumb to my needs last night. I check my phone just to see if Mom's either texted or posted something else. Neither thought is a comfort. And there is nothing on my phone.

"Two against one," Luis says, hitting play on the black-and-white film.

I get up and walk to the wall, my left hip screaming persistently. The dull ache wraps itself around my body. Luis eyes me as I back up against the wall until my heels touch the baseboard. Caitlin ignores me. What I'm about to do she's seen a hundred times.

On a normal person, hips would sit flush to the wall when you do this. For me, my right hip meets the drywall while my left juts out.

Ready to take on the pain, I inhale, put my hand on my left hip, and shove it back toward the wall to square them off. Pain tingles up my spine as bones are forced back into its regularly scheduled S-curve. Muscles and tendons scream and stretch.

"Whoa whoa whoa, what are you doing?" Luis asks. The panic in his voice is a response to the pain written on my face.

Pain crests and my hips re-form, muscles contracting to pull them back the "right" way. Or at least my normal way.

I relax against the wall, going from a six to a three on the pain scale. Luis is still caught in a state of shock. His response doesn't surprise me. Maybe it should, but it's just a reminder of why I keep a lot of things from my friends.

Caitlin looks up from the screen. "She's just straightening her hips." She says this like someone might say *She's brushing her hair*. It's just something we do.

Body back in order, I flop back on the couch. We layer ourselves there like lasagna, oozing everywhere but knowing that this mess will ultimately be good. Hours pass as we cycle through movies, sending

Luis to get new ones. I'm not to be trusted, and Caitlin's body has turned on her—everything hurts and swallowing is hard. She sips hot tea and takes the smallest mouthfuls of smoothie.

All our snacks and meds are spread out on the coffee table. We should clean them up, put them away, maybe not have them out for the world to see, but then again that's a lot of work.

"Has anyone seen Kim?" Luis asks, looking for the next film.

Caitlin looks pointedly at me. "Yes, Ellie, why don't you tell us where Ryan is?" Her words are pointed as if she knows something happened last night besides the fight with my mom.

"How should I know?"

She needles me with her foot. "Because you two are basically the same person."

"We're just friends," I say firmly.

"So text him," she says, her tone making this a challenge.

Fine.

I pull my phone out. Time to be brave. Maybe we can both just agree that nothing happened.

It was a fluke.

A mistake.

We're just friends.

It's fine.

> **Ellie**
> Where are you?

I can't hide my smile when his response is almost immediate.

> **Medical Coach**
> Why do I feel like I have a hangover?

I laugh; it never occurred to me to compare this feeling to a hangover. I've been to a party or two where there's alcohol, but I don't drink.

Not because I don't want to or whatever, but who knows what I would do while drunk? And who knows who would be around to call the EMTs if I got hurt? There's just a whole other level of concern when it comes to underage drinking for me.

Ellie
Welcome to the club.

Medical Coach
Did I black out?
Did we drink last night?

Ellie
We did not.

Medical Coach
I would like to return my membership to this club.

And just like that, we're back to our old rhythms and I ignore how it makes me a little sad. But it's better this way, I tell myself. Ryan is just helping me get back to Jack.

Ellie
If you figure that out let me know. I'd like a refund
and a get out of jail free card.

Medical Coach
About yesterday I just

His text bubbles disappear, like he's waiting for me to fill in how we're supposed to feel about the kiss. This is my chance.

Ellie
I'm sorry.
I shouldn't have done it.
Can we just pretend like it didn't happen?

There's a long pause where I hold my breath, waiting for his reply.

Medical Coach
Sure.

Ellie
Great!

I respond, but strangely I don't feel it the way I expected to.

Ellie
Meet us in the 3rd floor living room.
Bring BSG.

Medical Coach
Ugh.

Ellie
Just do it.
We have painkillers.

Medical Coach
You know that's not funny, right?

Ellie
Also not a lie.

"Annnnd," Caitlin says, and she claps to get my attention. She looks at me as if she can see my feelings plain as day. I don't want to explain to her what's going on with Ryan. We're ignoring it, moving on! No one needs to know this—it's just for us.

I sit up and nearly drop my phone. Sitting up was a mistake. My whole body tenses and grabs on to pain like it's a lifeboat on the *Titanic*.

Then, because they hate to be left out, my lungs chime in.

"He's coming, if he knows what's good for him," I say, and sink back into the pillows. A cough singes my chest and I turn into the pillow to cover my mouth while my arms cradle my chest. *God, that hurts.* Mom had better be right—this surgery *has* to work. I leave my phone on my chest and cover my face with the one hand that can still touch my face.

"I've been summoned?"

I tilt my face away from the pillow so that I can see Ryan. This position usually hurts, but now it seems to stretch out my entire back, so I relax into it.

"And I brought entertainment," Ryan says, holding up my box of *BSG* DVDs.

"So that's why you texted him," Caitlin says, turning to me, eyes narrowing as if she's trying to judge my level of betrayal. I flip around and resettle on the couch.

I shrug. It was a benefit. But Caitlin continues to look at me like I'm purposefully keeping something from her.

Luis takes the box from Ryan, who limps to a chair and just collapses into it as if whatever strings that held him up were suddenly snipped.

"I've heard good things about this show," Luis says, heading to the DVD player.

Caitlin makes a noise of protest.

"Three against one," I say, and I don't even try to hide my smile.

"I'm being tortured," Caitlin says, mock agony dripping from every word.

"I believe the term is educated." I give her my best smile. Ryan angles himself so he can look at me. He smiles at me and I meet his gaze, seeing the tiny flecks of black in his eyes that make his gaze so rich and warm. We're still just friends.

Just the way I want it.

"Anything new on the mom front?" Caitlin asks, trying to draw me back into conversation.

Whatever was definitely-not-building between Ryan and me goes out as I focus back on Caitlin. "Mom? Oh. Nope," I say, trying to put my thoughts back in order.

Ryan looks away and Luis looks confused. "Why do I feel like I missed something?" Luis asks. And I can't tell if he means the blog or the kiss.

Ryan gives Luis a look that could cut through glass.

"It's all terrible," I say. The last thing I want to do is explain to them what's going on with my mom.

"But?"

"Look, I don't want to talk about it anymore." Ryan looks at me with concern in his eyes.

But Caitlin is not done yet. She blinks at me, like she can't believe the words that just came out of my mouth. Last night she was understanding, but in the daylight she wants answers. She flips back the quilt and launches herself at me. She may be small, but she is fierce.

"I'm so proud of you. You actually replied to me when I asked this, not just deflected or changed the subject."

"Really?" I say, blowing her blond curls out of my face.

She pulls back and settles down, ready for the full story. Luis and Ryan hold still, afraid any move might startle a beast.

"I know it was bad—"

I shoot Caitlin a look that I hope says *Shut. The. Fuck. Up.*

She doesn't take the hint.

"But this is a great first step. She actually got the message? You set her straight, right?" Hope hangs on her last word. When I can't meet her gaze, she looks to Luis and Ryan as if for backup, but they're confused and silent.

I press my lips together. Didn't I make myself clear—this topic is off-limits. Caitlin tips her head at me, her joy vanishing as quickly as it came.

"Hit play, Luis," Ryan says, shutting down the conversation.

I smile at him, grateful for the distraction.

Caitlin looks between us. "Oh, I get it now." She makes a sound somewhere between a roar and a sigh. She stands up, anger pouring off her.

"What?" I ask, not able to keep up with her emotional tailspin.

"You've found a new hospital friend. Good luck, Ryan, she doesn't last long," she says. She looks pointedly at me and walks off.

I'm the one who says things through looks and glares, but I don't know how to deal with this. Caitlin and I may have different approaches, tiny skirmishes, but we don't leave each other. We don't do stuff like this. Last night she was supportive, but when I want to just keep things to myself she gets angry at me?

I want to run after her and ask what happened. What did I do wrong? But my body is too tired, and my lungs say *Don't even think about running.*

You did nothing wrong, I tell myself even as my stomach sinks. This time, I'm not sure my body is telling me the truth.

Chapter Twenty-five

I stare at the screen, trying to decipher the messages from Caitlin that came in late last night. Unsure how to handle her big emotions when they're directed at me.

> **Caitlin**
> Ugh. I . . .
> look I was in the wrong
> Can we just talk about this Ryan thing?
> About the Mom thing
> Can you please just answer me?
> Don't do this whole not speaking thing

Her messages don't make much sense. Yeah, sure, she never came back to hang out with us, even when I texted her. She was angry and no one knew how to explain it. Sure, *she* can drop off the face of a text thread, but I don't respond at three a.m. and I'm suddenly being a bad friend? It's not like I didn't answer intentionally. Caitlin pecks at sleep like she's five and sleep is spinach. I'm the one who needs a full eight hours.

I shake my head and toss my phone onto the seat next to me.

All my emotions seem to be in chaos—Caitlin's anger, my kiss with Ryan, the agreement to forget it, not to mention Mom and me—I'm almost grateful for the marathon of surgical prep appointments.

Cardiologist.

Internist.

Nephrologist—if you can't pee, you can't get out of the hospital.

Spine.

And, of course, more Darlington.

Each of those doctors comes with a specific set of tests.

Blood work.

X-rays.

Ultrasounds.

Mom and I did not deal with our argument, and we seem to have come to a mutual understanding to act like it didn't happen. Just shove it in a mental closet and let it be. There's surgery to deal with, and she's already brewing, a storm of emotions, bouncing between anger and fear. With every test I wonder, *Will this be the one to crack her calm exterior?* But she holds it inside, leaving me to walk on eggshells, waiting for Dad to show up and become a barrier between us.

We're confined to yet another waiting room. I've chosen a seat across from her but have my phone out just to make it clear I'm not here to interact with her.

"Everything all right?" Mom asks, her voice trying to melt the ice that creeps into her words. She fails. Real hard.

It's then that I realize I've been staring at Caitlin's message for the last five minutes. "Fine," I say, hating the meaningless word.

We're called back to see yet another doctor. They check my vitals—which haven't changed since the last appointment. I cough and they all wear that concerned look. I guess everyone read my file and they're just hoping that Darlington comes through with answers. One by one, Mom and I shuffle through the phases, collecting sign-offs for this next hurdle.

Tomorrow is the blood work and final set of X-rays. Dad's driving up after he gets off work.

Relieved and somehow even more exhausted than I am on Benadryl, I make my way with Mom into the subway below Coffman. There's a patient café we've gone to since I was a kid. A long line of small plates where you can pick and choose your breakfast or lunch. When I was a kid, Mom would also grab small packets of cheese for snacks during our long waits on doctors.

Skylights and a lot of marble make the whole space feel airy. Nostalgia for happier times overrides the anger still brewing in my chest. This is something familiar, something stable that I understand.

"Caitlin's out of surgery," Mom says—with a shred of hope in her voice. I suppose a day of silence and one-word answers has gotten to her.

She can try to patch this all up, but I'm still not interested. Phone it is, then. I scroll through different feeds as I pick up plates at random. Mom shifts a few things around, and I don't even mind. Her small annoyances don't even compare to whatever is going on between Caitlin and me. She pays and we go to find seats.

I hold my tray, feeling like I'm back in high school. Clumps of people are all in their own world, held together by a common place and circumstance. Everything else, how we got here and where we fit in, is arbitrary.

I spot a familiar head of black hair in the crowd. Ryan sinks low in his chair, the food in front of him barely touched.

"Mind if we sit with Ryan and his mom?" I ask. Without waiting for an answer, I cut through the crowd toward Ryan.

As we approach, Ryan sits up. Our moms drop into easy conversation. A subtle look passes between Mom and Mrs. Kim. She's hovering close to Ryan, and I know from experience that is no way to get your kid to open up.

"I was thinking of getting some coffee," Mom says despite her tray of food, and invites Mrs. Kim to join her. They leave. I know Mom's trying to make up for what's happened between us, and I'm grateful to her but haven't forgiven her by a mile.

I didn't go to medical school. I am not board-certified. Do not leave me alone with this brooding teenage boy. We might do something stupid.

Like kiss again?

And all the confusion and guilt over our kiss comes rushing back. *Forget it*, I tell myself. Clearly he's had a hell of a day, and all I want to think about is . . . well, it was a great kiss.

If I could, I would put my head in my hands.

Leave me alone hangs on Ryan like body spray in a boys' locker room. I sit across from him, unsure how to proceed. I'm usually the angry one. While that tactic may work on moms, it's not exactly scaring me off.

"Hey," I say, because what else is there to say?

Nothing. Not even an attempt at moving.

"Make any more progress in *BSG*? You were, what, almost to the end of the third season? Personally, the beginning of that is one of my favorites. I would have even been okay if they spent more time . . ." I let my voice trail off because he's not even pretending to pay attention.

He's sunk so far into himself that I may need a bomb team to help me get to him.

"Are you gonna talk?"

Ryan picks at his meal. This is not the Ryan I'm used to. The one who will defend his point even to the extreme and call you out no matter what.

I didn't think I'd ever have to pick him up like this, not Team Doctor Boy. I've been in this hospital so long, I should know that nothing stays on course forever.

I stab at my cake with my fork. There's only one reason you go this quiet in the hospital. "So how bad was the news?"

Ryan's head shoots up like a meerkat's. I guess he wasn't expecting me to just go in for the kill. Sometimes movies and stories like to take their time and draw people out; we don't have time for that.

"This is the part where you say I told you so?"

"We're approaching that, but I thought I'd give you about five minutes more." I smile and hope that he grabs hold of it, but he sinks deeper. "What'd they say?"

"My endocrinologist at home did all of these tests. Muscle, nervous—but there was always this understanding that I could be referred here at any time." He seesaws his spoon over his fingers. "The best in the world. I thought . . ." He looks away with a small shake of his head.

"You thought they'd fix everything."

"How could they not?" His gazes slices into me, hot and angry. If I could take away this part of the process for him, I would. It's a deep sense of betrayal when doctors can't figure out what's wrong with you. Sometimes it feels like you've been stranded in the ocean and then there's a ship, but they promise to send someone back for you. The doctors move on, but you, you're just stuck.

"They don't know." Ryan picks up his fork and stabs a hard-boiled egg. "All these tests. All these doctors. Millions of dollars in research and they can't tell me anything."

Bang. Bang. Bang. Again and again, Ryan drives his fork into the egg.

"Sucks, doesn't it."

"You're loving this, aren't you." His voice is cold, and I can't help but wonder if that's how I sounded that first night.

"I go under the knife Wednesday. This is the last thing that I want. Sometimes you have to have a little faith."

I am grateful that looks don't kill because not even the high-tech docs and all their equipment could save me from the look Ryan gives me. "Don't you love it when your words come back to haunt you?"

The egg is practically mush now.

I reach across the table and place my hand over his, because I need him to stop.

He jerks back as if burned, but I hold on. I'm not letting this come between us.

"Look at me," I say, my voice firm. He did this for me once, and now I'm here to repay the favor.

"I would give anything to be fixed." His statement hits me below the belt. Not a surprise. Well, not really. We've all been there. What would I give to be healed. To be normal. To not exist in this state of disrepair. "How can you live like this?"

His words cut deep. They're as much an accusation as they are a question. But what threads through all of his words is the underlying belief that the way I live . . . is wrong. Is somehow subnormal and therefore worse.

So glad we've reached that stage. I try to shove my feelings aside, but they cling to me like tape around an IV, holding me in a place that says my life must be so much less than everyone else's.

Ugh.

I shake my head as if that will clear my thoughts, but even still they crowd in on me.

"Come on," I say, and start eating as fast as I can.

"What?"

"Eat, we have somewhere to be."

I can't pull Ryan out of this state because he'll just push me down further past him. And at least this way I can maybe fix my relationship with another friend. Because no one does this better than Caitlin.

Chapter Twenty-six

It takes some doing to get us from Coffman to St. Joe's—the only hospital in town that handles pediatrics. Unfortunately, of the two hospitals it does not connect directly to Coffman's main complex. The moms are skeptical, but Ryan complies and even helps convince our elders that this is going to be worth the short bus ride.

Oh, the joys of being underage.

We drop into seats on the bus and our moms give us some space.

"You know your way around this place," Ryan says, his voice catching an edge that feels like sandpaper and judgment. I don't snap at him.

I think on some level this is why people fear hospitals. That doctors will fail—whether that means death or a worse life like mine, it's hard to say. If I had a dollar for every time someone told me they'd rather kill themselves than have my life, I'd never have to worry about medical insurance again.

Where Caitlin would give me tough love, I decide to take Ryan's advice and *be a team player*. Open up to him, if only to prove that I can. "This was like my summer camp," I say, leaning in when everything inside me says *Pull away*. "It's never like the movies—summer camp, I mean. Like, you know how even high school isn't like the movies? But that doesn't make it bad. It's just a shift in expectations." Unable to look at him, I focus on my hands, my normal thumb running over the scars of my surgically created one. Lots of people see only the bad, and I guess we're trained to, but there's something good here.

Ryan says nothing. When I finally gather my courage and look up at him, he's just staring at me. Like I'm the first snowfall of the year—something beautiful and magical. I wiggle in my seat.

The bus pulls up to St. Joe's and we all get off. We pass through the large stained-glass doors, our breath coming out in puffs of white. The cold air makes my lungs scream and threaten to cough, but I shove it down. While Coffman feels like camp, a hospital still feels like . . . a hospital. A place to cut and stitch and hurt.

I swallow, and as if he can sense my fear, Ryan squeezes my hand. This is supposed to be for him, not for me.

"Caitlin's in room two oh five," Mom says, reading my thoughts. I haven't exactly told her why we're here, but it's pretty obvious all things considered.

We check in and I lead the way to Caitlin's room. I'm surprised she's even in a room; her surgery is outpatient. I guess they just want to make sure she can check off all the things to be released.

"Knock knock," I say, pushing open the door to her room. I should have waited, probably, but there's very little I haven't seen of Caitlin over the years. Postsurgery Caitlin isn't something new for me.

Her hospital room is private—like all ped rooms—and looks the same as every one I've been in. A bench that turns into a bed against the far wall, a green pleather rocking chair by the large bed. Dim lights and so many plugs and wires coming off the walls that it looks like the back of a TV.

Caitlin sits up in bed, her phone in hand, fingers going a mile a minute. It's a gut punch, a reminder that we're caught between not okay and okay. Caitlin and I haven't really talked since she blew up at me and then texted me, but if I know anything, it's that she'll be there if I need her.

I hope.

The parents fall back, clustering by the door. I want to kick them out, but hospitals, surgery, and general concern will keep them glued to the room.

Ryan seems scared to even come close. A curtain divides the entryway from the rest of the room, but it's mostly pushed back. I nudge Ryan toward the chair and try to tell Caitlin with a look what's going on with him. He needs it more than me. He brushes his hair out of his eyes and sits.

Small miracles.

"What are you doing here?" Caitlin's forced disinterest, bordering on hope. Her question is directed at me and meant to feel out the edges of where we left off. I still don't know why she was mad at me, but I need her right now.

"Ryan needs a medical coach," I say. Caitlin's eyebrows shoot up. This isn't about me; we can deal with our relationship later. This is about Ryan.

"I use my powers for *good*." The implication somehow being that Ryan is evil? "Don't twist my words, don't—"

"I haven't—"

Caitlin holds up one IV'ed hand to silence him. With her other, she reaches for the table that extends partially over her bed and grabs a skein of yarn and a crochet hook.

I smile; she's on board.

"Ellie, you want to go grab some Popsicles?" Caitlin nods toward the door.

I see myself out as the interrogation starts. Ryan needs a taste of his own medicine, and there's no one I know better who can dish out medical advice than Caitlin.

She's the best at reading people into the hospital, a guide of sorts. Hospital living is like someone makes you a superhero just for a few days. You get the taste of it, the ups and the downs, but in the end, you don't stay like that. You can walk away. The only difference is that people usually want to stay a superhero; no one seems to want to stay like us.

At least that's what I've gathered about superheroes from Jack. The thought of my maybe-boyfriend stings. I wait for the surge of panic, the feeling that any form of communication with Jack about this part of my life would be catastrophic, but it doesn't come.

There's just relief that I found someone who might be able to get through to Ryan. To explain to him what I'm clearly failing at. I don't want him to hate this place that feels like such a part of me.

The nurses' station is easy to find and better equipped than when I was having the bulk of my surgeries. The nurse goes to find the Popsicles and I'm left to wait.

"Here you go," the nurse says, lining up three cups each with a Popsicle sticking out. I maneuver my hands to carry them and head back for Caitlin's room.

I push open the door and find Caitlin's crochet project growing by the second as she listens to Ryan. I can feel the stares from our moms, the way they seem to lean toward us as if they can be protection from this storm. But perhaps instead of protection, they could learn that this isn't a storm to be waited out but a place for us to learn to live.

"Do not," Caitlin says, and for emphasis she points her hook at me, "let this one corrupt you."

"Hey, I'm having the surgery, thank you very much," I say.

Both of my friends exchange a look.

"Be careful," is all Caitlin says with a very pointed look at Ryan. What is she talking about? Why would Ryan need to be careful, other than the obvious, of course, and Caitlin isn't into stating the obvious. She sees pieces and makes them a story that she reads, filling in the gaps with too much personal knowledge.

"Don't worry." Ryan reaches out and takes my hand.

What did I miss?

VATERs Like Water

This is how you fix a child

Age: 7 yrs, 6 mos. Entry #532

Comments: 2.6K   Bookmarks: 250   Shares: 40K

Ellie was six weeks old when she had her first surgery. She looked so small when she was first loaded onto a child gurney and taken through those double swinging doors to the OR. Strangely enough, although she was tiny and this was her first—this was the easiest choice.

Easy because there was only one choice: life or death.

And there was only one way to fix her heart. Balloon valvuloplasty.

We chose her life.

It came with plenty of fear—I don't want to make it sound like this was easy-easy. Like ordering take-out for dinner easy. There was plenty of fear that this choice, this decision, wouldn't work, but without it she wouldn't make it. I sat on the edge of those hard plastic waiting room chairs for hours until Ellie was brought into recovery. But it was a different kind of worry. It was the worry of losing my child. The idea that I would never see her eyes blink blearily up at me. That her gummy smile would slowly fade from memory. There was a promise in me to always find her the best doctors, to make sure no matter what happened she had the best of everything.

Surgery was a defense, a way to keep her here, to give her life.

Once we succeeded in keeping her stable . . . things got complicated. Ellie's lower right arm was . . . in layman's terms—a mess. She only had her ulna, the tissue below her elbow was shot. She had three usable fingers and an extra one that was stuck somewhere between a thumb and a finger.

Her back also wanted to compete for attention with malformed vertebrae and every possible presentation of scoliosis.

Internal organs were there, and mostly functional. Missing kidney, extra-large liver, ill-placed heart. The laundry list went on and on.

The problem with all of these VACTERL pieces is that none of them were going to kill her in six months, in four weeks, in a few hours. We were no longer playing a game for her life; we had entered the arena of quality of life.

That's when choices really hit the fan. Let's take her right hand, for example. She's missing her radius, the larger bone in your lower arm, as well as a thumb. Because the ulna wasn't strong enough, it curved, placing her hand at a ninety-degree angle to her arm. Of the four fingers she had, only three were really functional—and I use that word loosely. Her fourth was completely useless.

Choices of what to do for her abounded.

We could amputate the partial finger/thumb and leave her with three (mostly) functioning fingers.
We could take a toe and use it to substitute for a finger.
- *But then whose toe? Hers? Was it worth it to mess with her normal feet?*
- *Could my husband or I give one of our toes?*
- ~~*If we had other children, they would probably be a better match—could we force (a nonexistent) other child to give a toe for their sibling?*~~
Should we do thumb pollicization?
- *If so, when?*

What about hand straightening?
   • *And if we did this, then did we fuse her wrist?*

And let's not forget about timing . . . doing this sooner rather than later wouldn't allow Ellie to build up bad habits. Habits she was already developing, such as using her pinkie and what should be her ring finger to grab things, like a crab claw because there was no thumb for her to pinch with!

Weighing over all of this was the biggest question: How would Ellie react when she's older? Will she hate the decisions we made now?

There was research and sleepless nights and so many what-ifs. . . . I used to rock Ellie late at night trying to get her to sleep and think, *All I want is for you to be happy. I want you to be normal.*

And so I made a choice.

Just keep moving,

Gwen

Chapter Twenty-seven

With the surgery looming, I pretty much turn into a hermit, surviving on Ryan's stream of commentary on his *BSG* progression. I want to go watch a few episodes with him, but by the time I get back from my final tests I'm too tired to even think about dragging myself to the family room.

Mom is the one who chooses to leave me alone. Not actually leaving, just not talking. Her worry barely filters through the room as she works on her cross-stitch project by the window. Between my phone and some comedy on the TV, there's plenty of entertainment.

Veronica texts every now and then to complain about school. Finals. All the things that seem so far removed from me. Sure, I brought my textbooks and teachers sent along assignments, but I've barely felt the urge or had the stamina to actually tackle it.

TUMOR SQUAD
Veronica
Ugh can you all chill while I'm at school?

I'm not sure a break from texting would do her any good since most of it was about procedures. Luis has been a constant upbeat jokester. Part of me knows I should worry about this because there's nothing more dangerous than when a kid like him finally cracks. But also maybe that's just the way he always is.

Medical Coach
Starting the last season.

Ellie
I have to say this is impressive. Jack couldn't even
manage one season while he was at debate camp.

My message glares at me, another sharp twist in my gut. Mom's blogging pushed away all thoughts of what happened at Morelands between Ryan and me. We both are in agreement that the kiss didn't happen and we've gone back to whatever we were before that.

Ellie
You are not allowed to finish while I'm in the hospital.
Medical Coach
Then I may need another show.

Ellie
I've created a monster.
Medical Coach
So say we all.

He also asks me other things and we continue to leave our hospital lives behind, exploring life beyond Coffman. Classes. What I'm thinking about for college. And surprisingly, I want to know about him too. I want to see his life beyond these walls.

We get in a long fight over Ivies vs. state schools. He tells me that he wants to be an engineer, but not the boring kind. Or even the kind that goes into space.

Truthfully, I don't even know what that job entails. I'm pretty sure there's math involved.

Medical Coach
Roller coasters.

Ellie
What?

Medical Coach

I want to design roller coasters.

That launches into a whole thing about Ryan wanting to help design and engineer amusement park rides. It's part of the reason he's considering schools on the West Coast—they feed right into places like Disney and Six Flags.

Medical Coach

Aren't you like a nationally ranked speech person?

Ellie

What's your point?

Medical Coach

Why can't you go on Broadway?

Or move to LA and come hang with me?

Ellie

Do you see people like me in the movies?

Medical Coach

So you'll be the first.

I sigh and drop my phone on the bed. Just thinking about the future like that makes my thoughts run together. How can I think about what might come in the next five years when I'm just trying to make it to the end of this one?

Ellie

I don't think it's that simple.

Medical Coach

What dream is?

Ellie

Yeah, but it's not like normal hard.

It'd be like extra hard.

My brand of hard.

Medical Coach
Your brand of hard?
You lost me.

                                            Ellie
                                      Like hard plus.
                              Yeah, it's hard to be an actor.
                        But like when you're one of the first.
              When you've gone your whole life seeing yourself
                                      only in the mirror.
                                      Not on-screen.
                                      Not in books.
                              Not even in my family.

I stop there and stare at these words, realizing I sent them. These thoughts I've kept hidden, swallowed down because they were probably *too much* for anyone but me to understand. Wrong. Ugly. And I just told them to Ryan. I panic, unsure if I should backtrack and try to make him forget he ever saw this hidden part of me.

Medical Coach
I guess I never thought of it that way.

The group chat has continued without us and I get some emoji eyes from Veronica. So at least one person has clocked that Ryan and I are not participating. I try to add some thoughts, weigh in on the conversation, but mostly I sleep and text Ryan. My whole body feels wrung dry and I've been left to salvage enough to keep surgery ready.

Dad finally arrives, just another reminder of my impending surgery. Mom practically flings open the door, and he comes in, tie undone and suitcase in hand. I smile and hold my arms out for a hug. He sets his bag down and comes over to give me one. I take a deep breath and relax, not realizing until now how tense I'd been with only Mom for company.

"How you doin', kiddo?" he asks.

I shrug. "I'm having surgery soon. Sooo probably not great?" I add a brilliant smile so he'll get my joke.

He chuckles and Mom coughs, drawing our attention back to her and the grave face she wears to remind us of the severity of the situation. We forgot how Mom reacts to surgery—how she's panicked and any little thing can set her off.

Dad backs up, placing himself between Mom and me as if he knows the fight that's about to erupt. "We talked about this," Dad says quietly to Mom, as if he can keep the peace this way.

Mom bites her lip and I think this whole moment might pass. Surgery's close now; we're all in hell. Then she opens her mouth and out comes her frustration. "How can you joke about something like this?"

I blink. What?

Of course I should be thinking about *her* feelings.

Is she serious? I'm allowed to joke; it's my body. Dark humor is the only thing standing between me and absolute depression.

"Gwen," Dad says, trying to cajole Mom and pen her in so she won't explode.

"Probably the same way you can write about it," I say. The words leave my mouth and I don't even try to stop them. Normally I would. Hold them in, pin them down, swallow them, but I'm done stomaching her feelings.

Mom looks like I slapped her, even going so far as backing up and cupping her cheek.

"How can you say that?"

I struggle to free myself from the nest of pillows and blankets I've lived in all day. My feet shake under me, but I stand my ground. "Because I asked you to stop writing about my life. You agreed."

Dad looks first at Mom then me, trying to read between the lines of what's happened. *So Mom didn't tell him. . . .*

"You asked me to not write about you anymore. But this is about all of us." She looks between Dad and me, searching for teammates.

Maybe Dad is on her side, but I am squarely on the opposition. "People have always wanted to know how we're doing, how they can support us. I wanted to be able to give them that. I wrote about what I was doing—how things were going."

"This is not a team sport," I shout. Despite what Ryan thinks, I am in this alone. "My life is not yours. You do not get to make my life about you. What else do you need me to say? I can't say it much clearer. I want this to stop. No more posts about me going into surgery. Nothing about me at the doctors'. No photos. No nothing. I don't just want to be removed from this narrative. I want this narrative to end."

"All right," Dad cuts in, trying to be the peacemaker. "I think we're all running a little hot tonight and could do with some space. Ellie, we understand where you're coming from." Mom fists a hand in her hair like she's trying to hold something together or perhaps rip it all apart. I suppose my words—my request—is doing both.

Mom and I mutually agree to ignore Dad. He's here, but he hasn't been *here*.

"We're doing important work raising awareness and money for families to learn how to deal with this curveball life's thrown them," Mom says, her voice rising.

"Why do they need every detail of what I'm going through? For years, I have lived under this cloud of a girl you've made me out to be, and nowhere in this have you seen me for who I am." Tears cool my heated cheeks. I reach up and wipe them away, unsure when I started crying.

Ready to butt in, Dad faces Mom and plants his hands on her shoulders, trying to calm her down. She brushes him off and he's back to playing referee between us. He looks at me and I glare back. If he tries the same tactic with me, I will not be able to hold it together.

"Okay," he says, his voice firm. I imagine this is the tone he might use with his employees. "Let's all just take a moment. We"—he looks at Mom—"understand what you're saying, Ellie." Mom looks ready to start round two. My family may not survive this request. Here I was believing that maybe—just maybe—things could be different. But I had to make them different. Ryan taught me to ask the hard questions and hold out for answers.

"I don't think she does," I say, standing my ground.

He holds up a finger to silence me, a gesture that I know means I am skating on very thin ice. "We know that surgery is part of your life. But," he says to cut Mom off, "it has also been a major part of *our* lives. Through the work your mother has done, we support others. It was a way to build our own version of hope."

And here I am smashing that fragile hope to pieces, to burn the world down that she has worked so hard to build.

"It's not that I don't appreciate that—I just . . ." I look between them—they mean well, but right now it's hard to see beyond my frustration. "I just can't stay her defenseless little girl forever."

"There is so much I gave up for you."

"Gwen," Dad says, an edge to his voice that hasn't been there before, one that distinctly says *Stop*.

We ignore him, and there's no way for Dad to stop this fight. It's been brewing for too long.

"Oh sure. What could you have possibly given up for me?"

"I lost friends. My career. Your father and I got divorced—" Mom cuts herself off and her face pales, like she didn't mean to say that. I stand there, my anger and frustration completely driven out by shock. *Divorced.*

"That's enough." Dad's voice is sharp and cuts through the messiness we've ended up in.

Wait, what?

"What?"

Dad's face crumples and Mom smacks a hand over her mouth like she can't believe what she just said. He holds out a hand as if to calm a wild animal, but I pull away. I thought it was just a feeling that I ruined my parents' lives.

"You're divorced?" I somehow get the words out around the dread pooling in my chest. "Does that . . ." I look to Dad, not wanting to put the words to breath.

"Ellie, it's not what you think," Dad says.

"I'm sorry, I don't . . ."

"It's complicated—" He reaches for me and I jerk away. No, this is not what I want.

"So you're not married?"

"For where it matters, yes—on paper, no. We didn't have good insurance at the time. And—"

"And I needed a lot of insurance." You don't get forty-plus surgeries in by sixteen and not rack up some pretty impressive hospital bills. "So you got divorced?" I don't understand it. "I ruined your lives. . . ."

"Ellie," Mom says, her voice full of regret and pain. I want nothing to do with it. No wonder she doesn't care about what I want.

"We are still your parents and we love you very much."

"At least that's better than Darth Vader," I mumble.

Dad presses his lips into a fine line. "Let's sit down and talk. It has to do with a loophole in qualifying for Medicaid. Let us explain." Dad walked in on a minefield and probably didn't know it. Mom and I have been good at avoiding the dangerous, fraying edges of our relationship. This just severed the last threads holding us together.

I cross my arms over my chest. "I'm good standing." Just when I thought the hospital might not break me—I get hit with this. The hospital and all the medical care—me, it all destroyed my mother's life.

"We love you," Mom starts, and that's it, I can't hear it anymore. Her voice is abrasive on my skin, peeling away the hard coating I need to get through the next twenty-four hours and surgery.

He takes a deep breath. "We're all tired and on edge—"

"I guess I'll wait to read about it on her blog."

I take off, pushing past both of them, crushed under the weight that the hospital really does break everything.

Chapter Twenty-eight

We're trapped in the Home—Mom, Dad, and I are stuck here. That's the whole philosophy of this place. Put all the families with sick kids together in the hope we can get through by supporting one another, but when we are ready to break there is no place to go and lick our wounds.

Mom and Dad are going to come flying out the door any moment now. I run, even as my body screams that this is a bad idea. I just keep going, letting my feet carry me to Caitlin's door for the second time. She pulls it open as if expecting me.

I push through her, pacing the room like a caged animal.

"Well, this is a surprise—I like it," Caitlin says, trying to lighten the mood. But then she sees me, like really sees me, and her mood shifts. Even her curls seem to deflate. She drops out of her annoyance, drops any petty fight we may have had, and instantly switches to friend mode. I'm numb inside and out.

Everything that happened comes out in fits and bursts, but finally, I've relayed the whole story and stand there waiting for Caitlin to say something.

Her mom comes out of the bathroom, cleaning rag in hand. I look around, realizing that their suitcases are out. The room is being prepped for them to leave.

"Ellie—" her mom starts.

"I got this, Mom," Caitlin says, and inclines her head toward the door. Her mom doesn't look convinced, but she ducks out. "Pretty sure she just bought us some time," Caitlin says.

I don't say anything until the door closes and Caitlin locks it.

"I told you this doesn't work," I say, new tears already coming. "The hospital destroys all relationships." Just when I was ready to believe otherwise. When I thought that maybe, just maybe, there was hope. But no.

With a sigh and an eye roll Caitlin pulls me back to earth. "Oh please." She puts her hands on her hips and tosses her curls back, ready for this fight. This was not exactly what I was expecting from my friend. I thought she'd be a comfort to me, put on a Marvel film—help put me back together. Just like last time.

"What?"

"Ellie, I love you, I do, but this . . . this is unhealthy. 'The hospital destroys everything'—what exactly are we?" She motions between us.

"That's different."

"How? Because you definitely cut me out once you found Ryan." Caitlin squares her shoulders, ready for a fight. She never has been one for bedside manner. "Your parents still live together, right? It was probably a divorce in name only." I stare at her. What would she know? Her breakups happen so often that she must be used to reining in her emotions. "Perhaps the hospital is not the cause."

"But she blames me," I say, ignoring whatever she said about Ryan.

She sinks to the edge of the bed, as shocked by the news as I am. That gets Caitlin's attention. "What she just said . . . She told me how much she's given up for me. That this was all that she had done for me." My worst fears about the blog, about why I let her do it, are real.

"Well, that was a bitch move," Caitlin says. She sighs and picks up a pile of laundry next to her suitcase. "Here's the thing: you think that because all this happens at the hospital, then the hospital is to blame. But a place cannot make things happen." She pauses and drops down next to me, her face softening. "You have to stop pushing people away. Stop replacing your hospital friends. You have room enough for all of us."

Her kind tone punches through my walls, her words slam into me and steal my breath. "Did you just hear what I said? I know I'm a problem—or rather my body is, hence the hospital."

"Yes, and your mom has issues. There is no denying that. But that statement—the hospital ruins everything—is not something you pulled out of thin air in response to her terrible move." Caitlin looks like she's pulling out her own teeth to say this. "If I didn't fight tooth and nail to hold on to you . . . you would have lost my number years ago. And even now you tried to replace me."

"You think you have everyone figured out." I lash out because it feels good, and because how dare she suggest I would lose her number? I have made it through this with her. She's always been here when I am here. "But you'd rather insert yourself into my problems than deal with your own."

"I am fine," Caitlin says, her tone bordering for the first time on real anger. Before she was annoyed, maybe even hurt, but now this—she's ready for a fight. "You think a breakup is gonna end me? Someone breaks up with me, I cry. I curse the universe. I shake my hands at the sky and then I move on. But with you, someone breaks up with you and no one would know it. At least not here. You keep everything and everyone in a neat box. If they escape that box and try to fit in with another, then you cut them off. You bottle up not only your emotions, but also your friends. No one can know you because everything you are, you keep under lock and key."

"I do not." I grit my teeth. What good would telling people about certain things do anyway? Then I'd have to explain my whole life to people like Brooke and Jack, which would only serve to remind them that I'm different. And maybe they'd start to think I was a freak too.

"Oh yeah? And so that's why you don't tell your friends at home about your surgery? Or why you and Jack were having problems? Instead of telling anyone, you just sewed your lips shut. Or you and Ryan—how long until he figures out you two aren't built to last?"

"So it's always about me, but why don't we talk about you—about your TV appearance? I offered to help you—to do something for you for a change—but all you want is to fix me and how I deal with my life."

"Friends are there for each other."

"All you know how to do is push. Push me to be on *A Patient Life*, push me to talk to my mom, you pushed me and now I know that I broke up my parents' marriage."

Caitlin takes the news like a slap, and every word I said sinks into her. Concern is written into every line of her face. This isn't meant to be harsh, but I'm crumbling under the weight of it all.

Tears slip down my cheeks because of course now I'm crying.

"Ellie—say something—what are you feeling?"

I fish for words. Here, Caitlin is a lifeline, an essential person I refuse to live without. And yet I cannot find the words.

"I know it's hard, but I get it—probably better than anyone." She reaches out for me, but I pull back.

"No," I say when she tries it again. Can she not see how wrong she is—Caitlin's made it very clear whose side she's on. I back up out of the room. This was supposed to be something different. I came here for help, for a place to hide and lick my wounds, but instead I got this.

None of this can be my fault.

This was not what I was looking for when I came to see Caitlin. Unable to go anywhere else, I head back to my room. I hold my breath, hoping for the best but prepared for a "family talk."

To my surprise, no one says anything. I slip back in, refusing to look either of my parents in the face. Mom seems like she wants to say something, but Dad holds out a hand to stop her. Silence is our agreed-upon reaction. We tiptoe around one another as if one false move will plunge us all to our deaths. And so we ignore it.

Their eyes scrape over me and several times I catch Mom looking like she might say something, only to have Dad silence her with a look. Small blessings.

There's still surgery in the morning. Too bad shattered friendships don't count as a get-out-of-surgery-free card.

Ryan texts me. Again and again my phone pings. I curl up in the twin bed, unable to sleep and refusing to leave this room. I can't take meds to knock me out and my lungs are having a field day. But I know Ryan is just outside, waiting for me. But what's just happened isn't something he's prepared to handle—even with all his medical coach knowledge. What could he say about my parents' divorce? It's not like they did it because they hate each other, they did it because of me.

I'm the problem. And I should just be left alone.

Mom too seems to be restless, her nervous energy crowding the room. Mom the worrier. This time there is no place for her to put her fears. No place for people to tell her things will be okay in the end, that they are rooting for us, or praying for us, or any manner of things. Here we are finally alone. Three people, one family against an unknown force, but our cracks show, and we are not built to last. Love was never meant to survive the hospital.

I turn on my side and flip my phone to night mode. I don't want to see any more messages. I don't want to hear the vibrations. This— whatever I was building with Ryan—stops now. How foolish I was to think that it could be more.

I'm a case in point for that.

And isn't Caitlin? Who runs through relationships like she's an Olympic athlete?

Eventually they all reveal what I've known for years—that this place will tear them apart. My parents are just another strike in the hospital's favor.

Curled up in blankets, I let tears stain my cheeks. I didn't think there were any left. I thought I had gotten rid of them all, and yet my body continues to surprise me and push for more.

Chapter Twenty-nine

*T*he sun's not even close to being up yet when Mom, Dad, and I enter the hospital. There's something quiet and eerie about this place at such an odd hour. Doctors walk at a leisurely pace. Some in suits and ties—off for rounds, maybe. Others in full scrubs and white coats—off to the basement where the ORs lurk. It suits my mood just fine.

No one's talked about last night. In fact, we've barely said two words to one another.

My stomach grumbles, deprived of food since midnight, even as it flips with unease. I sit on the edge of a chair as Mom checks us in. I should be up there, but I can't make myself move. Disinfectant stings my nose and I take shallow breaths, trying to avoid the fumes.

"Ellie . . ." Mom calls me over to the desk. "They need your wrist."

The nurse behind the counter is sweet as she double-checks my ID numbers with me. DOB. The usual. Just to be sure that I am who my parents say I am.

I find myself rattling them off automatically when all I really want to do is turn around and walk out of here. I do not want to have surgery, I don't want to be this mistake in my parents' lives, but still I find myself extending my left arm, letting the nurse slide on my hospital bracelet, effectively accepting my imprisonment.

They call me back—or rather up—to my room. I flinch at the sound. Dad wraps an arm around me as we ride up, but Mom keeps her distance.

I change out of my sweats, the things that keep me feeling connected to something outside of these walls. On goes the hospital gown, on go the scrub pants.

Ping!

My phone goes off. It's still so early, so I don't know who it could be. Mom and Dad both look at me expectantly.

I dig out my phone from where it sits hidden by my clothes and skip straight to the latest.

> **Medical Coach**
> Good luck?
> Break a leg?
> Caitlin didn't tell me what the correct saying is.
>
> **Ellie**
> Any of the above works.

The nurse comes and we leave my room behind. I'm in a wheelchair, because from now on I won't be allowed to go anywhere on my own. As if they think that the anticipation of surgery will make me sprint for the door.

They're not exactly wrong.

A new set of elevators, these wide enough and long enough to fit a gurney. This early in the morning we're alone. Down we go, to the basement. I don't know why they choose to keep the OR in the basement. Maybe they wanted it to be a dungeon. Maybe the equipment and building materials are so heavy they need to be down there. Or perhaps since it is the anchor of this place, they want it there to weigh down the whole enterprise.

Mom creeps closer, standing next to me, not so close that she can touch me but close enough that I can smell her shampoo. The child in me wants to reach out and take her hand. We've been in this together, and I hate that I'm angry at her when she's been through so much for me, but for once, I hold on to my anger and the accusations that lie under her confessions: all the things she gave up for me. The thing she started for me, to give me access to a world of my true peers, ultimately separated us. There's probably some poetic justice in there, but it stings too much to think about.

My wheelchair stops by a bed and I climb up, curtains pulled up to give us a semblance of privacy. Just me and my parents. No one talks because we're all still chewing over what we said last night. The last thing I want is for another fight to happen right before I'm going under the knife. My chances of making it are really high, but with surgery there is always a chance of death.

I swallow.

I've done this forty times, what's one more? I'm practically ready to go pro. And yet that fear, that anticipation, sucks me down.

"Ellie," Mom says. I snap out of my daze, realizing I've been completely out of it and lost in my own thoughts. Mom, Dad, and some medical professional are looking at me like I should know the answers.

"Forty-two?" I say as a joke.

Only the guy in scrubs smiles.

"IV time."

Panic cold and hot runs through me in waves, and I lock up. I hate needles. I've gone so many years having as few sticks as possible. Surgery has and always will be done with a mask to knock me out. That's when they can stick the damn thing in my arm.

I wrap my arms around myself protectively. Nope nope nope. Not happening. Dad looks confused, but it's Mom who steps in.

"She doesn't like needles. I know we didn't talk with the doctor—"

The nurse seems to get it instantly. "Oh, no problem. I'll make a note on her chart. We can insert it once she's asleep."

Mom and I both breathe a sigh of relief. Dad is clueless to the mini-drama that almost played out in front of him, and I love him all the more for it. He's spared this intimate knowledge of my life—something that I should have gotten over a long time ago. Because really, who has my medical file and is still afraid of needles? The nurse moves on, leaving us once again to our own devices.

Should I say something? Break the silence that's encased us since Mom blamed me for their divorce? I'm sure Dad knows Mom's version of the past few days—but is he even interested in mine?

"Ellie, your mom and I," Dad starts, because of course he does. "We want you to know—"

Mom is giving him a face that says *What the fuck are you doing?* This time we're on the same page.

He wants to talk about this *now*? As if this might be the last chance to speak their peace.

"Dad," I say, cutting him off. Nope, I am not having this conversation here. "Let's just not until I get through this."

Mom takes my right hand with both of hers like we're a team on this. I want to pull back, because we aren't a team and I'm not sure we ever will be again. No matter how nice it is to have backup.

But I don't need her. I have my own team.

I pull out my phone, surprised at seeing so many messages in our group chat. My friends are awake and eager now. Lots of well-wishes. Caitlin's sticks out with, Just make sure you moon them at least once. That makes me smile.

My team has changed—grown, certainly. I click over to Ryan's contact information. It's still labeled *Medical Coach*. I make a quick edit, just to prove Caitlin wrong, and swap out his title for his real name. It's a small gesture and maybe stupid, but the change seems bigger. More permanent. He's not just here to see me through this, he's here to last.

Perhaps friendship can exist in a hospital.

Ryan
Don't forget those of us stuck here when you're done there.

I stare at his message, trying to shrug off the joke, but it stabs close to home. Is he trying to start the separation between hospital life and real life? This whole time it's always been about the doctors, but he promised we could still talk.

I take a screenshot of his contacts page and send it to him and start a new message.

Ellie
Sorry, you're stuck with me.

Another text message distracts me before I can hit send.

Jack (1)

We haven't talked since he showed up. I just haven't known what to say. Or how to even start explaining the hospital so he sees it like I do. Exchanged texts, sure—every now and then. My responses were bland as I tried to find the right ways to show him this world.

Two more messages pop up as I try to figure out my feelings about this latest development. First it's like a boob punch, totally underhanded and a pain you didn't quite know could exist. But it's also a surprise, a friendly face showing up to your hospital room when you're stuck there.

Is this what hope feels like?

Leaving my conversation with Ryan, I open up Jack's.

Jack
Hey—I know you're having surgery. And I wanted to
say good luck.
I hope everything is okay.
I miss you.

Yup, that's definitely hope. It fills my chest and brings on a cough. Mom and Dad don't even look up, they're so used to me being face down in my phone.

For once I text back.

Ellie
Thanks—I'll let you know what happens.

The read message is almost instant. Followed by another smiley face from Jack.

My first thought is to text Ryan. I click over to our conversation, and there's the photo. The switched profile, his actual name. Warmth spreads into my chest. I shouldn't be in this conversation, not with Ryan. I should be engrossed in my conversation with Jack.

The interns come to take me down and it's time to leave the parentals behind. Despite our arguments and the fights, I give Mom a hug. Fear overrules anger. We may not speak it, but the fear of death, of not coming out of this back to my same self, is so foundational and we both feel it. Mom wraps her arms around me and Dad just pats me on the shoulder.

I grab my phone for one last text. And on the off chance that it will work, I text:

Ellie
Going under now. See you on the other side.

Hopefully, I made the right choice and the boy gets the message.

Chapter Thirty

*A*cute. Sharp. Driving. Pain shoves aside the anesthesia. It sprints down my left arm, and I practically come up off the gurney. Gentle hands push me back down, all the while pulling my left arm up.

Why does my arm hurt? Wasn't this supposed to be about my side? My lungs? Reminded that those organs exist, my nervous system kicks in with a dull, stabbing pain from three points on my side. The world swims around me as I try to remember where I am and what has happened.

Here the light is white and the world is a wash of blues. Nurses in full scrub gear dance around me and blend in with the background as if I'm in the middle of a Degas painting.

I pull at my left arm. *Give it back, make it stop.* But the hands grip tighter and raise it above my heart. Then comes a new pain that slithers between layers of skin. Tubing being extracted from deep in my body, igniting a fresh wave of pain.

"Please . . . ," I say, wanting them to stop and let me go. My right hand is basically useless, kept trapped under the stupid heated blankets.

"Ellie, I need you to relax," the nurse says. Her voice is calm even as it feels like she's wrenching my arm out of its socket. Why is this happening? What went wrong with my arm? I can feel the IV tube and tape farther down from the pain site.

"What happened . . . ?" The words swim in my mouth. My head can barely keep track of what's happening between the hands on me and the pain.

"Just relax," the nurse continues.

Pain congregates in my left wrist and drips down my arm. One thought breaks through everything: *That is not where pain should be.*

I blink and then my parents are there in recovery. Familiar faces among the chaos still whirling around me. Mom leans over the side of the gurney and Dad hovers in the background.

"Mom?" What's happened doesn't matter, I just want Mom to make it all better. To make it stop. She can go back to blaming me for ruining her life tomorrow as long as she fixes mine today.

"Oh, sweetie," she says, and I can hear the sadness in her voice. She strokes my cheek. Anger mixes with pain, leaving me feeling more drugged than usual. I just want everything to be normal, at least as normal as it ever is in surgery.

Panic spikes and I quickly test each appendage. Two hands. Two legs. Yup, I can feel everything, so not a spinal cord injury. I force my eyes open. I am awake. I didn't die.

"Did they get it?" I say, but the moment I hear these words I know I'm still under anesthesia's power. It sounds more like "Diths zhauy geth ehth."

She smiles, but it doesn't reach her eyes. She digs through the blankets so that she can take my right hand. The head torturer is still busy with my left arm. Mom smooths back the hair from my face. "It'll be okay." Down here so alone, I try to shove aside the anger pounding in my chest, because I want an ally. Even one who is only partially on my side.

Her eyes tell me a different story, and she can't lie to me. I look around at the bright lights, the beeps and bops from the machines. Recovery is that strange place and I'm never sure how long I stay here, but it always feels like both forever and the blink of an eye. These things that dot my childhood, this was once my playground. Now everything hurts. My arm in particular, my good arm. And no one will answer my questions.

As if to prove that something went drastically wrong, my lungs seize and I cough. The nurse still has hold of my arm and won't let it go as my body deals with my lungs.

The coughs force me to suck in air, which clears out the anesthesia. It hits me: the surgery did not work. And no one wants to tell me why. My side burns with pain and all I want to do is sink deep into the haze of medical-grade painkillers.

It's a while before my senses return and they wheel me up from recovery to my room. Once there, Dad hands over my phone. "I think you have a few messages," he says, planting a kiss on my head. Surgery and Darlington's failings seem to have fixed everything for them, while I'm drowning in both.

He's not wrong. There are several.

Jack (1)

Ryan (5)

Tumor Squad (111)

I click over to Tumor Squad first. I'm slow going, trying to navigate my phone with my right hand as the nurse finishes putting the bandages on my left.

TUMOR SQUAD

> Ellie
> 111 messages? Really?
> Sum up.

Text dots appear almost instantly. Congrats on getting out of surgery pour in and I almost drop my phone. Their well-wishes are sandpaper on my skin. They all think this worked, that I'm better now, because that's what Ryan has led us all to believe.

Anger flares in my chest and makes it hard to breathe. All I want is to scream. To bang my phone against the side of the bed until it cracks and I don't have to talk to anyone ever again. I'm going to have to relive and manage all of their disappointment before I can process my own. Why did I ever listen to him?

Ping!

Ryan
Hey—glad to hear you're out.

It's so strange to look at my last text message to him. I wanted Ryan to be the one to know I was going down over Jack. I wish I could go back in time and tell past Ellie not to waste her time. Ryan had me believing that doctors could do anything. He's lucky I can barely text.

This is why you don't hang on every word that doctors say, because then you start expecting things to work out and it's all the more crushing when they don't.

I swallow, trying to push everything down. All I get is the scratch all the way down my esophagus like when I dry swallow big pills. No, I don't want any of this. My phone goes off, more pings as my group chat tries to catch me up.

I want none of it.

I flip my phone to silent and bury it in the covers.

Mom and Dad still won't tell me what happened—mostly, I think, because they're not sure themselves. When things go right, we know how to explain them because that's what the doctors have briefed us on. But when they go wrong, we're in the dark.

Dr. Darlington comes late in the afternoon in scrubs and his white coat. Mom and Dad have retreated to the edges after I snapped at them. No, I haven't forgotten what Mom said or what she blames me for. I'm furious, but anger sits differently in a recovering body. It weighs on me, pressing me into the bed. Normally anger seems to give me fuel, make me rise.

But now, I'm drowning under the weight of it.

"What happened," I croak out, my voice still hoarse from the intubation.

He has scans with him, because of course he does. Interns cower in the corners, eager to learn about what happens when things go wrong. I want to yell at them to get out, that I am not here for them to ogle at. I am not a public subject.

Then again, maybe I am. What does it matter if Mom stops writing about me? Doctors still see me as a case to present to the world, one that can fuel papers and win awards at that. I'm just a piece in their lives to be picked up and discarded as necessary. My value is linked to what I can provide or what I take away from people.

He pops the scans into the wall lights. For all the high-tech equipment in the offices at Coffman, there are still wall lights to display scans.

He traces the wisp-like fibers that blow across my lungs like spiderwebs. I've seen a million X-rays, MRIs, and CTs and nothing about this seems abnormal. It just looks like lung tissue.

"What the scans didn't show us—couldn't show us—is that you have lots of tiny blood vessels that run from the back of your lungs to your rib cage. We couldn't get the lap around them without breaking them. The only option would have been to completely open up your back, which would have necessitated a full blood transfusion."

I squirm in my bed, and pain spikes. Those three tiny incisions are a bigger issue than any other surgery I can remember. He may say they're small, but I don't believe him. I'm never going to believe anything that comes out of his mouth ever again.

"So why didn't you do it?" My voice hits like acid, and everyone flinches.

Good. I want them to feel it. They all deserve it.

I stare around the room at the doctor, my parents—why am I here with this thing still inside me? I went through all of this pain, and for what? There was a backup plan. The thoracotomy. I was ready. I signed up for this. I listened to the doctors and they can't even do their job when I did mine.

"*I wanted it out, why didn't you do it,*" I scream, because that's where I am. I'm angry and hurt and everything is always against me. For once could Mom have just done what she wanted? This was her idea.

Darlington steps up as if he's ready to take the brunt of my anger. "Because when your parents and I discussed it, they asked if I believed this was the cause of your illness and how sure I was of that."

I turn my head and body slowly toward Dr. Darlington. This is my worst fear—I knew he couldn't be trusted.

"And?" I ask, fear spiking in my chest. This was what I was afraid of, a scalpel-happy doctor. Someone who wanted to cut me open just to poke around.

"And I think there is a twenty percent chance your cyst is the cause of your illness."

I'm angry, furious. With myself and the hospital. But mostly with Ryan. Wasn't it his fault I decided to try this out? To trust doctors? If Darlington all but knew this wasn't the cause, then shouldn't he have said so before I even went under the knife?

"We wanted answers. Laparoscopically, if it could have been removed, it would have been for the best. There was a strong case for it—to try."

Right, because medicine isn't about answers, it's about guesses. Hypotheses—that's what science calls guessing, isn't it?

"But it wasn't worth ending up in the ICU, Ellie," Dad says. Mom looks down at the floor, and I wonder if she would have been game for it if he weren't here. We would still be locked in silent battle and she would be free to write about my full thoracotomy all she wanted. Maybe what started with the best of intentions hasn't continued in that way.

"And now what, I just go back to where I was?"

No one wants to answer that question because no one likes to say they've failed. That's what happened here today: we failed.

No, *they* failed.

Dr. Darlington tries to make some excuses, some plans for the future. But what does it matter? My life is just going to play out like this. "Am I just going to be stuck like this?"

"We hope that when the weather changes, you will be able to get better faster. There won't be viruses or colds that can agitate your lungs."

"So for like half a year I'm just"—I look around the room, my parents worn out from worry and Darlington trying to be sure—"sick?" This illness will lay me out. I won't be able to go to school. I'll fall off the face of the earth. Then, for six months, I'll live again. A never-ending half-life.

His smile consoles no one. He nods to my parents and backs out of the room.

Chapter Thirty-one

Two days post-op, Darlington has no idea when I'm leaving. My whole rib cage is on fire and Mom, Dad, and I are still not on speaking terms. Things are great.

I swear my ribs are about to snap from the pain, my whole chest cavity is waving the white flag. Who knew how painful three tiny incisions could be? To top it all off, I got stepped down to Tylenol with codeine. There's been a standing order on my chart that I get morphine for forty-eight hours after surgery. *Minimum.* They stepped me down after less than twenty and they wonder why I am still at an eight on the pain scale.

Between the arterial line they pulled out of my left arm and my three incisions from the lap, the weak shit that is Tylenol with codeine can't keep up.

Dad brought DVDs of his newest sci-fi TV obsession. It's a needed distraction to keep me from focusing on the pain.

A knock at my door is quickly followed by my current nurse. It's too early for a vitals check, so she must be here to announce someone. She's a rule follower, hence why I decided not to learn her name. Nurses aren't here to buddy up to you. The last thing I want is another person meddling in my life and another tie to a place that tears relationships apart.

I expect to see my parents for their daily visit, or maybe Darlington checking in again. *Please let it be morphine orders.* Or maybe he thinks that's all in my head too?

I don't expect Ryan.

My friends—hospital and high school—have texted, but what is there to say? *Everything is terrible, your well-wishes are not working?* So I "lost" my phone. It's easier than telling them the truth.

Ryan just stands there, leaning on his cane, his black hair still falling in his eyes, and my heart leaps for my throat and lodges there, too scared to beat. He smiles and the hospital falls away around me. We could be back on the couch watching *BSG*. All I want to do is tell him to get out. He shouldn't be here. I hang on to the rails of my bed, trying to remember that there is ground underneath me.

"Hey, Ellie."

I nod.

My nurse looks at me but doesn't see me. I've had nurses who were near telepathic and would have whisked Ryan out of the room and made excuses—recent pain med dose, exhaustion, not up for visitors. They would have had my back.

Instead, my nurse just turns on her squeaky white sneakers and walks out, closing the door behind her. Ryan and I don't say anything until the door slinks closed. We're cocooned in here and I don't think we're going to transform into anywhere near a butterfly.

Ryan just stands there, as if to defy what I know. He almost had me fooled and believing that I was wrong about the hospital—that maybe, just maybe, this place wasn't a life ruiner.

With an easy motion that he's picked up pretty fast, he goes to the TV and pops in a disc.

"What are you doing here?" I should have just started with *Get out.* My voice rasps still from surgery, but Ryan doesn't seem to react. He sits in the chair next to my bed, as if nothing is wrong, as if nothing has changed.

"You haven't been responding to anyone's texts. Plus—last episode." He clicks a few buttons on the TV remote and the disc's main menu pops up.

"So they sent you?"

"Well, Caitlin's home already, Luis is in surgery, and Veronica's got school. That leaves me, but I would have volunteered anyway."

He says that last part quickly and I want to hold on to the feeling it gives me. That I'm lighter than air, better than what might follow. But I know how this turns out. My life is like surgery: the process is painful and something always has to be removed, restructured, and fixed.

This is a place where the fixes are sometimes too high a price, and that price always seems to be my friends.

"I'm not really up for visitors."

"Oh?" Ryan says, and reaches in for the call button. "'Cause I thought we could catch up. You promised I had to give you final thoughts, so I thought I might as well come here and experience them together."

"You're not staying."

"You said, and I quote, I was not allowed to finish this series without you being present."

"I was wrong, okay?" My voice cracks into desperate. I just want to be left alone, but the emotion feels too raw and so I pull back, closing in on myself. "Go back to the Home and watch it there. I don't want you here." It's what he's going to do anyway. Go home, be free, leave me behind.

Ryan holds my gaze, refusing to let me off the hook with this one. It's like we're back on that first night. I should have told him to pack up and go back to his room, but instead I invited him in to wreck my life.

"I'm not leaving."

"Get out!" My scream is hoarse and rips through my chest, pissing off every nerve ending. Pain twists my face and pushes my resolve. This isn't how it's supposed to go. I don't need Ryan here as a reminder of what might have been.

The nurse opens the door and hovers there like she's not sure whether to intervene.

"Caitlin said you might be like this," Ryan says.

For his part, Ryan looks like he's been hit with a sledgehammer.

I'm glad. I want him to hurt, to know what he suggested was wrong. Doctors are not here to heal me. They're not going to fix anything or change things or make me better. If I had stuck to my guns—if I had done what I thought was right—I wouldn't have wasted my time here.

But you still wouldn't be healed, a small voice in the back of my head whispers. I can't slug myself, but I can rage at Ryan.

"And what did she tell you?" My voice is venom and I want to see him hurt, even as I want to save him from the anger that breathes inside me.

"That if I wanted you, I'd have to fight for you." His response takes me down a notch. A chink in my anger that I was not prepared for. I was calm, knew what to expect and the story that fed my ire. But not now, with the knowledge that Caitlin kept my secrets.

"I don't want you here," I bite back. I want him gone, even as I want him to stay here and fight. It's so stupid to want that because he's going to leave, float out of my life. Nothing here is permanent.

"I think you do."

"You're just going to leave like everyone else. Caitlin likes to say that I'm the reason our friendship's a struggle." This has been the thing I have clung to my entire life. How many times have I been through shit because of the hospital, because of Mom's posts? It has to be true.

My life isn't understandable unless pared down and spoon-fed by a normal person.

"You're so afraid that everyone will leave you."

With that, I erupt.

"You think you know things because these doctors have fancy degrees and are the best in the world. You think that means you follow them blindly, but you're wrong." Tears run hot down my cheeks, but I don't remember starting to cry. Ryan reaches out as if to touch me, but I pull back. My stitches scream. Three little cuts and so much pain. "You told me this would work."

"I am here, Ellie. You want to be angry at this whole thing, fine. Be angry. I'm angry for you, but don't you dare say that this is what is pushing me away. What pushes Caitlin away. I came here to see you because I wanted to keep a promise: to watch the final episode of *BSG* with you. You dropped off, just stopped talking to any of us, and none of us knew what was going on. You say we all leave—but you're the one who's already gone. Not your doctors and not VACTERLs. You."

I open my mouth to tell him about my parents, how they got a divorce. How the hospital just tears everything apart. But I can't. Because maybe he's right . . . maybe it is me, and that thought scares me even more.

"Come on," the nurse says, trying to place herself between me and Ryan. Her movements set him off. He ducks under her arm and his legs betray him. He steadies himself on the bed.

"I wanted to see you. I missed you. Because I—"

I don't want to hear what he has to say. "I have a life. But it's not here."

Ryan stops and pulls back against the nurse helping him out of the room. "No, Ellie. You have a dream of a life. Always wanting to get there, but never actually arriving." His words are a slap, hard and visceral. My chest heaves; every breath makes my stitches hurt.

I want to yell at him more, but he cuts me off.

"You've made it pretty clear that you think I'm doing this wrong. That I listen to doctors, that I think they're always right. Well, they've earned that respect."

"What have they done for you?" It's a question he doesn't know how to answer, and I watch him fish for words. "Exactly," I say. I wait for the triumph, the feeling that I won and how great that is, to settle in on me. But instead I watch his face harden. "You want to place all your faith in them, but you choose not to be active in your own treatment."

Ryan stops. I want him to keep going, to yell at me, and to come back to this argument. But he doesn't. He raps his knuckles on the bed and then backs up.

"You're leaving?" I say, stunned that he's just giving up. I want to rip the IV out of my arm and run after him. He doesn't get to leave this fight. We are not done here.

The nurse shepherds him out the door like she can't get free of this room fast enough. Ryan pulls away for only a moment. "Why should I stay? It's not like you're going to keep me around. Isn't that how this works?" He raises an eyebrow in challenge, but I look away.

And just like that, cold settles into my bones that would rival the temperature outside.

My chest heaves as I try to catch my breath, each inflation of my lungs sprung on more pain and more hatred. For this place. For my so-called life. For myself.

Chapter Thirty-two

If I thought yesterday's nurse was bad, today's is worse. She won't let me stay in bed in the one position I know is comfy. She gets me up in a wheelchair and takes me down the hall. My whole chest burns and I cough a handful of times, each one stretching the few stitches that line my side.

The pediatric floor is actually not a bad place to be as far as hospitals go. Bright colors, artwork everywhere — even on the ceiling, which, when you stare at it for hours on end, you start to appreciate.

But the crowning achievement is the kids' activity room at the end of the hall. It's either busy or empty. Cushions on the floor, tables wheelchair height, a crayon box that looks like it exploded on the walls, and crafts of every sort can be found here. We may be stuck, but like hell will we be bored.

Nurse Overlord parks me at a table and sets a dish of beads and string in front of me. There's a call button just in case we actually need medical attention, but the look she gives me makes it clear I am to use this only in an emergency. Like, a real one.

"Can't figure out a pattern you like?"

My head snaps up and I turn, wincing at the pain in my side. Luis rolls up to my table. He's still wearing his signature beanie. Besides looking a bit tired and sporting a bandaged scar — he looks great. There's still that trademark humor shining in his eyes. "Luis? I didn't think they'd let you out and about so soon," I say, remembering Ryan said Luis was headed into surgery yesterday.

"Fast recovery."

"I guess that explains the million texts?" I feel bad if I missed them. My phone is still buried in my bed, barely touched. I don't need that device or the people in it. I'll just end up saying something I'll regret.

"None of which you've replied to. We thought you might hate us now." Luis pulls a stack of construction paper toward him and grabs a stray crayon. He lays down line after line on the paper—not actually creating anything worthy of a museum, just something to do with his hands.

"It's better for me to be alone." I don't even try to stop that coming out. Normally I would keep those ideas to myself, the ones that say wouldn't it be nice to have something that people knew and were primed for instead of me explaining what I have to every single person who asks. They all regret it. Almost instantly you can see them start to backpedal, to pull away. And then there are the things that are impossible to explain. Like how a fucked-up insurance system forces your parents to get a divorce. I spent a lot of time on the internet, searching for reasons. The main takeaway: insurance companies don't want to cover kids like me. So you're left with the state-run insurance, if you qualify. When you're married, you usually don't. So, divorce. It makes Mom a single parent of a kid with a disability, and suddenly she has access to life-saving medical care for me. And that's how I became the reason for every decision, taking over their lives like a tumor.

"Oh really? That's why you didn't tell your friends back home any of this?" I glare at him. "Face it, you need people."

"Did you get that out of a fortune cookie?"

"Shut up, I have cancer, that means I'm real deep."

"Says who?"

"Every YA novel ever written."

"Lay it on me, then. What am I missing?"

Luis crunches up a piece of paper and chucks it at me. "I will not tolerate that attitude."

I plaster on a cheesy smile and wait for him to go on.

Luis seesaws the crayon on his fingers, waiting for me to get myself in order. He doesn't ask if I'm okay. Once I'm back to some kind of working condition, he goes on as if nothing happened.

"People."

"The majority of them suck. Next question."

"Let them in."

It all comes back to me, crashing in on me. Why am I like this? Why me? Why did I break up my family?

"Are they going to understand how my parents got divorced because of me? That I'm the reason my mom lost her job? How I've ruined her life?" I say these words to the table, finally giving breath to what's been living inside me. Saying it out loud just pushes it down on me even more. There's no lightness in sharing because maybe this is all my fault. Maybe I should just let Mom do what she wants because I've taken so much from her?

Luis lets out a long, slow whistle. "Damn, that's a lot. I did the same thing to the first person I told that I had cancer. Unloaded like that. It's like a smack in the face. But that's not on you. You deserve to be happy, and the only person stopping that is you."

His words dig under my skin, pushing between muscle and dermis, trying to make me a host. To turn me into the girl who should not ask why but just live in the unknown.

"This place takes away everything I want."

"And what does it give in return?"

"What are you talking about?"

"First law of science. Matter cannot be created or destroyed."

"You made that up."

"Not possible, I'm an honor roll student." He pushes on, not daunted by my silence. "The hospital can't kill something. It can change something, but kill it? Nah."

I stab my plastic string through the beads. There is no way I am going to admit he has a point. None.

"Ellie?" He says my name a few more times, and I want to respond. I should respond, but the anger in my chest chokes my words. I can't get them out. All I can do is keep stringing beads, until finally he gives up.

He hits the call button and a nurse comes to help him leave. Before he goes, he looks at me one last time. "Maybe it's not the hospital but your fear of it that's doing this. That's what makes you clam up. Keep to yourself. Why not let people in instead of holding them at arm's length?"

I stare at him.

"A *Patient Life* is actually pretty great." And the nurse takes him away.

Caitlin. An ache lodges in my chest, pushing against my heart at the thought of her and the words I said. I move to wipe invisible tears away and my side lights up again with pain. Perhaps this is just life.

Life is pain . . . I doubt *The Princess Bride* knew just how right it was. I wonder if they were thinking specifically about doctors in that moment.

No one else comes to visit me. Luis takes to his room, and only through our group chat do I know he made it out of the hospital. I read the messages but don't respond. That lifeline too seems to have dried up. Texts went from hundreds if not thousands a day to none and I feel the loss like a missing limb.

One I didn't know I needed until it was cut off.

When the pain gives up and I just grin and bear through the bulk of it, Dr. Darlington signs my discharge papers. Mom keeps her distance, but Dad is trying to put things right with a one-armed hug as he helps me from the car into the Home. We won't be here that long, and I can't wait to escape all of my missteps here.

Veronica sits behind the counter when I walk in. She smiles and gives me a shallow wave, which I don't return. Why should I? There's nothing permanent here. Nothing to hold on to.

I curl up in our room as Mom and Dad go through the motions of packing up and cleaning. I pull out my phone and stare at the list of text messages. Should I reach out to someone? Tell Caitlin how I really feel? That I'm sorry? She's always been there. For a moment, I was sure she was going to be the thing I could take across that hospital line. A friendship built to last.

Look how that turned out.

Luis's words come back to me. *Maybe it's me. . . .*

What a hot mess I have made of my life. I drop my phone onto the ground and then roll over toward the wall. Dad covers me with the quilt from Veronica and asks if I want anything to eat.

Nothing. I want nothing. At least nothing he can give me. I want to take it all back, gobble up every word I said so they cannot fracture my world anymore.

Ping!

This time I don't reach for my phone.

My lungs still keep me up at night, and now they bring a friend—pain! I gladly swallow the Benadryl and I'm dead to the world in less than thirty minutes.

Chapter Thirty-three

I sit on the couch in the front room of the Home, waiting for my parents to settle the bill. Technically, there is no bill. Or at least there doesn't have to be. Families here pay what they can, and if that's nothing, then that's nothing.

Sinking farther down into my hoodie, I try to block out the world. Still caught in a Benadryl fog from last night, plus the fights of the last week, I shove in my headphones and take in the world through sight alone.

This is a place threaded through my childhood. Friends were made and lost; it's a place where I knew time stopped. I could walk away from here unscathed, back into the real world where life-life waited for me with open arms.

"Ready, kiddo," Dad says. He's taken over the talking to me since Mom and I had our big fight. Every now and then I'll catch her, mouth open, as if she's willing the right words to come out. All I want to tell her is there are no right words, except *I've deleted my blog and started new social media accounts that are all private. Also your father and I are getting remarried.*

I don't expect her to tell me that. Those things are her way to connect. I'm asking her to cut off her life support. I wait for the guilt to settle in, but it doesn't come, burned away by the constant anger.

The car is packed and the room cleaned. It feels like we've never even been here, despite everything that's changed.

Mom's going through the trunk. "Rick, have you seen Ellie's *BSG* DVDs?"

I'm right here, I want to shout.

Dad turns to me, knowing that I heard her question. His look says this has to stop, but our family is good at digging in our heels, refusing to give up. After all, that's how we ended up here. Mom was so stubborn at getting me the best care, the thing that would keep me alive.

"I gave them to Caitlin," I say. A lie.

Ryan still has them. And no way am I going to retrieve them. Perhaps he'll burn them in effigy. I smile at the thought. It would be nice to destroy something. Anything.

Be the destroyer and not the destroyed.

Except maybe I am both.

Soon enough Ryan will understand what I told him. He'll feel the sharp sting of the hospital, and then . . . I'm sure someone else will pick up the pieces. Or maybe he'll text me. I hate my heart for jumping at that thought, hanging it among the stars with my other wishes.

I crawl into the back seat and lie down, struggling to adjust my seat belt so it falls just right. My lungs still burn with coughs and I can feel the large bruise from the arterial line that takes up most of my lower arm, stretching out yellowing tendrils into my elbow.

My phone is strangely silent. The hundreds of messages a day, just gone. I achieved everything I wanted.

Go me.

Mom climbs in the front seat and Dad slides behind the wheel.

"Don't you want to say goodbye to your friends, Ellie?" She strains for neutrality, but I can still feel everything she's holding back. Tension clings to each word as she tries to make them sound like she cares and is not still furious with me.

I stare at her. Did she just say something, to me? Like, directly? The roof of the car isn't as interesting as hospital ceilings, so I close my eyes, not replying. I haven't checked to see if she took the blog down, mostly because I don't want to be disappointed when I see that it's still up, cataloging my life like I don't exist apart from her words.

Dad turns around. "I heard you had quite the friend group—certainly some of them are still here. Your mom and I would happily wait for you to—"

"No." I open my eyes and look at him. "They have their own appointments." All of the pain I feel pours into my words, and I hope that they extract it from my body. Take the pain away and leave me in peace. But they don't.

With a sigh, Dad turns back to the wheel and my parents exchange a look. The car starts and I don't watch the Family Care Home fade. I don't count down the number of blue-and-green signs denoting Coffman's reach.

I pull out my phone and delete every conversation.

Our group chat. Gone.

Ryan. Goodbye.

Caitlin. Done.

I delete so many that I end up back at my friends from home. Jack. Brooke. A few others from the speech team. I swipe into Brooke's chat, and start the message, my fingers flying over the keyboard. It's not a full rundown of events, but enough that I hope she'll say something. Anything.

Unwilling to stare at my phone, waiting for Brooke to forgive me, I stuff it back into my hoodie pocket and lean back.

The drive to Coffman is quick. There's just one last appointment before we head back home. I sit silent, letting Darlington talk to my parents. I don't care anymore. Shock and anger insulate me from whatever follow-up he prescribes.

We stop at the coffee shop in the subway before we head out. Dad sets my cup in front of me and Mom pulls him away.

"Ellie?"

I look up and see my internist and possibly all-around favorite doc—Dr. Carlyle. There's a strange moment where I see so many images of him superimposed one on top of the other. I've known him my entire life—he's still mostly the same. Sandy-brown hair, but it's starting to thin. His face is mostly unlined, but the wear of a surgeon's life seems to have polished his face to an even shine.

"H-hi," I stammer.

He motions to the seat across from me. "May I?"

Relief crowds my chest—and for once I welcome the burn. How long has it been since a doctor asked for permission to do something for me? I guess that's what comes from being there at the beginning, and Dr. Carlyle has seen it all.

Several patients give us side-eyes. Normally you don't see doctors and patients interact outside of Coffman's floors. We all inhabit areas of the subway, but we really don't speak, both living in our personal worlds.

Dr. Carlyle takes a seat across from me and smiles his warm, quiet smile. "I talked with Dr. Darlington," he starts.

I curl farther into my hoodie. What good ever came from talking with Darlington?

"And I know his theory that this might be psychosomatic."

I sit up. Darlington can think I'm an idiot for all I care, but I need Dr. Carlyle to like me, be on #TeamEllie. He can't believe I would fake something like this. . . . "I swear—"

Dr. Carlyle holds up a hand and I fall silent, gulping down the words wanting to escape.

"He's new, and while that shouldn't be a factor, sometimes even doctors forget there are other possibilities."

"I don't follow."

Dr. Carlyle rests his elbows on the table and leans forward. "Your mom called me. And we had a very long conversation. We talked about what's going on in your life. Where you go, the different places you go every day. She thought Dr. Darlington may have missed something."

"My mom talked to you?" I pick at the edge of the cardboard sleeve of my coffee cup. What he's saying doesn't filter through the correct neurons in my brain. He has to be mistaken. Mom thinking anything other than Darlington is a gift from God? No.

"Your mother was quite specific that she doesn't think this is all in your head. Up until you got sick, your life seemed pretty great. So either something happened and you're not telling anyone, or Dr. Darlington is wrong."

My mouth falls open. Someone finally said it. "My life was pretty great. . . ." The words sneak out and Dr. Carlyle raises an eyebrow, asking a silent question. There are lines that you can cross as a doctor and then there are *lines*. We're more like distant family, close but not that close.

Brooke and Jack—my whole crowd of speech friends. I haven't been happier than when I was at school and hanging out with them. Going to speech tournaments, even homework felt like something I was normally good at. My life was on track, and then . . . it wasn't. "Is it really in my head?" I ask, and fear gums up every word.

"Dr. Darlington, for all his awards and expertise—sometimes overlooks things. I wanted to know more about the places you went, and your mother mentioned your school building is older, doesn't have a lot of windows. And I looked through some other files—you've had quite a few illnesses since you started high school."

"I guess." No one has ever quizzed me on my cold and flu history. Surgery, sure. Common colds—not worth noting.

"Can I share what I think might be going on?"

I nod, too afraid to speak. He has a theory. One that doesn't include me being wrong?

"I think—and there really is no way to prove this—but I think it's the school building. Perhaps poor ventilation. It probably wouldn't affect the students with a normal lung capacity, but for someone—"

"With shitty lungs?" I fill in for him.

"With compromised lung function," he amends with a stern look at me. I hold in my eye roll. "It can be. I think when you get an average cold, like anyone else, your lungs flare up. You're well enough to go back to school, but the building with so many kids packed inside, unable to go out, few windows—virus gets in the air and aggravates your lungs."

"But it doesn't happen in the summer."

"Because you're outside, the doors are open, there's airflow. Flu season is over."

"Oh . . . kay."

"She shared with me that while you did have a few 'down days' after going to Morelands, you bounced back faster than before and didn't have nearly as many attacks as you did when coming back from school. To me, this suggests environmental factors. It's not you, it's where you are."

"So I just have to live with this?" I want to believe him, in his theories, but I've been let down by so many doctors over this. Believing what he's saying is like stepping on ice—you have to trust that it will hold. The lake is beautiful when frozen over and you can stand in a place where normally you'd sink, but it won't last, it's not permanent. This is an answer, and in the moment it's everything.

"We'll do some monitoring, but I think next year—if this happens again—what is important is calming your lungs down. We know there's nothing in your lungs and the cough is not productive. We know it's not the cyst on your bronchial tubes. I would have to talk with Dr. Darlington about this, but we could try nebulized lidocaine."

"You want to numb my throat."

"And your lungs."

"And that will help?"

"We'll have to wait and see."

He stands up and offers his hand to me. "Take care, Ellie."

"Do you really think it's my school?" I ask, taking his hand.

"It feels like the best hypothesis. Your mom was adamant it wasn't in your head."

I snort. *Sure, it's Mom. . . .*

Dr. Carlyle levels another stern look at me, as if he knows what's gone down between me and Mom and he doesn't approve.

Too bad his opinion doesn't count in this. He can counsel me on surgery, not me being the cause of my parents' divorce.

"Take care of yourself," he says. "The golden doctor is not always the answer to everything—that's what your mother told me." He nods at me again and heads off back to Coffman.

Mom hovers at the edge of my vision with Dad. Sometimes I want to believe the worst about Mom. I hate her blog so much, but it started as a way for her to find out how to help me. Mom's eyes are full of love and care, and I look away, still not quite able to reconcile our fight with what Dr. Carlyle just told me.

She was so adamant that surgery was the only way, that Darlington would fix me—I never thought she would look elsewhere. But she did for me, because she knew I wasn't lying that something was wrong with me. In that moment, all I want to do is hug my mom.

Chapter Thirty-four

I've never missed my hospital friends. I've learned to let them go, to treasure the moments because the future was too uncertain. Letting us drift apart was easier than finding out someone else died. Caitlin refused to become a statistic in my life, forcing herself in at every possible moment. There is something in how we helped each other through difficult times, but the constant reminder of that fight is just too much.

I'm home. I have my friends. Jack—I think. I'll be able to go to Brooke's party.

Why do I still feel so lost?

Mom and I are just slightly misaligned and it makes us bump into each other. She's hesitant and it makes me want to reach out and say something. She fought for me. I can't remember the last time I truly believed Mom was on my side. This thought wedges itself into my chest, refusing to budge even when I list the numerous times she failed me. Mom cared about me beyond what she could do for my illness.

I wish I could talk to Caitlin about this. Several times I pick up my phone to text her, only to remember we're done. Still, I try to force my way back into Caitlin's life, unable to let the hospital take her from me.

Ellie

Made it home.

Miss you.
Hope everything is okay!

There's no instant reply or even a read receipt. I know because I stay there, huddled under the blanket that Veronica helped me get from the Family Care Home, and stare at my phone, willing Caitlin to respond.

She doesn't.

Social media gives me only a small window into the lives of any of my hospital friends, and Ryan went to private. *A Patient Life* is updated regularly and now includes a whole series with Luis and the different experiences of BIPOC people as patients.

I'm curled up with Tok'ra trying to catch up on my homework when Mom knocks on my door. I've been in bed most of the day, being tortured by a book for English. Mom leans there in the jamb just like she used to, her head cocked to the side, a small smile in place. Casual, like we're okay. An ache forms in my chest for what we once had.

"Dad's going to be late tonight."

I nod.

Mom seems to hold her breath, as if waiting for me to go on and invite her in. But I'm afraid of opening my mouth because who knows what might come out of it.

She starts to back out of the room, but she stops, and instead of leaving, she crosses the demarcation line. With quick, practiced movements, she stacks my stray books and sits on the edge of my bed.

Anger flashes in my chest, but it's old and dying like a security blanket I've held on to for too long. *Let it go,* I tell myself. My feelings knot themselves up and I'm not sure which to trust. "What?" I ask. The word comes out harsher than I mean it to and I flinch.

Mom gives me a warning look. I can be angry, I can be cross, but she is still my mom and that position demands respect.

And she fought for you.

She presses her lips into a thin line and takes a deep breath. I know this routine; it's the same one she uses right before I go into surgery. The same grim determination that everything is going to be okay—if only by the sheer force of her will.

"When you were born—"

"Mom," I start; I do not want to go through this with her.

"Please. When you were born, I would have given anything to keep you safe. To give you a life that you deserved. And yes, there have been hard choices that your father and I have made for you."

The weight of their lives presses down on me. "Mom, you don't need to explain this to me." I struggle to get out of my blanket nest. *Distance:* I need physical distance from this, from her.

"I think I do—what you said—"

"*Mom.*" Now it's my turn to make a warning. I don't want to discuss this.

"I know it may not always make sense, but I would do anything for you. I love you," she says. Mom kisses me on the head and I accept it because I'm trapped in a straitjacket of blankets of my own making.

She pulls back and stands up, nodding. This is not the time, and yet I want to reach out and say yes, it is. She pulls her phone out of her pocket and closes the door to my room.

A few seconds later my phone dings with a link.

> **VATERs Like Water**
> **[Private Post]**
> *This is for my daughter.*

I push myself into a seated position, wincing as the movement stretches the incisions on my side. At least that's better than the itching. Nothing worse than when a scar or stitches itch. I click open the message, trying to prep myself for whatever comes next.

Dear Ellie,

Welcome to my last post. This one's entirely for you.

    When you were born, another mother told me that I would dream new dreams for you. That I had to let go of the dreams I had for my child. I laughed and thought, No, I will not find new dreams for my child; I will fight for her dreams.

    All I ever wanted was for you was to find your dreams, to help you achieve them, to make sure that your disability didn't stand in your way. As a mother, the scariest thing is when your children are sick and you feel helpless. I found the best doctors, your father and I fretted over every surgery, what would be best for you, what would give you the ability to reach your dreams? That's all I ever saw the divorce as. It changed nothing about my life or your father's. It only meant that we could get you the best medical care.

    When you were small, people would ask about you. They meant to be supportive, but the question came up after every surgery. Well-meaning but exhausting. Giving them the rundown of your surgeries felt like a chore. Perhaps because they weren't asking about you, but they wanted to know a piece of you. Not the brave, funny girl you were growing into but the intricacies of your surgical life. I put up walls against them, unable to cut them completely out, but forcing them behind a blog. Writing everything that happened, trying to show them who you were. Chronicling your life for them became a balm for me after long days at Coffman.

    When you said stop—I was scared. I've hidden behind this for so long that to reengage with people, well, it terrifies me. But that is for me to figure out. You should have a say in your life, and I'm sorry if I ever made you feel like you didn't. There are excuses I could make, but please know I have only ever wanted the best for you.

When Dr. Darlington came out and explained what was going on, I took a step back. Before you asked me to stop, before we fought, maybe I would have said do the thoracotomy. This would have crossed out another issue for us not to face again. But I thought about you, how determined you were to get home, to get back to Jack and your friends.

Your father and I made a call that we thought you would agree with. If you are angry at it, that is your choice. I am still your mother and I want what's best for you, but I am ready to listen to your voice. It is your life and they are your dreams.

As to what you read on this blog, it makes me sick to think for a moment that you think you ruined my life. This blog is no longer public and I will delete it after this post. I wish there was more I could do to take back what you saw. I love you.

Perhaps I shouldn't have disagreed with the other mother for asking me to dream new dreams for you, but because she thought they were my dreams in the first place.

I no longer need to be the general in this fight. It is time for me to take a step back and for you to tell me where I can fight. For you, Ellie, I will move mountains.

Tears well up and I tilt my head back to keep them from falling. So many things were messed up in the hospital. One of them was my relationship with my mom. But as much as it broke us, it brought us back together stronger than before. Suddenly I don't want to be alone, and struggle to get out of my blankets.

Mom sits in the family room, lit only by the glow of the TV program she's watching. It's a show we used to watch when I couldn't sleep. There are, like, a million seasons and the plot has doubled back on itself so much that even I can't keep the mythology straight anymore.

"Hey," I say, my voice surprising in how quiet it is. Mom reacts to it like a nuclear bomb just went off. My face is wet from crying.

"Ellie," she says, starting to get up. But I beat her to it. I walk forward and don't think about it, I just wrap my arms around her. The vanilla in her shampoo is a comfort I didn't know I was missing. I hold her tight even though I should be too old for this. Too grown. But I don't mind being a child again.

She's stiff at first, unsure how to respond.

"Thank you," I say.

Her arms come around me and she holds me in a hug. Strange how much I've missed this.

She pulls back first and there are tears in her eyes. "Ellie . . ." She brushes a strand of hair out of my face. "I'm so sorry."

"Mom," I say, "I think I messed up."

"What—what happened?" she asks, pulling back so she can look at me.

Trust people, be a team player. Ryan's words come back to me.

"With Caitlin, Veronica, and . . . them," I say, my throat closing up around Ryan's name. "I just . . . the hospital ruins everything." Mom said she would fight for me. I need her to tell me how to fix this. All of this. So I tell her everything.

"Kiddo . . ." Mom's voice is a comfort, but there's also an edge of a lesson in it. I brace for what she's about to tell me. "The hospital cannot break or fix everything—that is entirely up to you."

Her words are heavy and take time to sink in. I don't know how to ask what she hit on—what if it is me? What if I'm the one too broken to be fixed?

"Have you talked to them?"

"Caitlin won't answer my texts."

"Have you tried again?"

I play with the tassels on the throw pillows. No, because I thought once might even be too much.

"How many times did she reach out to you?"

Just go in for the kill, Mom. Sheesh. Caitlin texted me a lot. Every week, sometimes more if she just wanted to talk. Message after message that would pile up until I responded. That girl doesn't know how to give up.

I fish out my phone and turn the camera on, take a selfie, and then send it to Caitlin.

Ellie

I'm not going anywhere.

Chapter Thirty-five

Minutes tick by, and I retreat to my room, working on a longer message. Different apologies. Several life updates. Even a simple *Hi*. But all of those seem foolish. Getting nowhere, I make a big move and start a video call.

Time doesn't mean a lot to Caitlin—she's up at all hours, sleep being an option for her most of the time. Holding my breath, I wait either for it to ring into eternity or for her to answer.

"Do not think . . . ," Caitlin says as her picture forms from a pixelated mess. She stabs her crochet hook through the hat she's currently working on, and I can imagine that she's picturing it as my face. "That I answered because I forgive you."

"You answered because you want to see me grovel."

"Get to it," she says. Her words remain stern, but her eyes flash off her work to the camera, and for a second, I see hope.

I take a big breath. Only I can fix this. "I'm sorry. I've been a bad friend. I just . . . I don't know how to mix everything. I thought keeping it separate would be better for us—for me."

Caitlin holds up her hook.

"You cut me out," she says. "Chose a boy over me. Me. Who understands better than I do? And then on top of that, you think you need to fix me. We're broken together," she says. A kernel of hope grows in my chest. Broken together. That's our phrase—and no one, especially those who count themselves as "normal," are allowed to use it. Reclaiming words and all that.

"I didn't—"

"I'm not done yet," Caitlin says, and her hook goes back to whipping through the project, going round and round. "Do you know how many hats I've made? My mother has practically cut me off. If you hadn't called . . . I would have . . . started to crochet the carpet."

I laugh.

"You are never allowed to do that again."

I nod. And then I work up the courage to ask, "What did you decide to do about the morning show?"

Caitlin blows an errant curl out of her face. "Nothing. I just . . . I don't like it. I know—I *know*. But I just don't want it comma however . . . ," Caitlin says, making me die from anticipation. "I offered to do a six-month Instagram takeover with them on the lives of disabled teens by and for disabled teens."

"*And?*"

"And they agreed!" Her smile is infectious even across the airwaves. And even as I'm so happy for Caitlin, I can't help but feel the fear and pain Mom's blogging has caused. I pick at the ties of my hospital quilt, trying to put together the shame and fear inside me. Shame of wanting to be seen and fear of what that will bring.

"What about you—what's next for Ellie Haycock?"

"Speech, friends . . ."

"Acting . . ."

I look down, ready to be told it's foolish. Wanting to be an actress.

"What's wrong?"

"I just . . . I can't do it. I'm not brave enough and it doesn't matter how much I want it in my bones, I can't . . . I'm too scared. It's too much of a fight." Bravery has been my default setting since I was a child, but I'm worn thin and all I want is for something to be easy. But this dream, it's like wanting to go to the moon. It's possible, but it's a really, really, *really* hard possible.

"People are terrible, we know that. But you are allowed to want those things, just like anyone else. Don't let assholes on the internet stop you. There will be enough assholes in the audition rooms. Save your ire for them. And their names, because I will put them all on blast." There's metal in her voice that would build the world's tallest building. She's a rock, much more into the whole "community" thing than I am. Still, no matter what, she's there for me.

"I'm sorry." The words sink into my bones, and I feel certain in our friendship. We are not sand on a beach to be thrown about by the tide; we are trees firmly planted and growing together.

Caitlin sighs and blows a stray curl out of her face. "Good."

We chat for a while, catching up on things. Caitlin's various channels have grown, especially since her last surgery. There's maybe someone new in her life, and I smile at the normality of our conversation.

"Oh, tell me everything!"

"I just . . ." Her hook stops dodging in and out of her project. "This is going to sound stupid, but I go in and out of the hospital so many times and I just want something more permanent. Like what I thought you and Ryan were working on."

My eyes snap open.

Caitlin chews on her lip and slowly pulls stitches through her project. This is the divide for us. Either I can step back and remain how we were friends only in the hospital or I can be true to my apology.

"Have you talked to anyone?" I ask. I'm desperate for news. I don't want her to mention Ryan, but I also don't know if I can handle her talking about everyone else but Ryan.

Caitlin's stitches grow progressively faster. As if she's pulling petals from a daisy trying to find an answer. *Tell her, don't tell her, tell her . . .* Finally she reaches the end of the row and a decision has been made. "Yeah." Caitlin focuses on her project. Her hook retreats to a steady, precise rhythm. "Luis started radiation. As he predicted, the doctors are saying full recovery. His classmates sent him a whole series of get-well junk. He's really insufferable about all of this."

"Hopefully the docs have it right."

She raises her hook and points it at me through the phone, as if to say *Correct*. "Eh, I think he's gonna make it." In, out, in, out. "Veronica and Luis are official. . . ."

"*Finally*," I say, and flip over onto my back.

"This makes the group chat awkward sometimes. When they really get going, Ryan just ducks out altogether. . . ." Her last word slowly grounds to a stop and her fingers still, the crochet hook halfway through another stitch.

That's a gut punch I wasn't ready for. Yes, I had deleted the chat, but it never popped back up on my notifications, which meant they had started it over without me.

"So that's enough about our love lives."

I laugh to close the topic and so I can ask her to weigh in on my level of bitchiness.

"Oh, on a scale of one to ten, you were a flaming twenty."

As expected. What I hoped not to be but actually was.

Caitlin looks up from her crocheting without raising her head and gives me the death glare. "Didn't we cover this? Not everything that starts in the hospital goes up in flames."

I bite my lip. Logically, I believe her. I can just look at our friendship for proof. We're still here. The hospital failed to destroy us and that might take some getting used to.

"So Veronica's his radiation buddy?"

Caitlin shrugs. "Did I not say this topic is closed? She's still in town, so the group chat goes off the hinges when they're planning to get together."

I look away from my phone. I wanted so bad to be free of the hospital, and now I'm craving the very conversations I once thought split me from the world.

"If you want back in, you need to apologize to them," Caitlin says. I'm pretty sure she can read my mind. It's one of the advantages she has from having VACTERLs, just a direct line into where my brain likes to wander.

The weight of what I said to everyone, from Luis to Veronica and even Ryan, sits beside me in bed, suffocating me.

"I'm not doing it for you," Caitlin says.

"I'll handle it."

"You don't have to."

She's offering me an out, if I want it. I could let them go like any number of friendships I've formed over the years; let their memories fade to ghosts and then vanish in time. The sharp stab in my heart seems determined to anchor the shades of their friendships to me.

"Yeah."

Happy that she's delivered her message and that it's been heard, Caitlin lets the conversation drift to other topics. School, friends at home, world politics.

"So when is Brooke's party?" she finally asks.

"Tomorrow."

"And Jack is gonna be there?"

"Yeah," I say. "Jack is gonna be there." I wait for the light to fill me, the hope that I once had at the very mention of his name, but there's nothing. I force myself to smile, to act happy as Caitlin offers advice.

"I think you should just be direct, and you can blame me if you need to—be like 'I had to take care of my friend.' Chicks before dicks and all that."

I laugh.

"Just practice what you're going to say. You got this," Caitlin says as a sign-off.

Hanging up, I lie back in bed and close my eyes. I try to think about what I'll say to Jack, but every time I start all I see is Ryan's angry face yelling at me.

Chapter Thirty-six

I reposition my headband in the mirror, trying to tame my brown hair into looking as normal as possible for Brooke's party. I've been out of school for so long, it feels like I'm stepping into a new world. Like I went on summer vacation and they were still stuck in classes. They've been doing something that brings them closer together while I've been drifting further away.

That Mom is letting me go is a minor miracle, especially when I haven't even been back to school, but I am not questioning her. I snap a selfie of me and a cup of tea and I send it to Ryan.

Ellie

Rule #2.

I stare at my phone, willing him to pick up. The irony isn't lost on me. This was a Jack tactic. Photos of my life, texts checking in. That done, I start a new thread—and type in three names, leaving Ryan out because, well, I'm not sure I can handle that rejection.

Part of working my way up to seeing Brooke is to start with smaller apologies. Or rather, apologies I'm pretty sure are going to go the way I want.

I hope.

Please. *Please* let them go over well.

TUMOR SQUAD—TAKE 2?

> Ellie
>
> Hey—I hope everything is going okay.
>
> I know I fucked up.
>
> I'm sorry.

I stare at the messages, hoping for something, anything. Caitlin's separate message pops up almost instantly.

Caitlin

Well done.

> Ellie
>
> Think it'll work?

Caitlin

They're in post-radiation food comas.
Give it time.

Time. I had plenty of it, but that didn't make enduring it any easier. Maybe because luck is finally working on my side, the texts start coming in.

TUMOR SQUAD—TAKE 2?

Veronica

I'm clueless about this—so no apology necessary.
Also Luis says all good but wants to know if you're letting people in?
I demand someone bring me up to speed.
Luis is taking too long.

Caitlin

Ellie yelled at us all when we tried to be there for her.

> Ellie
>
> Just rip the Band-Aid off.

Caitlin

You're welcome.

Veronica

Luis is also asking about Ryan?

Should I add him in this chat?

Caitlin

ABSOLUTELY NOT.

A separate message pops up almost immediately.

Veronica

I knew it!

YOU ARE DATING.

> **Ellie**
>
> We aren't.

Veronica

Ahhh

So that's why he's not in the Tumor Squad. . . .

Because I don't know how to talk to him? Because while I was angry with Luis, he seemed to expect it. With Ryan I had been so . . . it had been a bad time. I was angry and hurt and everything just felt like it was falling down around me. The thing that no one thinks about when you blow up is that you're bound to get caught in the rubble. I was just now trying to climb out. I wasn't sure Ryan would be there when I finally did.

I grab my keys and head for the door. Mom stops me and gives me a hug and a kiss on my head and I am forced to remind her that I am a teenager.

"*You are great,*" she reminds me, and there's a pang in my chest because it sounds like something out of a book of quotes for coaches.

Like something Ryan would say. He still hasn't responded. Not even when I reminded him of Rule #4.

Nothing.

I park outside Brooke's house and walk to the door, unsure if my friend will actually let me in.

I ring the doorbell and wait, bouncing on the balls of my feet until the door opens and we stand there face-to-face. Brooke just hangs there in the doorway, her chestnut-brown hair hanging in loose curls. Shock and surprise color her features, but she quickly puts on her debate badass face, her blue eyes going hard, shutting me out.

Say something! I scream inwardly. I was jealous of Ryan and his friends—how easily their lives flowed together even as they now had vastly different experiences. *Say anything.*

"I had surgery."

"I heard." She crosses her arms as if to punctuate the fact that she heard and not from me.

Let.

People.

In.

"It didn't work." Her arms drop and her mouth opens, my words knocking the anger right out of her. No one in life-life is used to medicine not having the answers, not working. "They don't know what's wrong and . . ." And it all starts to come out. The last weeks of my life. The story that friends like her, my best friend, don't even know. I pull out everything that I've ever kept from her. The surgeries, the doctors' visits, the pain and fear I didn't think she could handle; it all comes out in one continuous wave.

Brooke holds up her hands and I keep going, because she wanted this. And I'm not sure I can keep it all in my head anymore. Then she starts waving them. "Why are you telling me this now?"

I look around at the snow-impacted yards.

"Because I didn't know how to explain to anyone what my life was like there."

"And now you just want to get rid of it in one go?"

"I'm so tired of trying to pretend it's nothing. I felt so alone."

Brooke lets out a heavy breath. "I'm glad you're back." I tense, waiting for the *but* I know will come. Maybe I deserve that. "And Jack is here and I did some minor probing . . ."

I shoot her a look. "Brooke—"

She waves away my words. "I am taking things into my own hands." She pulls me into the house and waits patiently as I struggle with my coat. Stitches stretch and I wince. I can either continue with the pain or ask for help. Before, I would never have asked anyone for help, didn't want to call attention to my differences. "Can you—"

The question is not even fully finished before Brooke is there, helping to ease the coat over my shoulders. "Jack is apparently *miserable*."

We share a smile, because this is what I've waited for, what I've worked so hard for. As Brooke takes me to the basement, she gives a rundown of the rest of our friends. My stomach does flip-flops and my chest suddenly doesn't feel like it can hold my lungs. And it's not my illness.

Friends mix in Brooke's basement. They hold cups of soda and examine the different packages they've brought. A sharp laugh punctuates the general hum of conversation.

"Hey, everyone," Brooke says, "look who's back."

Color drains from my face and I grab Brooke's arm in a viselike grip reserved for nurses who need to give me my next dose of morphine. This was not planned.

Eyes focus on me. I am sure that I am going to throw up. The moment hangs heavy in the air, every second dragging out to a year. The shift happens on their side first. Smiles bloom along with small cheers. My friends push closer to the edge of the stairs to welcome me first. Jack hangs back and we lock eyes. A spark crisps my chest and I offer him a smile.

He returns it.

Maybe this will work out. Jack and I will patch up everything and life will go back to how it was. I want for that feeling to sink in, that everything will be okay. But I feel like I'm walking to my execution.

We skirt around each other, finding ourselves in different groups, trying to work up the courage to talk. My friends provide a great distraction. They fold me back into their lives, gently turning over the last several weeks and months, catching me up, waiting for me to reciprocate. I add a few things, testing the waters. It's hard, not being with my hospital friends. Being here, with Brooke and my friends—this feels normal. But thinking about telling them about Caitlin, Luis—Ryan . . . My heart tightens and I can't breathe.

A cough helps me find breath again and my friends look worried.

"So are they going to do another surgery?" Brooke ventures. She's bringing it up. Not me. She's never asked me a direct question about the hospital before. I guess it was another unspoken rule, that I just didn't want to talk about it. But maybe she did and she was just protecting me.

I wrap my hands around the can of Coke and pray this caffeine will help silence the cough in my lungs. My bruises from surgery still linger, the stitches . . . Maybe the hospital is grafted into me and I will never be free of it. Things still haunt me. The look in Ryan's eyes, the pain as the nurse pulled out the arterial line, telling my mom to stop owning my life. Things that I want to forget, need to cut out of my life so that I can get back to what and who I really am.

Who I want to be.

"No," I say quietly. I want to look at my phone, check to see if there's a message from my medical coach. Even though I know what his advice would be, I still want his message to be there. *Talk to them.* "They thought it might work, to help me get better."

Every instinct in me screams to pull back. Stop before they get too freaked out. Before they leave me. But wasn't this what Luis said—I have to trust people? I can't grade them on just a few moments. "But it was too complicated."

I pull my elbows into my sides, wanting to disappear. I'm scared to look up and see pity on their faces, to hear the inevitable *I'm sorry*, and then watch them move on in the conversation back to happy topics, things in their lives that will go on as normal. Things that aren't failures. But that's not what happens.

"So that's it?" Brooke says. "They just gave up?"

"I mean, there's nothing more they can do."

"They just cut you open and now are like *Well, sorry, we're done.*"

"Yeah." This time I do look up, prepared for the pity I didn't get the first time. For the sad and secret *We're so glad it's not us* looks. But again I'm shocked. Every one of them looks furious.

"Fuck them," Brooke says. And the others raise their glasses in agreement. I don't know what to say. Tears hit the backs of my eyes and I want to say more, to say something to mark what just happened. Instead, I take their anger, their comfort, and pull it inside, wrapping it around me like a blanket.

I lean into the conversation, suddenly feeling myself slide back into their lives. We are not perfect, but I no longer feel like this is something I have to keep from them. Something that I need to conceal.

Focus, Ellie, I tell myself, *this is your life-life*. I worked so hard for this. I hang in there. My cough gets a little worse and my side aches, but I forgo medication, willing my body to heal.

Jack comes up to me, as all-American as he ever was, and Brooke checks in via a look with me. I nod and she backs away with a warning glare at Jack. And then it's just us.

"Hey," Jack says. He seems surprised that I'm here. I suppose I'm not the girl he saw a few weeks ago.

"Hi," I say. We both stand there, neither sure what to do next. Some of our friends look like they're ready to intervene.

"You made it back," he says. I wait for hurt or anger to slice into me like a surgeon into a patient, clean and precise and knowing exactly how to inflict only intentional damage. But I find it easy to meet his hazel gaze because I don't care. It doesn't hurt to be here with him. And I don't want to lean into him, to kiss him.

"Yeah, it was . . . umm . . . The surgery didn't work out." I dig my hands into the back pockets of my jeans, refusing to shrink with the admission.

I brace for his reaction. The pity. The sympathy. The confusion on how he should feel about this. Things I've feared almost as much as I've feared surgery itself.

Jack looks down at his cup again, trying to make sense of everything. "Oh," he says, and that one words carries with it confusion, fear, and sympathy. "That sucks, I'm sorry."

That's when I realize I don't want anything from him. Not an apology, and certainly not to take me back.

"Yeah," I say. Maybe it's the simple expletive from Brooke, but it's not what I was expecting. There's no spark here now. Nothing that reminds me of why I did everything to try to get back to him. Instead there's just a dull glow from the memories that were good. Something to remind myself why I worked so hard to get back here.

"I can't imagine." His tone is cool, reserved. If he were Ryan, I would fight that tone, push until I broke through, but now . . . I don't want to.

There's only a scar there, where our relationship used to be. Old wounds healed and newly shiny. I have lots of scars. The thing is, sometimes they make you stronger. That's when I know I'm ready to let him go. I had surgery because of a boy. But maybe not this boy.

"I'm sorry," I say. The words feel right in my mouth, their shapes filling in the holes I realize I tore in my own heart. I've done a lot of apologizing. Maybe it's like doing surgical prep. All the tests are roughly the same, and they lead to one outcome. The actual surgery — the change — comes later.

Or maybe I'm still the same and just living through all these stupid mistakes, letting them heal. Closing them up to make way for something new. Something better — or at least functional.

"I should have told you about what was going on. It's never been easy for me to tell people — because it's too much to explain. Mom was always the writer about my life. People who were there in the hospital, they didn't need me to explain."

They usually already have at least a one-way ticket. Passengers have a very hard time on this train. "I clammed up about it because it's . . ." My voice trails off because I can't decide if it's a curse or a blessing.

Jack nods. "You should tell people more often. Let us be there for you." There's no forgiveness in his voice. I duck my head; it was a shitty thing for me to do. Perhaps if I could do it all again, I would do it differently. But there are no redos—we are stuck with the surgeries and lives we have.

Yesterday's miracles.

Jack falls in with some of his friends from choir. There is no good-bye, no understanding or meeting of the minds. His brush-off stings, but it doesn't kill me and it definitely doesn't inspire me to go after him.

"I can't believe he would do that," Brooke says, materializing by my side as if by magic.

I worked so hard to get back to Jack, but now I'm surprised to find I want to be at the hospital. I need to be there. I pull out my phone and look at Ryan's picture.

"Who's that?" Brooke asks.

"Can you do me a favor?" A weak plan is already forming. A treatment for a broken heart. I'm going to need a convincing lie, and I will probably end up doing one to two months' incarceration in my room, but what else is there?

"Have you finally found anger? Are we ready to take it out on him? I will throw him out of this party." Brooke is ready to pounce. Someday I should introduce her to Caitlin; they would be fast friends.

"I'm gonna spend the night at your place tonight." Brooke looks skeptical. "I'm not really spending the night. I mean, I don't think I will."

Chapter Thirty-seven

This whole plan is madness, but I suppose if I was going to back out, I should have done that four hours ago. I'm just reaching the outer limits of Coffman's perimeter, and turning back is not going to happen without a bathroom break. Onward it is.

I never thought I'd be back here so soon. In fact, I made it a priority to not come back for a very, very long time. Fate is fickle.

I have to Google Maps the Family Care Home because I don't know where it is. I only lived there for a large portion of my life but couldn't tell you the exact address to save my life.

Veronica is working tonight. I texted her the last time I stopped for gas, because I was going to need a way to get into the building. I pull into the circle drive and just sit there, my car turned off. This place has been a second home and nursed all my broken hearts, but now I'm afraid to walk in.

I worked on my apology for the entire drive here. What I would say and what I would definitely not say. Words lodge in my throat, and my heart is trying to slip through my ribs and escape.

Ping!

My phone goes off.

Veronica
I'm off in 10, if you still wanna do this.

"No guts, no glory," I tell myself. I grab my phone from the dash and struggle out of my car. Veronica lets me in and flashes a double thumbs-up.

Just looking at the stairs makes my lungs seize, so I opt for the elevator. I won't lie, maybe I wanted a little extra time before I had to admit my faults. The words I said to him still ring in my ears. I'm not sure he'll let me back into his life. I know *I* wouldn't be persuaded. Tears prick the backs of my eyes.

I'm not going to cry. I refuse.

Re. Fuse.

The elevator opens and I step on, bouncing on my feet. What if he says no? What if I came all this way and it doesn't work?

TUMOR SQUAD—TAKE 2?

Caitlin
Just tell him the truth.
Keep talking.
Give him no ground to intervene.

Ellie
And if that still doesn't work?

Luis
Tell him we'll let him have it.

Caitlin
Siiiiiiigh
Then you fought the good fight.
I have ice cream, FaceTime, and all the time in the world.

Veronica
I've got time tonight for movies!

Luis
I have nothing to offer but my sage advice:
If he rejects you—we riot.

My reflection greets me in the polished metal. What if it doesn't work out? Hasn't that already happened? Been there, done that. And I survived. You can't live life running from the things you're afraid of. Or try to live with your own bravado. At some point everything must be faced, and what you're left with is all you take with you. Things don't stay in the hospital or out in the real world. They move with you.

The elevator doors open and I suck up my courage. I've faced a lot between surgeries, treatments, and doctors, but apologies are right up there. *BSG's* title sequence rolls through the air.

He kept my DVDs.

Just like that, superficial anger flies up in me. I mean yes, everyone should get a chance to complete it, it's a great series, but those are mine.

Well, at least I have an intro.

Ryan sits, slumped on the couch watching the TV. The body count rolls across the screen.

"Were you even going to return those?"

His back goes from a gentle curve to straight before I can even blink. My heart jumps into my throat. I swallow it back down and step into the room. *I can do this; I can do this.*

Slowly, as if on a machine, he turns around to face me. I push off the wall and step into the room. Let's get this over with.

"What are you doing here?" he asks, pushing his black hair out of his eyes.

"Hi," I say, completely unprepared for how seeing him again would make me feel. Like he's a fire after a long day in the snow. Warm and welcoming, but I am a thief that has just snuck up here.

"Hi," he says, the word chopping off his tongue like a splinter. It stings as it wedges under my skin, making me want to bolt for the door.

Nope, I am not forgiven. And time has not softened any wounds.

"I wanted to . . . that is . . ." All of my carefully prepared speeches fly out the window. There is nothing I can say to him that will work.

Ryan struggles to his feet, his autoimmune disease getting the better of him. I move to meet him halfway.

"I'm sorry," I say. My own words cut me open, free the block that's been pressing down on my chest. "You were right. I was so upset about the surgery and what you said—I'm sorry I yelled—"

Ryan holds up a hand and I try to persist—to give him no ground.

"Ellie," he says. "Stop. I'm the one who should be apologizing."

His words hit me and I'm not sure what to do. My words tumble to a stop and I look between us. What did Ryan do that he would need to apologize for?

He leans heavily on his cane and limps toward me.

"I was so sure I could fix you—that I could fix myself. Follow orders, do the exercises, and get better. And then your surgery failed and I wanted to be there, but what you said . . . I shouldn't have pushed you."

"No, Ryan." I take a step forward. "I knew what could happen. But it's not your fault. It's not anyone's fault, and that's the hardest part. We want stories—we want enemies that we can face and defeat. But the enemy isn't a disease or deformity—it's not the hospital. Maybe we don't even have one. The hospital can't fix us totally—only we can do that."

Mom's advice comes out, and for the first time, I feel the words wrap around my bones and make me stronger. I can do this. I can change to meet the new and unexpected challenges.

Tears roll down my cheeks, big blobs that are for sure turning my eyes red. "I can go, I just wanted to say, in case . . ." But I can't say: *in case you want to take me back.*

The silence waits, as if it too is holding its breath, waiting to see what Ryan will say.

"Did you come all the way here to say that?"

"Yeah." I run my hand along my forehead, tucking my bangs behind my ear.

He steps closer. I only see his shoes move because I am too afraid to look up. Maybe he's going to walk past me, leave me my DVDs, and go. That's what I deserve. I roll on my feet, trying to hold myself to my spot.

Ryan stops in front of me.

"Ellie."

I start the babble again. Apologies, explanations, anything that might make him forgive me.

"Eleanor," he says, and I suck my words back in. My full first name. Is that a good thing? A bad thing? An I'm-about-to-get-yelled-at thing?

He leans in and kisses me, his lips soft. Fear loosens its grip on my heart and I feel like I can finally take a deep breath. I wrap my left arm around his neck, still unsure of what to do with my other. But Ryan has other ideas, he threads his fingers through my misshapen and doctor-formed fingers. Normally my instinct would be to pull back, but I want his touch. I taste the mint of his ChapStick and slowly sink into the feeling of us. I want to live in this moment, savor the places where our bodies connect. Those tiny pinpricks of sensation that ignite a fire in me. Hot enough to force my two worlds together.

He stops the kiss but doesn't pull out of my space. He's close enough that it's impossible not to meet his eyes. Close enough to count his eyelashes. Fear still prickles along the edges of my elbows and drops tiny bites on the back of my neck.

I squeeze my right hand around his fingers. My doctors used it as a test, and feeling his skin against mine is a pass with flying colors.

"Did you really drive all the way here to see me?"

"Kiss me again and I'll tell you the truth." I want to pull away, but instead I push myself forward. Ryan's hand skims down my back, brushing my spinal scars through my shirt. The tiny ribbons of skin that hold me together. That make me—me. It's not something I would have let Jack do. I wouldn't have let Jack even get this close. But Ryan knows all my secrets; I've always been willing to tell him.

Pacts are easily made and broken in the hospital, but there are few friendships that go beyond its walls. I don't know what the next steps will be or if Ryan and I can survive past his discharge orders, but for the first time I am willing to try.

Epilogue

Five Months Later

I pace back and forth between the tables in some lunchroom, waiting for the final scores to be tabulated. It took until spring for me to get really well, and now that Mom has so much free time she's become the local school board's worst nightmare in regard to the school's cleanliness.

Despite my fears that I wouldn't make state championships this year because I was stuck in the hospital or just out because of illness . . . I did. And now it's up to the judges whether I'll be a state champion.

Caitlin and Brooke both got to do one big *I told you so.* They repeat it every chance they get. I never should have introduced them to each other.

Brooke and Jack are both oblivious to what's going on, Brooke deep in conversation with a fellow debater and Jack lost in another comic. He looks up at me and gives me a weak smile—there was once a time when I would have sat with him. Our friendship, while not the same, is no longer on life support. There were a good two months where it was only Brooke and me hanging out at speech competitions.

My cell phone buzzes in my hands. I'm grateful for the distraction, because without Brooke or someone else, hanging out with Jack doesn't feel the same.

TUMOR SQUAD—TAKE 3

Caitlin
Results?

Ellie
Are not out yet.

Caitlin
Not state scores.
Read your email already.

Luis
We're dying over here!!

Veronica
The things you say in a chat called Tumor Squad. . . .

Luis
I put this chat together, it means I have power.
We talked her into applying.

Caitlin
Practically WROTE HER APPLICATION.

Veronica
I tried, Ellie!
But also . . .

I try not to feel a pang of sadness that Ryan isn't in the chat right now. Logically, I know he can't be tied to his phone all the time, but I want him to be the one telling everyone else to shut up. We have plans to talk later tonight, because despite not living in the same town, I talk to him more than I ever did to Jack.

Ryan was the one who finally convinced me to apply to the summer acting intensive. Like our nights in the Family Care Home he listened to every one of my concerns, and just like at the hospital he told me exactly why I was wrong.

I turn around, ready to do another lap.

Brooke comes up and grabs my phone out of my pocket. "Time to face the music." Before I can grab it back or stuff my fingers in my ears, she has my phone open and then is screaming, *"You got in!"*

Relief. Surprise. Adrenaline like I've never felt hits me hard. I got in. And then Brooke and I are jumping up and down, screaming. All eyes fixate on us, and I don't even care, because I got into the summer acting intensive. Maybe it's not Broadway, but it's a start.

"I expect to be thanked in your Oscar speech," Brooke says, one arm slung around my neck, the other motioning toward the crowd that's gathered as if she's knighting witnesses.

I do a double take, not sure if I'm losing it or if I've been struck by some sort of sudden illness. I wouldn't rule either out, honestly.

"Ryan?" I ask, pulling out of Brooke's grasp. "You aren't—What are you doing here?"

"Not every day your girlfriend makes it to state." He takes my hand and I can't help but look down at our joined hands.

He still uses his cane sometimes, the doctors are trying several different protocols, some cancer drugs, some lupus drugs—it's nothing solid. But it is enough. Some days.

Butterflies of excitement float around in my stomach from getting into the intensive. I'm at state. With my friends. And my boyfriend. I smile at Ryan. My normal may not be even close to anyone else's definition, but it's mine.

And those I choose to share it with.

Acknowledgments

So this is about to be a long list. Bear with me; perhaps by my fourth book I will be down to: "Strong power, thank you." But not today.

To start—the two people who pushed *Ellie* along the publication track—my agent, Alex Rice, and editor, Eileen Rothschild, who both read this book and saw something special in Ellie's story. You both had impeccable notes and really shaped me and *Ellie* into the writer and book we are today.

THE ENTIRE TEAM at Wednesday, with super shout-outs to Lexi, Cassie, Meghan, and Lisa!

Sarah Harden, who listened to me have a breakdown during our 1:1 and told me point blank this could happen. At every step of this journey—you have been there so proud and excited, and reminded me that this is important. To the whole Hello Sunshine team—Jane, Melissa, Olga, Cynthia, Hillary, Hilary, Joss, Joie, Kristin, Marissa, and anyone who I forget—your enthusiasm for storytelling and for my journey have kept me going. Claire Curly, who was the second person to tell me this should be a book!

Kara McDowell and Kimberly Gabriel are two of the best Pitch Wars mentors a girl could ask for. You helped me become a better writer, a better reviser—and cheered me along every step of the way.

Emily Wibberley—who held a fantasy writer's hand and told her she could write a contemporary book. And that that book had to be *this* book. (She is the first person who told me this should be a book.) You are *Ellie*'s godmother. Your friendship, kindness, and knowledge mean the world to me. Also a big thank-you to Austin Siegemund-Broka, who definitely called the cover first, and who always has the best candle and coffee advice.

DJ, Anna, and Eve—who each read the book and told me it was brilliant. You have talked me off ledges, discussed books with me, shared endless meals and cups of coffee.

Kristin, Mallory, Alexa, and Alex. There are zero words—and yet I will find some. You are my people. You call me on my bullshit. You welcome me—all of me and my weird emotions (you are probably reading and already reaching for the phone to tell me they're not weird). You make me a better friend, writer, ARMY, person. There is no group of people I would rather collectively MISERY with than you.

Rebekah, for inviting me over to your house and feeding me when I felt like *Ellie* would go nowhere. Your friendship and view of writing never cease to amaze me. Liz, while we are still new friends, I love the worlds you create and the time we spend together.

My LA writing peeps—Alexa Donne, Victoria Van Vleet—for constant coffee dates, dinners out, or just casual hangs. Melissa Seymour and Alyssa Colman, for your unwavering support, writing coffee dates, and friendship. Jessica Parra, I am so glad we connected over Disney and books—our days at the parks make the hard days easier.

Megan—whose weekly coffee dates got me through the pandemic and who celebrated every milestone with me. Our careers hit their strides at the same time, and I can't wait to watch your writing continue to soar!

Kalie and Amanda—my former bookseller friends. Your outside perspective on publishing is greatest. You are always willing to listen to me freak out, discuss the finer points of publishing, or just talk books.

Emily . . . the Caitlin to my Ellie.

My parents—this book is for you. *Ellie* wouldn't exist without you letting me spend eighteen months at home during the COVID-19 pandemic. Not to mention—Mom, you came up with that reveal.

(Yeah, divorce for insurance purposes . . . is a thing. The American medical system really is heartless.) Ben—who won NaNo now? JK, JK, there is no winning or losing, but our race to 50,000 many Novembers ago has kept me a writer even when I thought I'd set it aside.

And finally, I wrote this book for teenage me, who often felt alone and out of place. To every reader who's reached out to tell me they felt seen, understood, or just represented—thank you, it means the world to me. As much as Ellie had to find her own squad, I feel like I have found a space I've been missing.